THE AUTOBIOGRAPHY OF

KATHRYN JANEWAY

THE HISTORY OF THE CAPTAIN WHO WENT FURTHER THAN ANY HAD BEFORE

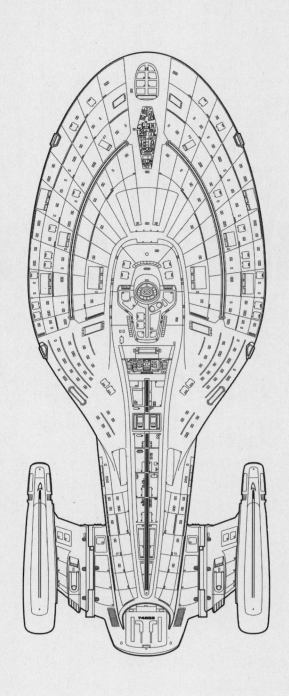

THE AUTOBIOGRAPHY OF
KATHRYN JANEWAY

THE HISTORY OF THE CAPTAIN WHO WENT FURTHER THAN ANY HAD BEFORE

BY
KATHRYN M. JANEWAY

EDITED BY UNA McCORMACK

Titan BOOKS

The Autobiography of Kathryn Janeway
Hardback Edition ISBN: 9781789094794
E-Book Edition ISBN: 9781789094800

Published by Titan Books
A division of Titan Publishing Group Ltd.
144 Southwark Street, London SE1 0UP.

First edition: October 2020
10 9 8 7 6 5 4 3 2 1

Illustrations: Russell Walks
Editor: Cat Camacho
Interior design: Rosanna Brockley/MannMade Designs

A CIP catalogue record for this title is available from the British Library.

Printed and bound in the U.S.A.

Did you enjoy this book? We love to hear from our readers. Please e-mail us at:
readerfeedback@titanemail.com or write to Reader Feedback at the above address.

To receive advance information, news, competitions, and exclusive offers online,
please sign up for the Titan newsletter on our website: www.titanbooks.com.

CONTENTS

For Daniel, for years of fun conversation, and the best ideas

INTRODUCTION
BY COMMANDER NAOMI WILDMAN

WHEN I WAS A LITTLE GIRL, I WANTED TO BE THE CAPTAIN OF A STARSHIP. I know lots of kids have the same ambition, but I wasn't planning to be the captain of any starship. Oh no, I had a very specific ship in mind. I was going to be captain of the *U.S.S. Voyager*.

The thing about this ambition of mine is that it wasn't so outlandish. Because I was born in the Delta Quadrant, and I spent most of my childhood on board *Voyager*, and as far as I was concerned, our captain was the best person in the entire Galaxy. I wanted to be her when I grew up. And in the meantime, I'd settle for being her assistant.

Most people my age grew up following the story of *Voyager*—lost in the Delta Quadrant, seventy thousand light-years away from home, trying to get back to family and friends. For me, this was everyday life. You may have thrilled to hear the news that *Voyager* had been found, or two-way communication had been established, or, most excitingly of all, that after only seven years, a Borg transwarp conduit had brought our ship home.

This might have been an amazing adventure for you, but for me it was—well, it was home. My mom, Sam Wildman, was serving as an ensign when *Voyager* was whisked away—and then found out she was pregnant. My birth story is one amongst many strange tales of those years, but it meant that growing up I knew no other life. Home was a little ship, a long way from where

1

it had started, full of Starfleet and Maquis and all sorts of other interesting people, which most of the time sailed quietly through space—and some of the time came under attack from Vidiians or Hirogen or Kazon. My childhood friends were a Talaxian, an Ocampan, and two decommissioned Borg drones learning to be individuals. I learned logic games from a thoughtful Vulcan, and how to fix anything in front of me from a half-human, half-Klingon. I played the *Captain Proton* holodrama before most people had ever heard of it. And I learned courage, and wisdom, and grace under fire from the very best captain of all—Kathryn M. Janeway.

Admiral Janeway, as she is now known, has been an inspiration to so many throughout the years. Who else could have held that crew together? Who else, through intelligence and sheer force of personality, could have made a group of Starfleet officers and Maquis fighters pull together and set course for home? Who else could have battled the Borg Queen, fought off the Hirogen—or played with such aplomb the part of holographic Arachnia, Queen of the Spider People, nemesis of Captain Proton? Who else would have taken time out of most days to check on her youngest crew member, Naomi, who loved her and admired her so much? Who else would have made that little girl her assistant?

When I was that little girl, I wanted to grow up to be Kathryn Janeway. But the truth is, nobody could replace her—and Kathryn's great skill is to persuade people to be the very best they could be. So many of us owe her so much. Thank you, Admiral, for bringing us home—but thank you, most of all, for the faith you showed us, and the way you brought out the best in us. There can only ever be one captain of *Voyager*—Kathryn Janeway.

Naomi Wildman
Executive Officer, Deep Space K-7

CHAPTER ONE

NO PLACE LIKE HOME—2336-2347

WHEN I WAS A LITTLE GIRL, MY MOTHER MADE POP-UP BOOKS. Do you recall the kind I mean? You turn a page and a whole scene springs up before your eyes. Even now, at this late stage of my life, I think these creations are miraculous. I guess it's something to do with the craft, the careful construction and—yes— the engineering that's involved. My mother's creations were sheer marvels.

My little sister and I each had our favorite. For Phoebe, three years my junior, it was *Alice in Wonderland*: an appropriate choice for a creative and artistic little girl, who seemed to inhabit a world of wonders. I loved that book as well: there was a little tunnel that my mother had constructed from card and clear paper, into which you had to peer to see Alice and the White Rabbit tumbling down. There was the house that sprang up with Alice's huge arms and legs sticking out that never failed to make us laugh. Most beautiful of all, however, was the grand display of playing cards flying up into the air when we—joining in with Alice—would say, "You're nothing but a pack of *cards*!"

Yes, I loved Wonderland, but my real passion was for *The Wonderful Wizard of Oz*. The story of Dorothy Gale, caught up in a tornado and torn away from her family to a strange land where she had to live by her brains, her heart, and her courage, making new friends, and finding her way home, appealed to me profoundly for some reason. My first glimpse of adventure. Safe at home, among my loving family, I dreamed of flying away to Oz. Mom's version of the

3

book was cunningly designed, from the cyclone that swept open on the first page, to the little pair of green glasses tucked into an envelope that you opened to explore the Emerald City, to the very last page where—most thrillingly, to my mind my mother's most elaborate creation was to be found: a cardboard balloon that lay flat between the pages, until lifted on a string between two straws and pressed out, to leave the tiny basket dangling below. I sat with that book for many hours as a small child, enchanted not only by the story, but by working out how my mother had put all the elements together. Mom used to say that Daddy was the one who gave me the flying bug, the desire to take wing and soar off into space. But a huge part was played by her most wonderful, wizardly, cardboard balloon, travelling all the way from Oz.

Looking back on my childhood, I see now that these books were the place where all our family's interests came together. My mother, born Gretchen Williams, was an artist. She was always experimenting with new forms, but illustration was her true talent. You most likely know her as the author of over two dozen books and holodramas for children. Two or three generations of children have taken her stories to heart. Phoebe followed in her footsteps by having an artistic bent: I have a holopicture of them standing next to each other, Mom with a brush in her hand and a dollop of paint on her nose; Phoebe, beside her, exactly the same. I was no artist: my houses leaned sideways; my cute furry creatures looked savage; my human beings something from a horror holo. I can, however, hand draw very clear schematics.

I was the scientist, the engineer, the practical one, the one who worked in numbers. I was the one who stared at the stars and mapped them, who wanted machines, who wanted to fly. In this, I followed my father Edward—Ted to friends, Teddy to my mother—who was an enthusiastic amateur pilot and astronomer. He was also a Starfleet flag officer, and this fact—which shaped our childhood through the sadness of his inevitable absences, and, at least as importantly, through the joy and intensity of his presence—was surely the defining feature of my life. More than anything, I wanted my brave, cheerful, wonderful father to be proud of me. More than anything, I wanted him to see me become the captain of a starship, exactly like him. It's one of the great regrets of my life that this didn't come to pass. Daddy saw me enter the Academy, but he didn't see me captain a ship, let alone bring one safely home from the furthest journey a ship has ever made. But I get ahead of myself. Let's go back to the beginning, back to a small country farm, in the Midwest, in the northern part of the continent of America, on Earth.

✦

Our family home was a small farm outside Bloomington, Indiana. My mother's family had been settled in the region for several generations—Midwesterners through and through. We knew the Williams family story (pioneers, settlers— the traditional covered wagons), and both my maternal grandparents and my mother herself made sure we knew the full history of this land that we lived on and not the partial account that had once been taught, in the old days of nation-states and manifest destiny. One of the peoples who lived here before my ancestors arrived were the Potawatomi, Native Americans of the Great Plains, forced out in the nineteenth century. They call themselves the Neshnabé, the original people. My mother made sure that both Phoebe and I understand that the land that we called home had been the home of many people before us and will be the home of many after us. We learned stories from other people too. A particular favorite of mine was a Cherokee story about the Water Spider; one of my mother's friends wrote and illustrated a book about it that I loved. The Water Spider goes on a long journey to find fire to help the other animals survive. The other animals boast that they will find it and laugh at her when she promises them that she will. But she weaves a boat from her own webs and sails across the water, carrying back with her a hot coal, and she is celebrated for her courage and her honor. I often thought of the Water Spider, on my journey home.

My maternal grandparents, Hector and Ellen Williams, lived on their own farm on land adjacent to ours, and Phoebe and I were often there. One of my earliest memories is of an old oak tree that stood on my grandparents' farm. I learned to climb on that old tree, and Grandpa built a swing for me on its boughs. It was a favorite playmate. One very hot summer afternoon, when the grown-ups were sitting sweltering in the shade, my demands for a playmate were rebuffed; after a tantrum, I took my grievances off to the swing, which I punished for a good hour or so. It's testament to Grandpa's skill as a carpenter that I didn't bring the whole thing down on my own head. When I got tired of that, I climbed up the tree, and sulked for a while. Eventually, still cross but now tired and hot, I repented, and went back indoors, where Grandma cheered everyone's spirits with slushes. An hour later, the inevitable storm started, and I watched from the window as the rains hammered down. The thunder started, then the light show, and I counted between lightning and rumble to see how close the storm was coming. And then—I can still see this in my mind's eye—a strike of lightning hit the oak tree, splitting it right down the middle.

The scream I let out brought the whole household running. Grandpa was there first, but he couldn't get any sense out of me. When I pointed out to the tree, however, he understood. He put his big arm around my shoulder and pulled me into a hug.

"Scary, huh, Katy? One minute a tree's there, tall and strong, and the next it's gone."

Yes, he understood. Lightning strikes so suddenly, so unexpectedly. An old tree that had been supporting you that afternoon could be gone by evening. Looking back now I see that this was my first sense that misfortune can hit even in the safest of places, that we cannot prepare ourselves for every eventuality that life throws at us. I can see too that it was my first brush with mortality, the realization that even old, strong things might suddenly be felled in their prime.

That night the house rattled in the storm, but the next morning was sunny and bright. Grandpa and I went out together and had a good look at our poor old stricken tree. I shed a tear or two, until Grandpa distracted me by saying we were here to find a present for my mother. And we did find a present, a good big piece of burned wood, and brought it back home for her, like proud hunters: a fine piece of charcoal for Mommy to draw me pictures with.

✦

My father's family, the Janeways, whose roots ultimately went back to the west of Ireland, were considerably more peripatetic than the Williams clan, but Portage Creek, Indiana was their base from at least the early years of the twentieth century. My paternal grandparents came back to Bloomington when my paternal grandmother, Caitlin Janeway, took up a professorship at the university: she was an aeronautics engineer, a materials scientist specializing in alloys for use in deep space, one of a long tradition of women in our family to devote themselves to exploring the stars, a tradition which it has been my honor to continue. My paternal grandfather, Cody Janeway, was Starfleet, reaching the rank of commander and serving as chief science officer on various vessels. Family legend has it that he once turned down the chance to serve with a certain Captain Kirk, but I have not been able to find any evidence to prove this, and Grandpa, the old rogue, would never tell the story past a nod and a wink. I'd love to find out the truth of things: family legends do have a tendency to exaggerate! Granddad took up a teaching post at the university when my grandmother took up her chair, and both seemed content to have put down roots at last, allowing their teenage children to attend the same school for several years in succession. Since they lived in the big city of Bloomington, Phoebe and I called our paternal grandparents Granny-in-town and Granddad-in-town, the Grands-in-town for short. They weren't daily presences in the same way as my mother's parents, Grandpa and Grandma, but they were still significant influences in our lives.

My mother and father, despite growing up so close to each other, did not meet at high school, nor were they even introduced to each other by mutual friends (and there were several, or so it turned out). No, they met in Geneva, of all places. How did that happen, when my mother did not willingly go further than Bloomington, and even then complained about having to leave her art and the farm behind? Well, shortly before graduating high school, my mother became deeply concerned with humanitarian issues: I think she had seen footage of the refugee crisis on Koltaari. Somehow, a teacher at school persuaded her to attend a youth conference being held at the old United Nations buildings in Geneva, where young people from across the Federation were gathering to learn more about how the Federation and Starfleet could assist in bringing aid to the refugees. My mother was not sure: the event lasted a whole month. But her passion won out over her domesticity, and she duly went along. Even my mother, a true home bird, had to admit that this trip—the longest she ever spent away from home—had been worth it. She brought home a young man, a Starfleet cadet, starry-eyed with love for this quiet and talented girl. They married the year they both turned twenty-two, when my father graduated from Starfleet Academy.

Knowing that my father's career meant that he would by necessity be away for long periods of time, but not wanting to delay starting their family, my mother and father decided that they would make their home close to my mother's parents. Mom was well supported when we were small, and able to carry on with her own work as an artist and illustrator. Grandpa and Grandma were therefore very strong presences in our lives; their wedding gift to my parents was the land next to their own farm, and there my parents built their family home, and established their own small farm. I know that many people are anxious to get away from their families as quickly as possible on reaching maturity, but this was not the case with my mother. She simply did not have the wanderlust of her husband and elder child. She was happy in the land where she had been born; she had everything she needed there. One of many ways in which we never quite understood each other—but I guess that this is the definition of true love, isn't it? It doesn't try to change; it accepts the other for what she is. Still, children are sensitive creatures. I knew that this gap in her understanding of me existed, and when I thought about that, it made me sad.

Don't let me leave you with the wrong impression! Most of all you should imagine a very happy, very loved little girl, who lived—in many ways—an idyllic childhood. The great grief of my early childhood—and Phoebe will forgive me for saying this, I know—was the arrival of The Baby. I was three years old, and had, until then, been the absolute center of attention for all the adults in my immediate vicinity. With Grandpa I dug in the garden and ate Welsh rarebit. With Grandma I baked cookies and other treats. As for Mommy and Daddy, they had surely been put on Earth to do my bidding. And then… Well, I knew something wasn't right when Mommy started to have naps all the time, just when I was giving up on them, and wasn't as eager to get down on the floor and play with me as usual. Then she started to get bigger and bigger… People said things like, "Are you looking forward to The Baby, Katy?" and "You'll have a playmate when The Baby arrives, won't you, Katy?" and "Do you want a brother or a sister, Katy?"

Well, I am here to tell you that I was not sold on the idea of The Baby: not one little bit. I was a bright kid, and I think I guessed what the score would be. Everyone would be fussing around the new arrival; nobody would want to play any longer with Katy. And when the darned thing arrived… Well, this was no playmate, was it? A tiny red screeching thing—Jeez! What a con! A noisy, troublesome, demanding con!

"Here you are, Kathryn," Mommy said, holding the creature in her arms.

"Meet your baby sister. Little Phoebe."

I eyed the new scrap of life suspiciously. "Mommy," I said, "can we swap it for a puppy?"

I have never been allowed to forget this. But I did get the puppy: Jess, a border collie of such perfection that even now I get a tear in my eye thinking about her. She came to me at ten weeks old, a warm little bundle of energy and love, and Grandpa helped me train her. We were devoted to each other. Jess trotted everywhere with me, and she snuck into my room at nights, despite stern warnings from Grandpa that spoiling her would ruin her as a working dog. (It never did.) In the holopictures that we have of that time, we are always together, and I loved her with all my heart. But in some ways, I knew that Jess was a consolation prize, and that with Phoebe's arrival, I had lost some little part of Mommy. My beautiful and elusive mother, always the first object of my devotion, was now shared. I was not wholly the center of her life any longer, and never could be again.

✦

This was my early childhood. We were a very happy, close-knit family, in which two little girls basked in the love of their various devoted adults and were encouraged to follow their own paths. Phoebe soon showed the artistic bent that rivaled even my mother's, permanently smudged with paints and modeling clays. My mother, around the time of Phoebe's arrival, started to grow roses, firstly for pleasure, but increasingly she became very competitive. This was most unlike my mother, although, as in all her endeavors, she excelled. There is a rose named after each one of her daughters. I recall one morning, not long after The Baby landed, when I was outside helping her, proud in my little blue overalls and my tiny spade and glad to be spending time with Mommy, when a man walked past the gate and stopped to watch me work. Mom came over to say hello, and he nodded at me and said, "Nice to see a boy helping his mom."

A boy?! This was intolerable. This was not to be permitted. By all accounts I gave that man the fiercest of stares—*skewered* him, as my mother tells it—and delivered the memorable putdown, "Katy not boy! Katy *girl!*"

"I've never seen a man move so fast," Mom said. "She more or less ran him out of town." I loved it when she told this story. I basked in the glow that came to her eye. Mommy was proud of me, and that was everything.

Let me describe my mother as she was in these years. A free spirit—but quiet, solitary. Still waters ran very deep in my mother; it was as if some kind of spirit of the natural world had been temporarily caught in a mortal body. By the sea, she would surely have been a selkie; here on the plains she was a genie of the river, perhaps, or of the lakes, some kind of spirit drawn to live among us ordinary mortals. She was outdoors as much as she could be—in the garden, or else working on the long porch at the back of the house. She had a shed which she used as a studio in bad weather, but rain did not daunt her and, in fact, often she would go out to meet it, walking around the farm and coming home drenched, her eyes shining. She was sweet-natured, funny, often absent in that way that very creative people can be, and endlessly creative with her two small children. Need it be said that I adored her?

People often ask me what it was like, having a writer of children's books as a mother. Truth be told, both Phoebe and I took it largely for granted. She had so many stories she wanted to share! Phoebe leaned toward fantasy: Wonderland, of course; later, she loved Meg Murry's journeys through the universe by means of the tesseract, Binti's career at Oomza Uni, Awinita Foster's slipstream adventures along the shining way. I tended toward more realistic stories: the Melendy children making a new home in the countryside, exploring the land and the people around them; Omakayas and her family of the Birchbark House, growing up near Lake Superior; Cassie Logan's struggles under Jim Crow; the stories of Mildred Jones and her friends, rebuilding the post-atomic world in the 2080s. Even my beloved Dorothy Gale was in many ways a practical child, focused on returning to her home at least as much as on the marvels she encountered.

There was one case I recall when Mommy did share her stories with us, and that was when she was invited to write for the well-known children's holoprogram, *The Adventures of Flotter*. I think it was a new direction for her—she hadn't written for holos before, although many followed afterward—but she was naturally drawn to a river creature. She was keen, too, to try out her ideas. Well, I loved them! Mommy had a flair for story, and an eye for detail. What a wonderful world that was: a truly magical space, a first encounter, for most children, of the possibilities of the holosuite: part play, part drama, all imagination. At first, this was something that only Mommy and I did: Phoebe was deemed still a little young even for the gentle perils of the Forest of Forever. Mommy and I wandered through the Forest with Flotter and Trevis, and built parts of the world together. It wasn't long before Phoebe wanted to take part though, and I have to confess I wasn't happy about that. But I swear, Phoebe, that flood was an *accident*.

Many people have told me how much they loved Flotter as a child (I think the only person I have encountered who didn't was a former CMO of the *Enterprise*, who called it 'that damn tree nonsense'), and many of them recall specific adventures that my mother wrote, such as the encounter with the fireflies, and the pebble house by the river. It was a delight to see the young captain's assistant on *Voyager*, the inimitable Naomi Wildman, take to the stories so much; yet another generation enchanted by them. So when people ask what it was like having a children's writer as a mother—well, here you are! But some part of my mother—a crucial part—remained forever elusive, out of reach. As a child, you try to bridge that gap; perhaps the definition of adulthood is accepting that some of the gap between you and your parents might well be forever unbridgeable.

Aged seven, and always eager to win her approval, I leapt at my mother's suggestion that I take ballet classes. Let me be the first to say that ballet did not play to my strengths. I was a strong and energetic child, and had a certain amount of athleticism, but not the kind that makes a prima ballerina. What I lacked in natural skill, however, I made up for in enthusiasm and hard work. My "Dying Swan" has become a family legend. I grasped at the time that it wasn't entirely for the right reasons, and I realized that if I were ever to become a star of the stage, it would be for comedy rather than tragedy. I kept up my dancing lessons for many years—less ballet and more ballroom and character dances—and I even picked up a bronze medal once for my Charleston, but let's just say that if ever I needed a new career, this wouldn't be the skillset I'd draw on. Phoebe refused point blank to learn ballet, and for this I am eternally grateful, since I'm pretty sure she would have been superb, outclassing me artistically once again.

Both Phoebe and I spent a lot of time out in the garden, not least because my mother—who felt such a strong connection to this place—encouraged us in this. I have to confess that I didn't appreciate this much as a kid: I'd rather have been building a model airplane, but Mom wanted it, so Mom got it. One summer, when I was nine and Phoebe six, Mom decided that we were old enough to look after our own little plots of land. She told us that if we cultivated them, we could choose where to visit next time Dad was back home. This was a big deal for us, to be given such a responsibility in Mom's beloved garden. I dutifully turned the earth and planted vegetables, many hours of solid back-breaking labor. Phoebe—clever girl—threw seeds in the air and told Mom she was growing a meadow. Given the hours she spent there, lying on her stomach staring at the flowers that bloomed, and the insects and wildlife that came to her wild garden, and the careful drawings that she made of them, Mom had to admit that she had kept her side of the bargain. We made biryani from the vegetables I'd grown and Grandma's special recipe, and we made postcards from the pictures that Phoebe had drawn. I earned my trip to the Smithsonian Air and Space Museum, and Phoebe her trip to the Van Gogh Museum. Boy, though, did I envy Phoebe her smarts!

Daddy, on his arrival home, was not the outraged ally that I had expected. When I told him the story, brimming over with indignation at Phoebe's cheating, he laughed out loud. "Work smarter, Katy, not harder!" he said. Not bad advice, and advice I took to heart—I am aware that sometimes I can be a little rigid in my thinking (not allowing deviations from Starfleet uniform regulations when you're seventy years' flight away from the nearest Starfleet base, for example), and I do try my best not to get overly set in my ways. I must say, however—since it is possible that some Starfleet cadets may well be reading this memoir—that hard work never did me any harm and those rules kept us together during some tough times.

I still have one of the postcards that Phoebe made. It shows *Dodecatheon meadia*, a type of primrose, native to our part of America, known more commonly as the shooting star. It's beautiful work for a six-year-old: she has captured the nodding petals with a sharp eye and painted them a delicate shade of lavender. Granny-in-town showed her how to imbue the card with the scent of the flower it depicted; this being Granny-in-town's work, it sure lasted. Phoebe and I joked about it, but the day came when I was grateful for Granny-in-town's skill.

Because that card went everywhere with me. It went to Starfleet Academy, and then onto the *Al-Batani*, and the *Billings*. And naturally it came with me on *Voyager*, and therefore all the way to the Delta Quadrant, and back again. I had it tucked away in my desk for safekeeping, but I brought it out very often, when I was alone and feeling bereft, and I would just catch the very last of the scent (it had mostly gone by the third or fourth year of our journey). Often, I would flip it over to read the message my sister had written. Just before I left for the Academy, she dug the card out, and wrote: "To my big sister Katy, may she always shoot for the stars." Those words kept me going through many a long dark night among unfamiliar stars, looking for the one that would lead me home to my beloved family: to Phoebe, to the grandparents in the country, and the grandparents in town, and, most of all, to Mom.

✦

Given that this account is about my early years, it's perhaps natural that I have written a great deal about my mother, but now let me tell you about my father. He was, after all, the great hero of my early life. Edward Janeway was Starfleet to the core: a first-rate cadet who became an officer of distinction, and who earned rapid promotion until, shortly before I went to high school, he became a vice admiral. As a child, like many who enter Starfleet, he had looked to the stars: he was an enthusiastic amateur astronomer, and he loved to fly. He began as a test pilot in his early Starfleet career, although, after Phoebe's arrival, listened to my mother's concerns about his safety, and agreed to move toward command posts. This, naturally, took him away a great deal, often to Starfleet Command, which wasn't so bad, as we could follow him there during school holidays for a week or so. But more often than not he was away from Earth entirely. Children accept what they are given, and both Phoebe and I accepted that Daddy would be away for long periods of time. Still, we didn't have to like it. Since Daddy was incapable of doing anything wrong, we needed to have someone else to blame —and blame fell squarely on the shoulders of the Cardassians.

Cardassians were the great ogres of our childhood, as I suspect they were for many of our generation, and given that the ongoing border skirmishes of the '40s and '50s eventually led to full-scale conflict, one perhaps can be sympathetic to that opinion. Much has changed since the Dominion War, of course, but to my sister and me the Cardassians—these aggressive, seemingly monstrous aliens—were also the entire reason that Daddy was so often away from home. It took me a long time to recognize the root of my hostility toward the Cardassians, and even longer to shake this off and reach a better understanding of them.

A little context is surely helpful here. First contact between the Federation and the Cardassians was many years in the past, but from the start of the twenty-fourth century, the Cardassian Union had become markedly more aggressive in its imperial ambitions, most notably its expansion into Bajor during the 2310s. We know now that conditions on Cardassia Prime were becoming increasingly difficult: intensive industrial farming on an already dry world was leading rapidly to soil exhaustion. The Cardassians were on the hunt for the resources of other worlds; this expansion led, ultimately, to the formal annexation of Bajor in 2328 (eight years before my birth). For my father, moving up the ranks, Cardassian ambitions and incursions into Federation space were his chief source of concern, as they would continue to be the concern of his daughter years later, at the start of her career. Starfleet Command, at the time, was chiefly trying to prevent the outbreak of full-scale war, while at the same time protecting our border worlds, and supporting the Bajorans without violating our principles of nonintervention. At this age, before high school, these issues meant little to me, but they created the condition of my father's continuing absences, shaping my early years and providing the backdrop for my own eventual decision to enter Starfleet.

When Daddy was at home, Mommy was happy, and when Mommy was happy, we could all be happy. Like everything else that he did, Daddy approached fatherhood with dedication, bringing his fullest attention to the task. He might not have been there all the time, but when he was, he was there completely. I see now how he must have been awake until the early hours of the morning to get through reports and messages before turning his complete attention to his girls. And when he was with us—oh, the fun we had! He combined the authority of a father with the mischief of an uncle, the curiosity of a child, and the instinct for guidance of a born teacher. Do I sound as if I idolized him? Well, of course I did. He was my wonderful Daddy, Starfleet captain and all-around hero. More and more, I wanted to be the apple of his eye.

Whenever he was home, he would devise some new project or excursion for the whole family. He would take us all camping—making sure we knew how to live in the wild, be self-sufficient, show us how to forage and find fresh water. He encouraged Phoebe in her interest in the natural world and helped me to understand what to look for, too, and why I should care about the environment around me. He saw that my eyes turned upward, and on inkblot nights beneath the heavens, he taught me the names of constellations. My first voyages into the stars, with him. Phoebe learned them too: he realized that that mythological names captured her imagination. We learned the name of Mars in different languages, some still living, some long lost. Mars, Huoxing, Nergal, Wahram… This, I realized, was a kind of different world that I could get behind: not made-up fantasy worlds, but real planets that I might visit one day. And indeed Daddy took us to Mars, when Phoebe got to high school.

Here's a typical project of Daddy's, from when I was about eight years old. He decided that what our farm lacked was a telescope. Well, of course! He was Starfleet, after all, he said. He always had to be keeping an eye on things, even when he was on leave. So we made one. The whole Janeway-Williams clan got together and built the darned thing. And not some small instrument, but the kind of telescope that would have been the envy of an Edwardian gentleman. Granny-in-town was brought on board, of course, this being something of a specialty for her, and I think she was pivotal in replicating the parts we needed. Granddad-in-town came in handy too, bringing along a couple of graduate students to help renovate the old pig shed that was to be the telescope's new home. Grandpa made them work for their supper: sawing and hammering, fetching and carrying. I hope they got extra credit for this, those kids; what a flagrant abuse of power!

We girls oversaw the process from start to finish: the tooling of the parts, the grinding of the lenses, the construction of the outhouse, the assembly of the device itself. Good lord, it was magical—no, better than that. It was *science*. There was no mystique to this, no trick. This was something that could be built, crafted, made—and yet once it was assembled, it could show the beauty and majesty, the awe-inducing grandeur, of the stars. Out on the porch, Mom lay out long sheets of black paper, and together she and Phoebe and I created star charts. At last we were done, and we went out late one night—well past our bedtimes—and Daddy showed us the stars. I spent many nights in there, learning the names of the constellations, much later than perhaps my parents realized, sneaking past their room to my own bed, head full of the wonder of space.

On my ninth birthday, Dad took me over to the local flying club, and took me up in a little plane. The thrill of this. At last I was in flight! We were up for about twenty minutes, and Dad flew us over the land that I knew so well. I saw my home, all these places that I knew intimately and up close—our farm, Grandpa and Grandma's farm, our school, the road to the city—but from up above, like a map, but real. This little trip changed my perspective on the world entirely. Earth was never going to be enough for me now.

✦

As we grew older, my father continued this new tradition of taking me and Phoebe on separate excursions. Good tactic for anyone in a parenting or mentorship role, I think; give someone your undivided attention. Phoebe, in general, asked for cultural visits: ticking off one by one all the major galleries on Earth, Luna, or Mars. Me being me, I skipped culture and ran for the hills. I wanted to be outdoors. I wanted to hike and climb and ski and whitewater raft and in general feel myself moving or—best of all—in flight. I nearly got him to agree to bungee jumping (he didn't take much persuading, if I'm being honest) until Mom got wind of my plans and absolutely, categorically forbade it, on the grounds that I should at least reach double digits before risking my life (I guess she had a point).

I still haven't tried bungee jumping. I should go and book a trip to Queenstown now, leap from a bridge and feel the air rushing past, and shout, "This one's for you, Dad!" as I head toward the water. One benefit of getting older is that you no longer care how eccentric you look. I have embraced this in recent years, and I intend to avail myself of this freedom indefinitely.

Such freedoms were not available to me in my tenth year, however, and after my father and I were thwarted in our plans to throw ourselves off a bridge, he suggested we go to the Grand Canyon instead—the biggest ditch on Earth, as Dad called it. While my first impressions were of a big, dusty hole in the ground, this fortnight proved to be one of the defining periods of my life. We transported to Flagstaff, Arizona, and then took a small flyer out to the north rim. We hiked a few miles every day and camped at night. When we were done cooking and washing up, Dad and I would lie on our backs and look up at the stars. Sometimes he would tell me stories of worlds that he had seen; sometimes we just lay there peacefully, quietly enjoying each other's company. I thought of what it had been like, flying high above my home, and wondered what other worlds might look like from a great height.

"I'd like to go there one day," I said.

"Where, Kitten?" he said. I think I hated and loved that nickname at the same time.

"Up there."

He looked up at the heavens. "What? Luna? Mars?"

"Dad!"

"Oh," he said. "I see. Starfleet."

"What's it like?" I said. "Not the stories. I mean *really*."

I watched a smile pass over his face. He seemed… transported is the only word for it. "Kitten," he said. "It's like nothing else. It's *wonderful*."

I looked back up at the stars. I have never felt so happy in my life. I thought about leaving home, going to the Academy. I imagined myself on the bridge of a starship, people calling me "Captain," being the one in charge. But then a cold feeling washed over me. "Do you think Mom will mind?"

"Why would Mom mind?"

"It's a long way from home… You know how she is. There's no place like home…"

I watched him from the corner of my eye, and I could see that he understood. "You know," he said, "all that Mom and I want is for you to discover your own way. Find what it is you were born to do. It might take you to places that you or I or Mom can't even begin to imagine, but that's the deal you sign up for when you become parents. You want to keep your kids safe, close by— but in the end you have to set them sailing off, wherever they want to go. You just have to show them how to keep their ship afloat." He smiled at me. "Wherever you choose to go, Kathryn—we'll support you."

Do I need to say how much I loved him? Do I need to say how much I loved them all: my clever, curious, excellent family; my beautiful, sensitive mother; my gifted, creative sister; my brave and brilliant father? When I think back to this time, I picture them like this: Phoebe lying on her stomach among the flowers, her sharp eye catching everything about the world around her; Dad gazing wide-eyed at the stars, longing for adventure, longing to see whatever was out there; and Mom, lying on the bed beside me, reading from my favorite book, and whispering to me softly: *"There's no place like home… There's no place like home…"*

CHAPTER TWO

REACH FOR THE SKY—2348-2353

IN MY EARLIEST YEARS, I ATTENDED A SMALL COUNTRY SCHOOL very close to the house, with a dozen other children of varying ages from the local area. Phoebe and I were able to walk there, and, later, we cycled along the country lanes. At the end of the school day, Phoebe and I would take our time coming home, stopping to walk our bicycles along back lanes, while Phoebe collected samples, or I explored a new patch of land. The school itself was down a long lane: a white wooden building in its own grounds, with a flower garden and a vegetable plot and a huge wooden treehouse and climbing frame, and even its own stage. There were three little classrooms where we split off into age groups after assembly, before gathering at the end of the day to say goodbye. Although I loved the place and the teachers, who interwove play and learning so cleverly and intimately that it was never a struggle to get me to my studies, by the age of ten I was chafing against the boundaries of this small safe world, and I was more than ready to move out.

High school was the biggest change of my life so far. The morning cycle was still there, but instead of turning with Phoebe down the long lane to the schoolhouse, I carried on along the road to the local transporter. There, in a bustle of noise and laughter and the usual teenage squabbling, the local kids gathered to head into Bloomington. The school I was attending was a small charter school, covering grades seven through twelve, but it was a huge step for me. I remember that first morning piercingly: standing by myself, clutching my bag and books, staring at the gang of kids gathered, and wondering what the school itself must be like, if this was just a few of its students... Then I heard a friendly voice call my name.

"Kathryn!"

It was Aisha, the other girl from my elementary school heading up that year, and with her was her older sister, Tamara, who had gone up to high school two years earlier. I ran over to them with relief. Tamara, who must have seen my wide-eyed look and guessed what it meant, put one arm around my shoulder, one arm around Aisha's, and said, "Come on, kiddos. I'll look after you."

Aisha looked disgruntled (Who wants to rely on their big sister's good graces? Ask Phoebe!), but it did us no harm having Tamara as an ally. She was an outgoing, generous-spirited girl who kept an eye on us while we found our feet in those first few bewildering weeks, while keeping a sensible distance that let us make our own way without relying on her. I have, throughout my life, been lucky in the mentors that I have found, and, looking back now, I can see how this was the first of many of these kindly and well-judged relationships. I got back in touch with Aisha after my return from the Delta Quadrant, when those old friendships took on great importance, after having thought that I would never see any of them again. She was living on Mars, a professor of the history of space colonization at the Sojourner Truth Institute, University of Tharsis. Tamara was still living in Bloomington and had just published her eighth novel—Regency romances, if you can believe it! Some genres never die. We went out for dinner when Aisha was back on Earth and what joy that was, seeing these successful women living life to the full. Champagne and conversation flowed. I am blessed in my friends.

But let's go back to young Kathryn Janeway, arriving at high school, smallest of the small all over again, but dead set on making her mark. High school, despite my trepidation, turned out to be a good time for me. I remember that Dad, just before I set off on my first day, said to me, "Try everything once, Kitten. New sports, new hobbies, new ideas, new everything. You never know until you've tried." It's been a good rule of thumb over the years, even if it meant I ate more of Neelix's cooking than I might have risked under other circumstances. But it was the philosophy that guided me through high school (and, eventually, through the Academy). I threw myself into life there—lessons, clubs, friendships—everything I could, and I found that the more you put into something, the more you get out.

Like most children, this is the age when serious passions emerge. It is also an age when one is first able to devote energy for extended periods of time to one's object of passion, pursuing it with single-minded intensity. My first year at high school is known by my long-suffering family as "The Year of Amelia." This was the year that I discovered the life and story of Amelia Earhart during a classroom project to research a pioneer that we admired. Naturally, I chose the history of flight (Grandpa used to say I should have been born with wings), and naturally I chose a woman.

Well, I went far beyond the call of duty. I started with the data banks, and the story captivated me. I learned that she was flying in a time when women were held to be inferior to men (That took some understanding. How had anyone ever believed such nonsense?), but that within her family no such backward views prevailed. Her mother was forward-thinking, and Amelia and her sister were not held back. I didn't miss Amelia's involvement in women's rights, but it was the stories of her flying exploits that truly captivated me. The courage to conduct those flights alone, and her good humor and practicality. And then, of course, the mystery of her disappearance, with the hint of espionage about it. I knew everything. I made my family quiz me on the details of her life, built models of the planes she flew, and would have built a full-size version if Mom hadn't forbidden use of the barn. I tracked her journey around the world, and even lobbied to visit Lae, in Papua New Guinea, where she and her navigator last set out from, only to disappear on that same flight, in order to pay my final respects. This went on well past the submission date for my class project. My Aunt Martha fueled the fire by telling me stories about our ancestor, Shannon O'Donnel, whom, she said, had been a pioneering astronaut. And I got from my father a promise that when I turned sixteen, he would teach me to fly.

✦

This intensity of mine sometimes manifested itself as a competitive streak, best shown by my tennis career. I took up tennis in my first year at high school (dropping, with some relief from all quarters, not least my teacher, my rather lackluster efforts at ballet). Grandpa, seeing how this was developing into a serious activity, quietly cleared an area of land to turn into a practice court for me. The problem then was to find a partner: Phoebe, naturally, was not in the least interested in having tennis balls whacked at her by her older sister. It was, quite unexpectedly, Grandma who turned out to be game: it transpired that she had been a keen tennis player in her youth, and she was delighted to have the chance of a game or two. I was all set to have family tournaments… Sadly, nobody else would bite, and I had to make do with competition at school and, later, as I improved, state tournaments.

This competitive streak led to one of the more notorious episodes of my high-school career. I had been participating in a tournament at our high school, and the truth was that I had overextended myself, playing not only in the doubles' tournament, but in the singles too. The doubles matches had gone well, although my partner and I had been outclassed in the semifinal by a hugely accomplished pair who later went on to represent Earth at the Federation Schools Olympiad (one of them ultimately becoming a top-ranking adult player). We took them to a third set, and felt pretty proud in those circumstances, knowing we'd acquitted ourselves well against real stars. But losing this meant I had my heart on bringing home the trophy in the singles, not least because this was a rare occasion when Dad was there to see me play. Sadly, I hadn't paced myself. I had not dropped a set in the singles tournament, and I threw everything into my singles semifinal to keep this up (a more experienced player would have conserved energy and been prepared strategically to sacrifice that). And then of course the doubles semifinal wore me out.

My opponent in the final was a good player who deserved the place but was one that I had beaten on each occasion we had met in the past—sometimes with real ease. But that day, however hard I tried, I could not get my limbs to respond to instructions. This quickly rattled me. I didn't know what was going on; I thought I was ill! But the simple fact was of course that I was tired: too many games, even for a teenager in her prime. I needed to rest, and instead I was trying to scramble together muscle strength and brain power to win a tennis match. I lost the first set and, when the break came, sat with my towel over my head, cheeks burning and limbs aching, and didn't make eye contact with my coach or with my family (most of all my parents). The second set was even worse. Thinking of it now I shiver for my younger self! I was demolished.

Game, set, and match to my opponent in two sets: 6–2; 6–1. The worst game of tennis I played in my life. In a daze, I managed to take my runner-up trophy, and watch my opponent lift the winner's trophy.

If this story ended here, it would already be a fairly dispiriting one for me, but the day wasn't over yet. I showered and changed, but not even that helped. Sulking—yes, I admit it—in the changing room, I was not ready to see my family or my coach, and when they all turned up, I reached my absolute limit. When Mom said, "Poor Katy! We know how hard you worked!" I picked up my racquet, threw it at the wall, and stormed out.

Not my finest hour: but even the most hard-working teenager is surely allowed the occasional temper tantrum. This being me, it had to be the finest temper tantrum that the state of Indiana had seen in some time. Dad, chasing after me, said, "Come on, Katy, let's go home—" And I turned to him—turned to my beloved Dad—and yelled, "I am not coming home! Leave me alone! I don't need *any* of you!"

Off I marched. Oh, how I cringe to think of it now! How brattish! How unsporting! What my plan was, I'm not entirely sure, but by this point I was committed to wherever it was taking me. Backing down was not an option. I got my feet somehow onto the road out of town, but there was a danger of running into people, and I was, to my credit, starting to feel both ashamed and embarrassed, so I quickly took a turn onto one of the country lanes. After about fifteen or twenty minutes, I was starting to think that perhaps this wasn't the best decision I'd ever made (I'd just played some pretty tough tennis matches, remember), but the stiff neck of the Janeways would not allow me to give up, turn back, and either find my family or take the transporter home. Instead, I walked on. Seven kilometers home. What could possibly go wrong?

Well, the weather on the plains can be a fickle thing, as Dorothy Gale can tell you, and summer, as well as being tennis season, can also be storm season. The heat gets up there, and something has to give. Four kilometers into my walk, stewing in the heat, and aware that the sky was getting heavier and darker, I felt the first spots of rain on my face. I gritted my teeth and walked on. The rain became heavier and heavier. The sky now was very dark. I heard a distant rumble of thunder. I knew what was coming. I was out on the plains, and a lightning storm was headed my way.

I had the good sense to look for cover, but places to hide were thin and far between this far out. I had to walk on at least another kilometer and a half before I saw a barn that might do, and by now I was seriously frightened. The storm was not lessening. The lightning was truly scary. And I was very, very tired. The barn seemed so far away…

Then I heard a dog bark, and the sound of a groundcar heading my way. It was Dad, coming to look for me, with Jess. He pulled the groundcar up alongside me.

"Excuse me, miss—are you by any chance heading my way?"

Jess barked. I burst into tears. "Oh, Dad!"

"Hop in, Katy. I don't fancy being out here much longer."

I climbed in, and hugged Jess to me. Dad pointed the groundcar toward home.

Let's hear it for my family, who at no point told me what an idiot I'd been, and how I'd brought this whole thing down on my own head. Once home, I was tucked up straight into bed. Mom came and sat down next to me, and before I knew what was happening, I was *howling* on her shoulder. Exhaustion, disappointment, shame, and the fright of my life… What else do you want to do but cry on your mother's arm? She stroked my hair and said all the right things, and eventually my tears reduced to sobs, which reduced to hiccups, which reduced to laughter.

"Oh, Mom," I said. "I'm such an idiot!"

"Kate," she said, "if this is the most idiotic thing you ever do, you'll be doing all right."

Well, I've done a great many idiotic things since then. But I will note that the following year I came back and took both trophies, the doubles with my fine partner, and the singles for my very own self.

✦

There was one last serious conversation to be had about this whole business, and that was with Dad the following day. Because I'd been making it clear for some time now that my plan was to follow him into Starfleet, and he had a few things to say about my performance the previous day. I was out on the porch, curled up on the hammock with a book, Jess snuggled beside me. He came to find me, bent to kiss me on the forehead, and said:

"Well, Kathryn. That's one hell of a stubborn streak you've got there."

I blushed beet-red. "Oh, Dad! Please don't—"

"And that's not necessarily a bad thing… except when it is. Because—as I think you might have learned from this whole escapade—a streak like that can lead to a person making bad decisions. Striking out on their own rather than looking to their team for support—"

"Dad, it was a terrible mistake, I know it was. I knew within ten minutes that it was one of the dumbest things I'd ever done—"

"But you didn't stop."

"No," I said. "I didn't."

We sat in silence. Jess, sensing my mood, gave a low whine. I stroked behind her ears.

"I'm not here to scold you," Dad said, after a little while. "But you've told me that you're set on joining Starfleet, and I want you to be very sure you understand what that means."

I looked at him, carefully. He was staring out across the beautiful countryside. This morning, you'd never have guessed there had been such a storm. The sky was clear and that fine bright shade of blue that you only see in the Midwest. The fields were green and bountiful. But my father, I thought, wasn't seeing this. He was seeing something else. For the first time, I saw him not as Dad, but as a person in his own right, a man with worries and concerns that went well beyond our family, well beyond my teenage dramas.

"You mean the Cardassians, don't you?" I said.

Turning his head to look at me, he nodded. His face was the most serious I had ever seen. I wondered, briefly, however he had concealed this from us in the past.

"Are they really that bad, Dad?" I said, quietly, just in case Phoebe was passing by. I had the sense of being initiated into something, into a graver, more sober, adult world.

"They can be," he said. "Have you heard of Setlik III, Kathryn?"

I thought. "Yes…" I said, slowly. "A colony world on the border. Wasn't there was a battle there a year or two ago?"

"Not so much a battle. A massacre."

Any reply I might have had stuck in my throat.

"The Cardassians thought the colony was the cover for a military base—"

"Starfleet wouldn't do that! Starfleet would never use civilians as shields!"

"That's one big difference between Starfleet and the Cardassian *guls*," my father said.

"*Guls*?"

"The captains in the Cardassian military," he explained. "The admirals are called legates. What do you know about how the Cardassian Union works, Kathryn?"

The truth was, very little. My interests were flying, tennis, and getting ahead in math and science. I was starting to glimpse that perhaps this wasn't going to be enough, if I was serious about Starfleet. "Not much," I admitted.

"Okay, then listen up." And he gave me a quick briefing on how the Cardassian Union worked: a government run by the military—the Central Command—for the benefit of the military, with laws rubber-stamped by a powerless civilian Detapa Council, and everyone and everything kept in their place by the shadowy, terrifying secret police—the Obsidian Order. Almost the very opposite of our Federation, with Starfleet's primary purpose of peaceful exploration, a culture that celebrated diversity and opportunity, and a Federation Council that showcased these values.

"What really happened on Setlik III?" I said.

"Cardassian Central Command sent a squad to destroy the base."

"But there wasn't a base," I said.

"No," he said, "so they destroyed the colony instead. Like I said—a massacre."

This was hard to wrap my head around at first. "Did they know there wasn't really a base?"

"I don't know. Either way around, it doesn't reflect well on the Central Command. Either they didn't know, which means they were expecting us to behave as badly as they would, or they did, which means they deliberately and ruthlessly attacked defenseless people."

He must have seen the look on my face, because he reached over to take hold of my hand.

"I don't tell you these things to frighten you," he said, "but because I think you're mature enough to understand, and because you're soon going to be making decisions that will affect the rest of your future. What Starfleet and the Federation are facing in the Cardassian Union is a cruel society that seems bent on war. You can bet your boots that our diplomats are hard at work trying to stop that from happening—but the reality is that it takes two sides to make peace. And I'm not sure that both sides want it. We do. But the Cardassians?" He shook his head. "I just don't know."

"I see," I said slowly.

"Do you, Kathryn?"

"Well, it's like you said, isn't it? If I really mean it, if I really mean to get into Starfleet and become a captain—"

He grinned at me. "Oh! *That's* the plan!"

I gave him a steely look. "Did you expect anything less?"

He patted my hand. "Not from you, Kitten."

"It's not going to be fun and games, is it? It's not going to be all exploration and new worlds. There's a hostile enemy out there—and it might mean war."

He nodded. "So that's why I want you to be sure before you decide completely that Starfleet is for you. And that's why…"

I groaned. "Don't say it!"

"That's why temper tantrums like yesterday won't be good enough."

Yesterday's performance seemed years ago, as if it had happened to an entirely different person. A child. I was older already. "I know. I understand."

"Wanting to win and strategizing to win—those are admirable traits."

"I know. But pushing when I can't win, losing *badly*… and, well, the rest."

He laughed. "And the rest!"

"If that's not good enough, it won't happen again. I want to be the best I can be."

"I know."

"And I'll work to achieve that."

He leaned over and kissed my brow. "I bet you will."

It's strange to think back on that conversation now. Exploration turned out to be a larger part of my Starfleet career than either of us could ever have guessed. As for the Cardassians—well, there were a fair few of those in my life too across the coming years, that's true, and little did any of us know that the border conflicts would not be fully resolved until the Dominion War—but fate ensured I ended up missing that whole damn thing.

✦

It did not escape my attention that after this we had many more Starfleet visitors than we ever had in the past. Dad had often brought colleagues home, so Phoebe and I weren't unused to captains and commanders and top brass. (Grandpa sometimes joked when we were small that we were in danger of seeing admiral's pips as signifying "someone who will give me a piggyback.") But often these people had come to our farm for the same reasons as Dad: to enjoy a break from command and high-level decisions. From this time on, however, there was less of a gap between the outside world and our happy home. We were getting older, and we stayed up now around the dinner table, and listened to the adult conversation, and sometimes we even joined in. I don't underestimate how much of an impact this had on my Starfleet career: I learned at fourteen and fifteen nuances about the working of Starfleet that some ensigns who have served under me were still only starting to learn.

I made these resources work for their suppers. With the single-minded intensity of the ambitious teen, I grilled these people not only about Starfleet, and contemporary thinking and strategizing about the Cardassian threat, but about how entrance to the Academy worked, what the tests were like, what the examiners were looking for. I was already specializing in sciences, and, quietly, with the guidance of my teachers, I began to take extra classes: contemporary galactic politics, advanced astrometrics, astral cartography, and so on. One weekend, when Dad was home, I presented him and Mom with the results from these and announced to them my intention to skip a year at school and go for entry into the Academy early.

Mom was not convinced. "This is so impressive, Katy, but what's the hurry?"

Dad didn't say anything. He just let me get on with making my case.

"I'm in a hurry because I know what I want, Mom. I can do the work—no, better than that, I can *excel* at the work. Why waste time?"

"I'm worried about burnout, that's all." Mom shot Dad a worried look. "This wasn't your idea, was it?"

"Nope," he said.

"Mom! This isn't anything to do with Dad! This is what I want!"

"What can we do, Gretchen?" Dad said. "I imagine if we said no, she'd just go off and do it anyway."

I nodded in furious agreement. I hadn't, in fact, thought of this, but now that the idea was in my head… Crafty Dad, huh?

"But you're right," he said, "about burnout. Kathryn, there's no point in being accepted at the Academy early if you're not able to function by the time you get there."

This, I had to admit, was true… I remembered that awful tennis match, and how badly I'd coped with being tired…

"How about we make a deal?" said Dad. "We let you start on this, but every eight weeks we take stock, and we discuss honestly whether it's working."

"That sounds good to me," I said quickly. I was sure I could convince them.

He held up a finger. "But Mom and I have the final veto."

I frowned.

"It's a good deal, Katy," he said. "And it's what's on the table."

I guessed—rightly—that this was part of the test. Did I know when to compromise? Did I recognize that I could get most of what I wanted if I was willing to give a little here and there? I stuck out my hand to Mom. "Deal?"

Mom took my hand and shook it. "Deal, Kathryn." She looked at Dad. "I hope you know what she's setting herself up for."

I remember now how sad he looked at that. "Gretchen," he said, "I know *exactly* what she's setting herself up for."

✦

So the deal was made. I would work like I'd never worked before, and I would aim to enter the Academy a year early. But at the first sight of overwork, or stress, or burnout, my parents would nix the whole idea. Good heavens, but I worked, and I wasn't going to skimp on extracurricular activities either. Every single minute of my day was scheduled: and I'll say now that this skill at timetabling that I developed at this point in my life stood me in good stead when the unhappy task fell to me of preparing ship duty rosters. (Not to mention that I was the kind of kid that loved a full-color three-dimensional organizational chart.) Everything was there: classes, private study time, and, of course, breaks. I meant to prove that I could do this, and that it wasn't going to burn me out.

The Cardassian War took ever-increasing prominence in our lives. I mention this because I think this happened in our family much sooner than with most others. My father's work obviously meant that we were more aware of what was happening along the border, and his increased absences meant that there was a genuine, direct, and piercing, impact upon our family. Around this time, my mother, aware of the suffering of the Bajoran people under the Occupation, began to get deeply involved in raising awareness of their plight within the Federation. By this point, the Occupation was long established, and the effects on the Bajoran people were becoming devastating. I remember sitting with her and Phoebe one evening (Dad was surely away), watching holo-images of a refugee center just within Federation space. Those images were dreadful; heartbreaking. I remember feeling Mom stiffen alongside me, as if she had come to some resolution. My mother was gentle, artistic, solitary—but she was not a shrinking violet, nor was she sentimental. She saw a terrible need, and a great injustice, and she did whatever was in her power to alleviate it.

Her public profile as a children's writer gave her a platform to speak, and she used it. For a woman who preferred to be at home, among familiar faces and places, this was a great sacrifice, although it was her consciousness of her great fortune in having all this that drove her. Many of the interviews she could give from her office at home, but speeches required her to be present in the hall to have the most impact, and she began to visit schools to explain the situation to children. How would they feel, to have to leave their homes? How would they feel, to lose track of family and friends? What could they do to help? There is a generation of Federation children who first came to awareness of the Bajoran Occupation through the picture books that my mother wrote at this time. Starfleet officers, specializing in humanitarian work, have told me that reading about the little girl, Amjo Jafia, leaving Ashalla to escape the Cardassians, and her journey to the refugee center on Metekis II, was the first crucial step toward them doing the kind of work that they did. I was so proud of her. I *am* so proud of her: my brilliant, gifted, fearless mother.

It might have been easy, in these circumstances, for Phoebe and me to form the idea that Cardassians were a species without any redeeming features. This is, of course, inaccurate—not to mention an insidious kind of racism— and Mom and Dad were scrupulously careful about how they spoke about Cardassians. I recall one or two conversations with university colleagues of Granny-in-town, specialists in Cardassian history and culture, who had many glowing things to say about Cardassian art and literature, and how it survived under difficult circumstances. I even read some, but I didn't understand much, and I didn't like it. Truth be told, it was many years before I saw Cardassians as individuals, as people who might be suffering on account of their own government as much as others. It was a lesson I learned in a hard place too… but I'll come back to that at the right time and place.

✦

My hard work paid off. By age fifteen, I had passed various exams and was well on track to graduate high school a year early; I also put my head down and started a two-year program of study to prepare for entrance to the Academy. The exams were notoriously difficult, and competitive, as were the psych tests. I meant to excel.

I don't want to leave you with the impression that all I did was study, although this naturally consumed a great deal of my energy at the time. My father, knowing that the years were coming to an end when we would be a family unit, made a point of taking a month of leave over the summer, and we had some fine holidays. Surely the most memorable was our tour of Europe: we visited Geneva, where they had met all those years ago, and my mother spoke to the Interplanetary Red Cross and Crescent about her work; we went up into the mountains, were Phoebe and I learned to ski; we saw Paris, and nearly lost Phoebe in the Louvre, and London, where the same nearly happened in the National Gallery; and then we went to Florence, where my passion for the life and works and sketches of Leonardo da Vinci was born. And the summer I turned sixteen, my father made good his promise and taught me to fly. I slipped the bonds of Earth and began my journey toward the stars.

But we all sensed that childhood was nearly over, and that my decision to enter the Academy a year early was hastening the day when family life as we had known it would come to an end. Perhaps some of this fed into the difficult relationship that Phoebe and I had at the time. She has said to me subsequently how she envied me being so close to getting away and leading my own life, while at the same time she resented that I was going, breaking up the happy home. Not to mention that my father's increased absences put a strain on how the family worked. We both knew that we had more in common with one parent than the other: Mom and Phoebe shared passions for arts and activism; Dad and I were peas in a pod. With my father away so often, I sometimes felt like the odd one out, and Phoebe and I were often typical teenage siblings, quarreling and bickering at the slightest provocation. It must have driven my poor mother mad!

Eventually, our sulks and quarrels ended in an honest-to-goodness blowup on my part. I would like to point out that at the time I was midway through studying for entrance to the Academy, and so perhaps I was more than usually stressed. I had taken a break from study and come down into the kitchen to get a drink and a snack. I brought some notes with me, thinking that I might sit in the kitchen for a while for a change of scene. I put the notes on the table, and then went outside for a breath of fresh air. When I came back inside, I found Phoebe, mopping the kitchen table, a guilty look on her face.

"Don't shout at me, Kate," she said.

I saw my pile of notes. They were covered in paint. My beautiful, hard-worked notes…

Well, I blew my top. "You stupid, careless, selfish little *brat*—!"

"It was an *accident*!" yelled Phoebe. "Why did you even *bring* them down here?"

Mother had to raise her voice to get us to stop—something never heard in our house. And I would not be placated. I packed my little bag and marched off to my grandparents' house across the fields, announcing my intention to remain in their attic until I'd passed these damn exams or the damn exams killed me. My grandparents—presumably forewarned by my mother that I was on my way over—didn't even blink.

"Bed's made, Katy," said Grandma.

"Get yourself set up," said Grandpa. "I'll bring you a coffee."

And that was that: I settled into that space, and put my head down to prepare for the entrance exams, and Grandpa, bringing up regular trays of snacks and drinks to get me through all-day and late-night study sessions, helped establish my addiction to coffee. Thanks, Grandpa. It might not sound like it, but I'm supremely grateful.

This whole period culminated in a three-day assessment at the Academy: written tests, psych evaluations, group exercises, interviews with panels, and interviews with individuals. Everything—all my hard work—narrowed down to three grueling days. Mom offered to take me there, but I knew she hated being away from home, and Granddad-in-town came up with me instead. A good choice on my part: I would have fretted about Mom, but Granddad-in-town was always cheerful, and he knew the area well, and always managed to find a good place to have dinner in the evenings. By the end of the third day, I was exhausted. I had no idea how well I'd done. Some of the other candidates were in their late teens, or even their early twenties, and had come to Academy entrance after study or travels or volunteer work. I had felt achingly young in comparison. After the last day, I went back to the apartment where Granddad-in-town and I were staying, fell on the bed, and *howled* into the pillow. Granddad, bless him, had predicted this letdown, and had spent the day making the best curry I have ever eaten in my life. The next day he took me on a tour of San Francisco, showing me his student haunts.

"You'll need to know these places," he said. He at least had no doubt where I'd be the following year. I was no longer able to tell.

✦

I came back to Indiana, spent a week mostly asleep in the attic at Grandpa and Grandma's house, and then I went back home. Results were due eight weeks later, and I had no idea what to do with all this free time. I sat and watched Phoebe paint and wondered when she had got so good, and whether anyone had noticed. I took old Jess for a few walks, but from the way she sighed when she saw me and hauled herself up, I got the impression that my lovely old dog was humoring me and would much rather have been snoozing in the sunshine. I wondered what I would do, if I wasn't successful this time around, and I decided that I would get some real experience, like those confident young people that I had met. I'd go out to one of those centers on the Cardassian border and work with Bajoran refugees.

Somehow, Dad managed to get home the night before my results were expected. I tried to sleep in—I had a whole morning to fill, of course, since San Francisco was on Pacific time; Bloomington on Eastern. But I was up by eight o'clock. Everyone tiptoed around me like they were walking on eggshells. I drank a strong cup of coffee and nibbled at some toast. I sat out in the hammock and cuddled Jess. I read one of Mom's books. But at last, at 11:00

a.m., the family communicator beeped with an incoming message. The others let me go over.

To my surprise, there were two messages: one for Ms Kathryn Margaret Janeway; one for Ms Phoebe Teresa Janeway. I forwarded Phoebe's to her personal comm, stared at the Starfleet seal on my message, opened it, and read.

"Well, Kathryn?" my father said, after a minute or two.

I cleared my throat. "Dad," I said. "I'm in."

He came to read the message. "You're not just in, Katy," he said. "You've been commended on your excellent results, and on your performance in one of the group exercises." I felt his arm squeeze my shoulder. "Oh Katy," he said, his voice breaking slightly. "I'm so proud of you."

I turned to look at Mom, and that's when Phoebe said, "Holy moly. They're going to show one of my pictures at the Met."

✦

Never has thunder been so effectively stolen. Honestly, I could have strangled her! Yes, my baby sister—at *fourteen*—had placed one of her damn pictures at a damn exhibition at the damn Met and had chosen the day of my early acceptance at Starfleet to receive the damn news! Well, I bit my tongue, and bottled it up, but it was always bound to explode. We spent a day with Mom and Grandma, preparing for a big party to celebrate our successes, both of us stewing. As the family started to arrive, we both dashed upstairs to get changed. I couldn't find a necklace I wanted. I went storming into Phoebe's room, where I found the thing on her dressing table.

I snatched it up. "Phoebe, you're *impossible*!"

"Kate, you haven't worn the thing in *years*."

"You're a *damned pain in the neck*!"

"You're not such great shakes yourself, you know—"

"Honestly—"

"If you could only imagine what it's like having you as a big sister, *Kitten*!"

"If you could only imagine what it's like having you as a little sister, *Feebs*!"

And then, my word, it all came pouring out! I told her just what I thought about this latest stunt of hers; always having to steal the limelight from *any* achievement that I managed, always trying to get one over me; Mom's favorite little girl; and she told me exactly what she thought of me, oh yes, the big sister, one step ahead, the apple of Dad's eye, always game for another road trip or a night in a stupid tent… You know, we were on the verge of thumping each other. We were all ready to restage the fight from the end of *The Quiet Man* when there was a tap on the door. We both shut up.

The door swung open. There, framed in the light of the hall lamp, stood Grandma, possibly our most formidable relative. She took a good long look at us, her eyes narrowed. She knew *exactly* what was going on in here.

"Young ladies," she said, "when you're ready, the rest of the family would like to toast your successes."

She left. We stared guiltily at each other.

One of us—can't remember which one—began to laugh. That set the other off. We collapsed on each other, in fits of helpless giggles. From the stairs, Grandma called, in her sternest voice, *"Ladies!"*

That nearly set us both off again. Stifling our laughter, clutching each other's hands, we ran downstairs, where we both graciously accepted the congratulations from our aunts and uncles and all the rest, and Dad made a very nice little speech. Later, each clutching a glass of champagne, my sister and I convened out on the porch. We both looked at each other and burst out laughing.

"Did you *see* Grandma's face?"

"I thought she was going to roast us *alive!*"

We laughed on for a while, and then I said, "You know I'll always have your back, don't you, Phoebe?"

"Back atcha, sis."

I lifted my glass to her. "Cheers, Feebs," I said.

She clinked her glass against mine. "Cheers, Kitten," she said.

Phoebe, I think we agreed years ago that I was a beast and you were a brat, and that neither of us would have it any other way. Little sister, you're brilliant. You take the arts, and I'll take the sciences, and together we'll conquer the world.

CHAPTER THREE

AT EASE, CADET—2353-2357

I WENT TO THE ACADEMY AT THE TENDER AGE OF SEVENTEEN, a full year younger than most of the rest of my freshman classmates. The first couple of weeks were a blur. Everything was a rush of new names: names of the other new cadets, names of professors, names of classes… Then there was all the new information: sorting out timetables, signing up for extra credit, taking up a whole new slew of extracurricular activities, and, of course, socializing. There were so many interesting new people and more species than I had ever seen before. Sometimes it seemed that every second I encountered something new. This was why I had joined Starfleet—and this was just the Academy! Imagine what the real thing would be like.

I ended up in the lower half of the room ballot, which meant that I was sharing a room. I didn't mind: it seemed like a good way to make a friend. As I had hoped would be the case, I hit it off immediately with my roommate, a quietly dry and extremely funny Betazoid named Nexa Ochiva who was specializing in xenolinguistics, and who persuaded me along to a huge number of extra lectures that I might not otherwise have even been aware of. Nexa came from a large family and knew how to share a room with someone else: we didn't encroach on each other's space, and, after a while, even our work patterns fell into sync. Thinking back now to those days, I smile to recall her quiet sigh, the signal for one of us to stand up and make a fresh pot of coffee.

We would then join each other to sit in the beaten-up armchairs in the middle of the room, and grumble about the latest set of problems in our astrometrics classes. Nexa and I remained good friends. We kept in touch during our various postings right up until *Voyager* was lost. It was one of the saddest pieces of news that I received on my return from the Delta Quadrant to learn that she had been killed during the latter stages of the Dominion War. I made it back to the Alpha Quadrant in time for our twenty-first annual reunion. There were a number of sad losses to our class, but Nexa's was the one that hit me hardest.

Back to those early days. I worked out quickly that being the junior Janeway at Starfleet could cut both ways. On the one hand, I was keenly aware that what I did—for good or ill—inevitably reflected on my father. He had made a point of saying to me that I should not consider this—but I knew that others did. I worried too, given my comparative youth, that any failure or lapse would make people assume that I had won my place through his influence, rather than on my own merit. It's a difficult situation to be in, and one that gives me some sympathy to others who are children of flag officers, following in the wake of successful and respected older relatives. My relationship with my own father was supportive, but I was still acutely conscious of his success ahead of me, and I did feel that I needed to prove that I was there because I deserved to be.

On the other hand, my familiarity with Starfleet procedure and protocol undoubtedly gave me a head start over many others. Such things were second nature: Phoebe and I had been present at many formal events from as soon as we were capable of attending without kicking up a storm. There were other benefits too, some of which I hadn't predicted but proved among the most useful. For example, Mom, Phoebe, and I had often come up to San Francisco to visit Dad, and sometimes Granddad-in-town liked to tag along to visit his old haunts, see old friends, and show us the sights. Thanks to him, I knew shortcuts, places to hang out, and, in general, campus felt like a familiar place rather than bewildering. Almost an extension of home. That kind of local knowledge is helpful in your first weeks (as long as you don't show off): it gives you confidence, and it's a genuine help to your new friends to be able to tell them how to find the seminar room they're anxiously hunting.

With Nexa as company and my first friend, I settled quickly in my room. I sometimes missed my home and family so much that I felt almost queasy with longing for them, while simultaneously luxuriating in the fact that I was an adult at last. Sure, the schedules of classes and other activities meant that the days were still thoroughly timetabled (very much like school), but otherwise my life was mine to lead as I chose: where and what I ate; whether or not to work on free days; how to spend my evenings, and who with. Nexa had a knack for one-to-one conversations, making people feel special and welcome. I was great with groups, making people feel like they were part of a great gang. The combination worked. We soon acquired a large group of friends, and a favored spot to meet for study and socializing. This was a coffee house slightly off the beaten track that Grandad-in-town had spied while we were in San Francisco for the entrance exams. It was called the Night Owl. You reached it via a shortcut behind the parrises squares courts: there was a gap in the hedge there (I assume this had been left there deliberately, out of pity for sleep-deprived cadets anxious to get their caffeine fix; the academy groundskeeper, Boothby, as you shall learn shortly, would certainly not have missed a gap in the hedge), then snuck two blocks along a back street, and there it was. Somewhat shabby, large enough for many tables where groups of cadets hunkered down to study or else irritate the life out of friends who were trying to study and didn't want to listen to your idle chatter. The Night Owl served the third-best coffee I have ever tasted. (For the record, the best was the espressos I drank on that family holiday in Italy; the second best was the cup I had on arriving back in the Alpha Quadrant. By any general standards, that was not a great cup of coffee but… Oh, the smell! The taste! Nirvana!)

Coursework was a heavy burden, but I stuck at it, and I did well in classes. In part, this was because I was playing to my strengths, specializing in the sciences, and also taking classes and lectures to help me onto the command track once I had enough experience under my belt (I have always enjoyed giving orders). In part, to give myself credit, this is because I worked damn hard! I didn't want to let myself or my father down; I wanted to be the best I possibly could be… and I also didn't want to miss out on anything. Nexa, knowing that I was fascinated with first-contact scenarios, persuaded me to come along to an advanced communications course run by Professor Hendricks, where each week was devoted to learning from scratch a nonverbal form of communication. This was my first introduction to gestural languages, including ASL, and chromolinguistics. I know that one or two of my professors looked askance at my taking yet another extra class, not least as my conversational Klingon remained something of a joke, but the principles I learned in that class turned out to be of huge benefit in the Delta Quadrant: how to grasp rapidly the fundamentals of a language, and use that knowledge to make grounded extrapolations about the culture within which that language was used. The Delta Quadrant was a baptism of fire as far as first-contact scenarios went: we were flying by the seat of our pants in so many ways. That extra class came in handy many times.

As ever, I tended to take on a great deal, probably slightly too much, often burning the candle at both ends and pulling all-nighters to get through study commitments while maintaining my social life. I did get a note from Dad, toward the end of my first year, that said: "Remember to rest. A Starfleet officer cannot survive on caffeine alone." And I had not forgotten our conversation after the dreadful tennis match, and I decided I should try to find a way to relax. The Academy grounds proved a godsend here, as I think they have for many overworked cadets, not least because being in the garden reminded me of home, and my mother. One summer afternoon, tired after a long morning's seminar on fractal calculus, and fretting about the forthcoming exam (Patterson's exams were the stuff of nightmares), I found myself sitting in the garden, simply trying to *be*...

My eyes closed, but still I couldn't rest. All I could see were those damn equations, flashing in front of me: fractals, never-ending, always getting deeper and deeper with no resolution... I was *dreading* the test... And then I heard a voice.

"Patterson," the voice said.

I opened my eyes and found myself looking at a small, white-haired man whose gnarled face and hands suggested to me that he spent a lot of time outside. A veritable garden gnome.

"I beg your pardon?" I said.

"You," said the gnome, "have the look of someone who is currently studying under Patterson."

I stared at him. "How did you guess that?"

He smiled. "I've seen a lot of cadets come and go over the years," he said. "I get used to their worries. And I know that the biggest worry for first years on the command track is passing Patterson's fractal calculus class, and I also know that the exam is coming up soon. Am I correct, Cadet Janeway?"

Maybe it was because I was still half-asleep, but I was starting to get very bewildered by this whole encounter. It was as if I'd woken up in a strange enchanted land—Narnia, perhaps, or my beloved Oz—and had found myself in conversation with a magician, who could read my mind and saw all my worries.

"Who *are* you?" I said.

"My name," he said, "is Boothby."

That broke the spell—a little. My father had mentioned Boothby, so had Granddad-in-town. Yes, I knew who this was—not a sorcerer or enchanter, but the gardener! I should clarify this—Boothby was not simply a gardener, but the head groundskeeper at the Academy and, given the size of the campus, this was a significant responsibility. How long had he been there? I don't think anyone knows for sure.

"You've heard of me, I think," he said. "And I hear your mother likes roses."

I was amazed. Dad had said that Boothby knew everything about everyone, but this was pretty specialist knowledge. "How on earth did you know that?"

"I keep my ears open," he said. He peered at me. I know that look well: it's the one given by officers when they're assessing whether you're fit for a task. It's a look I've given myself over the years. "Yes," he said. "I think you'll come in handy."

"Come in handy—?"

He started to walk away. "In the rose garden, of course," he said. "Come along, Cadet!"

Well, I did what I was told. Boothby had this way about him… Next thing I knew, I was hard at work in the rose garden. How he persuaded me of this, I'll never know: you'll recall that I wasn't much one for messing around in the mud. Still, you didn't grow up with my mother—or, indeed, on a farm—without knowing how to find your way about a garden, so I daresay I did come in handy. After an hour or so, Boothby stood up, grunted in satisfaction, and said, "Good work, Cadet. You'll do very well. I'll expect you back here same time tomorrow."

And then he headed off across the garden, before I could open my mouth to protest. I looked after him in horror. I didn't have time to come and play in the garden! I had work to do; I had a goddamn fractal calculus exam with goddamn Patterson to goddamn pass! Still, the next afternoon, I didn't think of disobeying. I left my friends in the Night Owl, saying something vague about an errand, and I went and spent a quiet hour in the garden, under Boothby's watchful eye. And oh, what a blessing it turned out to be! A rest for my poor overworked brain; a real balm for the soul! Just that hour, once a day, doing nothing but using my hands and letting myself get away from my studies—it made all the difference. I found my focus got better; my concentration improved. And when the roses began to bloom, there were fresh flowers in my room every morning, courtesy of Boothby himself, as a thank you, so the man said, for my hard work. Nexa appreciated them too: she loved roses. When I finally did take the fractal calculus exam, not one of Patterson's fiendish tricks could discompose me, and I did one of the best papers he'd seen. So thank you, Boothby, for helping me, as I know you have helped thousands of stressed cadets before me, and thousands after me, to get things back into proportion, and for all the wondrous roses.

At the end of the year, my marks in general were excellent: I was hardly outside of the top one percent, even in my weaker subjects. Altogether, when I packed up my room for the summer, and headed back to Indiana for a couple weeks, I was proud of what I had achieved. I could justly feel that I was at the Academy on my own merits, and not because of favors shown to me on my father's account. But boy—was I ready for a break!

Going home that summer, even for so short a period, was an odd experience. I was glad to be back with my family, back in familiar places, but everything seemed smaller than I remembered. Messages I received from Academy friends told me that this was a common feeling, as if we had in that year outgrown our childhood homes. Still, I was glad of the rest. I was glad to enjoy Grandma's cooking once again, and Grandpa's strong black coffee. Most of all, I'm glad to say, I loved being back with Phoebe. If our quarrel had cleared the air between us, my absence for all those months had sealed the deal: we didn't want to waste the time we had together on our old competition for attention; we wanted to be friends and counselors. Her art studies were progressing incredibly well; more and more she was exploring sculpture as her primary form, although I have to say that her watercolors and drawings of our locality—its wildlife, its landscape, not to mention its characters—were a huge joy for me. She was working on building a portfolio for entry to the Vulcan Academy of Art, with an eye on postgraduate work at an arts school on Trill. It was a pleasure to discuss her work with her, to see her increasing understanding of material form. What we both found interesting was how much my engineering interests overlapped with her hands-on approach to her artistic practice. It's easy to say that we were opposites, but the real pleasure for me—and, so Phoebe tells me, for her—was finding how much we had in common.

That short break was tinged with sadness, however, as we said goodbye to my lovely Jess. She was old now—fifteen—and she slept most of the time. When I walked through the door, she lifted her head and thumped her tail at me, saying "hello," and I had one more week with my old companion, sitting with her in the sunshine as I read and rested, and she lay beside me. I think she was waiting for me to come home again, because one morning, a week after I arrived, she didn't wake up. I cried a great deal, and together Mom and Phoebe and I buried her in the garden, near the roses. My lovely Jess. I knew that given that I was heading into Starfleet, I would be taking posts onboard ship that were going to keep me away for long periods of time. I was not likely to get another dog for many, many years, and I knew the next one would have to be special. I was right there. Saying farewell to Jess felt at the time like the end of childhood for me.

Then it was time to say goodbye to the old homestead once again. I had an internship that summer in the office of Councilor T'Lan (don't get too excited: mostly it was answering correspondence, although I did get some insight into the ongoing Bajoran refugee crisis); also a group of us were going hiking through the Andes. (My parents said, "Aren't you supposed to be having a rest?") And then, before I knew it, I was back at the Academy for my second year. More of the same—only more of it. Much more. More work, more exams, more coffee, and more fun, as much as I could possibly fit in between everything else. Time in the garden, decompressing, simply being among the roses. More and more complex equations, more and more complex command scenarios. They say about the Academy that the individual moments—as you're trying to get a piece of written work done, or you're fretting about a forthcoming test—pass extremely slowly, but that the months fly by. It's true. Before I knew it, the second year and the second summer were over, and I was heading back for the second half of my Academy career. It struck all of us, heading back for our third year, that we were on the downward slope.

In the third year at the Academy, the nature of your studies alters somewhat. The number of large lecture classes gets fewer and fewer, and the barrage of in-class tests and end-of-semester exams reduces. Instead, you find yourself in smaller seminar groups and, if you're on the command track, as I was, you do more and more practice scenarios. I did not fail to notice how many of these involved encounters with Cardassian ships. By this point, the border conflicts that we now call the Federation–Cardassian War were well established and showed no sign of slowing down. Our tutors were preparing us for this conflict. There were some practical additions, for example, field medicine and surgery courses. I have certainly used these in my later career (not to mention the memory-training techniques we were taught in H'ohk's physiology classes). This background rumble of potential conflict was something we were all keenly aware of, and I recall numerous late-night conversations among friends, as we pondered what it might be like on the battlefield.

Life was full, and busy, and we were far enough away from graduating to be able to put aside our worries for a little while. By this point, I felt that I had the right balance, combining studies and my social life, and keeping at or near the top of my classes, getting downtime in the gardens. As long as nothing happened to disrupt my equilibrium…

Naturally, this was the moment I chose to fall in love.

✦

What can I say? I was still only nineteen years old; gregarious, yes, but I was still very inexperienced when it came to romance. I concealed my tender heart beneath an outgoing demeanor and being part of the gang. I think it was inevitable that when I fell in love, I fell hard.

Let's leave names behind; that wouldn't be appropriate. Suffice to say that the object of my admiration was what Granny-in-town would call "a fine figure of a man"; a rugged sort who exuded physical confidence. I thought he was gorgeous. He was a friend of a friend of a friend who came along to the Night Owl one afternoon and found himself sitting next to me. We talked about the Grand Canyon and worked through the equations for our advanced spatial engineering class (he was taking the same course, but in a different seminar group). We agreed to meet for dinner later that week. After that, we were inseparable.

I grasped fairly quickly that Nexa was ambivalent toward him, and I have to say that I was not pleased. My first serious beau; surely my best friend should be delighted for me? About three weeks into the relationship, I remember a very unhappy conversation—no, let's call it what it was, an outright argument—between me and Nexa. She said she didn't trust him; I told her she was jealous that he was taking up all my time. It's hard to come back from that one, and things became briefly frosty between us. After a few days, we tentatively made up (you can't live in a shared room with a cold war, and, besides, she was my *friend*), but I could see that as long as I was with my beau, she was not going to be happy.

I had no intention of giving up this one. He made me feel desirable, and that was not something that Kate Janeway had felt much in her life so far. I was outgoing, a good sport, active, and more than a little tomboyish. Boys were friends, not lovers. I was beside myself with joy that I had attracted someone like this—and that made Nexa's reaction even more upsetting. But I was eager for him to meet my family, and I invited him home for a few days during the winter break. That was another huge disappointment.

The whole family was there: my father had leave, and Phoebe had managed to get back from Trill, where she was on a graduate arts fellowship that year. I was so excited to introduce my boyfriend to them. Oh dear. It was plain within a couple of hours that they did not like him, my father most of all. Oh, he made polite conversation—friendly conversation too; this was a young cadet, after all—but I could tell. After his visit was over, and he went back to his own family, I confronted my father.

"Not good enough for your darling daughter, hey, Dad?"

He didn't rise to my bait. "Katy, this is your life, and I'm not going to interfere."

I was furious. "Dad! That's not an answer!"

"I'm not going to dictate who you should and shouldn't see," he said. "But no. I don't like him."

"Why not?"

"He's a taker, Kathryn. He won't give you what you need. He won't give anyone what they need."

Just on departure he had given me a beautiful pendant. I showed this to my father. "How can you say that?"

"Oh, sure, he'll be good with gifts. He certainly puts on a good show."

"Dad, that's not fair—"

"But he's a taker. You've spent half your holiday helping him with his coursework—"

"I don't mind!"

"Well, you should. He's the kind of ensign that I would get off my ship as quickly as possible. He's the kind of ensign that I wouldn't put anywhere except behind a desk. I wouldn't put my life in his hands."

I stalked out of the room. I took my woes to Phoebe, but I could see that even my beloved sister was finding it hard to be supportive. "You know Dad," she said, rather lamely.

I was shocked. "You don't like him either, do you?"

She struggled to find the right words. "It's not me that has to like him, Kate."

What was the right response to this familial ambivalence? Naturally I dug in my heels. I went back to the Academy after the break determined to stick with this relationship through thick and thin, and I would make it a huge success. That would show them! We spent most of that year together, living in each other's pockets, and if I found that I was doing more and more of his advanced engineering papers and seeing much less of my friends, I didn't admit this to myself.

Six months to the day after our first meeting, we went out for dinner, traveling all the way to Paris. It was very romantic. A violinist came past, and my beau brought out a ring. A ruby.

Like a fool, I said, "Hey, anyone would think you were about to ask me to marry you!" I burst out laughing. I stopped when I realized he wasn't joining in.

What followed was even more painful. Because he was, of course, asking me to marry him, and I'd taken the wind out of his sails. He didn't like that, I could see. We were off to a bad start, although after a moment or two he began to get back into his groove. He had prepared a speech, you see, in which he laid out his plans for us. He wanted to marry me as soon as we graduated, and he wanted us to set up home right away. He'd had a bright idea. The idea was that I put my career on hold for a while so we could "do the family thing," and once he had his command, I could get back to my career.

I listened to him talk and I drank my glass of wine. I felt like someone waking up from a dream; not a nightmare, that wouldn't be fair, because he really was very handsome, and we really did have a good time, most of the time.

"What do you say, Kit?" He always called me that. I don't know where he'd got it from. Suddenly it struck me as deeply annoying.

I put down my wine glass. "Here's an idea," I said. "You put *your* career on hold, and when I have my command, you can get back to your career."

Oh, his face. He was outraged. He opened his mouth to reply, but before he could, I had stood up. I leaned over the table to kiss his cheek, for old times' sake, and I said, "Thank you. It's been fun." And I left and walked back through the streets of Paris to the nearest transporter, and I was back in my room at the Academy within the hour and talking to Phoebe over the comm.

"You'll never guess what just happened to me," I said.

"I hope you shoved that ruby where the sun doesn't shine," she said, when I told her. A huge cheer for my sister, my best ally. Talking it through with her that night, I realized I wasn't as upset about the whole thing as I thought I might be. I guess I'd known on some level that my friends and my family were right, and that this wasn't going anywhere. I won't deny it took a while to bounce back from the whole business: my confidence took a blow, and I found it hard to trust for a while afterward. But at least I had the good sense to get away when I did, and I'd only wasted six months. I could have wasted years. I could have wasted my career. The next morning, I caught up with Nexa, told her what had happened, and said sorry.

"Oh, Kate! There's nothing to apologize for! He was *very* handsome!"

Yes, he was; but he really wasn't right for me.

There's a side note to this which I should mention; after my conversation with my sister, and with her encouragement, I finally got around to doing what all my female friends and relatives did at some point: I had some eggs frozen. Well, a girl has got to think ahead, hasn't she?

✦

My third-year grades took only a small hit from this distraction, I am very glad to say, and I was not outside of the tenth percentile, but that wasn't good enough for me. I came back to my final year intent on getting as close to the top as possible. Our fourth and final year continued the smaller group seminars, role shadowing, and holodeck scenarios of the year before, as well as a significant amount of outdoor training. We were also assigned a mentor, and I was beyond lucky to find myself come under the wise protection of

Admiral Parvati Pandey. In my final term, Pandey invited me along to her Ethics of Command sessions. If she gave you this invitation you took it: it was a sign that you were being taken very seriously for command. That final term was crammed, but whatever else you had on, you found the time to go along to these discussions.

We were a small group, half a dozen of us, and the meetings took place at Pandey's home, in a large office whose huge windows looked over her beautiful garden. A lot of that final year at the Academy passed so quickly—cadets are conscious that the clock is now ticking—but those sessions remain strong in my memory. We grappled with questions of honor, integrity, loyalty, candor; how to know when an order was a bad order; what to do about that. We talked about respecting the ethics of other civilizations while upholding our own values of diversity and openness. We discussed the ethics of war; how to comport yourself in a combat zone; how to command in a combat zone. We talked about the trolley problem, and the principle of utility, and means and ends. I am grateful to Parvati Pandey for this space she gave us as we shifted from the protected world of the Academy to the real world of ship life. After I had my turn on the *Kobayashi Maru*, Pandey came to me and praised me for my grace under fire. "Don't forget this, Kathryn," she said. "This is a lesson about courage in the face of overwhelming odds."

She was a fine teacher. I'd like to think I learned well from her. I'd like to think I made her proud.

✦

One final memory of my time at the Academy, since I believe this episode has earned its spot in the legends of the place, and that is no mean feat when you consider the people who have passed through there as cadets. There was an informal custom—certainly not a custom sanctioned by the authorities—for the outgoing students to play some kind of grand prank to celebrate their imminent release. After many years of some very inventive young people coming up with ever more baroque ideas, it was our turn to think up something impressive. Flash mobs weren't our style; sowing wildflower seeds around companels seemed more in the line of a protest than a prank; dyeing the lake pink was an old one and far too easy. The nexus of students who formed to take up this task wanted a challenge. We wanted to do something that would never be forgotten. We succeeded.

I had, for various reasons, been reading about prisoners of war, and the kinds of schemes they came up with not only in their attempts to escape their confinement, but to fill the hours and prevent despair and boredom setting in. Digging a tunnel didn't seem much in the way of fun, so when our "escape committee" was formed to pull our stunt, I suggested something else. I'd been reading a very detailed account of some prisoners of war who had been held in central Europe, during the last big war of the pre-Atomic Age (the war that ushered in the Atomic Age, in fact). They were prisoners who had a reputation for repeated escape attempts: their captors, in exasperation, decided to lock them all up together—in a huge castle perched up on a cliff, no less! There was some wisdom to this idea—you had them all in one place, for example, where you could keep an eye on them. At the same time, you found that you had put all the most reckless, crackpot, and stubborn eccentrics in one place. They were not going to give up until they had made a home run. Reminds me of *Voyager*, now that I think about it.

These guys just kept the ideas coming—with limited success, it has to be said, but then the point was to keep everyone busy: themselves, to stave off boredom, and their guards, never entirely able to relax. There were various attempts to get out using disguises: in uniforms stolen from their captors, or else, inevitably, in drag. A smaller man hid himself in a tea chest, and, of course, there were several tunnels. The cliff beneath that castle must have been Swiss cheese by the end of that war. But I had another of their plans in mind. Two of the men held there were pilots, and they decided to build a glider. Once I read about this... Well, what else was my graduating class supposed to do? I put it to the committee, and they looked at me as if I had lost my mind, and then somebody started to laugh, and the next person began to laugh, and I saw in their eyes what I had been thinking: *We've got it!*

We used the plans that those two men had devised, and we decided to use the same tools that they had used. As a matter of principle—and bearing in mind that they somehow had to lay their hands on all this material—we decided not to replicate anything. The rummage shops of downtown San Francisco did good business that year, but do you have any idea how hard it is to find a gramophone spring? As for the prison sheets used to skin the thing, and the ration millet that those men used to seal up the pores of the sheets... Who knew porridge had so many uses?

There were times I thought we weren't going to be able to do it. As for finding a place where we could hide this thing while we built it... Let's just say in return for some extra labor, Boothby turned a blind eye on what was happening in one of the larger garden sheds. Eventually, we had it: a two-hundred-and-forty-pound, two-seater, high-wing glider. The day before our exam results were due to be announced, and in the dead of night, we hauled the beast across to the library, and up onto the roof. The next morning, as our year group gathered in the main campus square, finding solidarity in each other before learning their individual fates, my copilot and I launched our beautiful machine over their heads, landing it with perfect precision just beside the lake to rapturous applause.

It's not a final-year prank if you don't get hauled up before the president of the Academy, and indeed we were, and I took responsibility as the main architect and chief ringleader of the scheme. I looked the president in the eye and said, "And I'm proud of it, ma'am. We've shown initiative, technical skill, a substantial amount of guile, and we've fitted it all in around exam season. I think our final grades will speak for themselves."

I could see that she was having a hard time not laughing, and I knew we'd get away with it (more or less), not least because we were leaving campus the following week, and there weren't that many sanctions they could impose. Besides, we'd excelled ourselves. I'm about as proud of that glider as I am of just about anything else I did at the Academy, and given how often my father told the story afterward, I'm pretty certain he was proud of me too. All this time later, looking back on the whole escapade, I'll add that our make-do-and-mend approach to sourcing the materials we needed came in damn handy on *Voyager*.

✦

I graduated in the top four of my year (that means fourth, of course), and I was grateful for and pleased with this result. The people ahead of me were stellar students: you could see that they were going on to early commands. All three of them were decorated for valor during the Dominion War, although only two of them survived that war. Those two have gone on to great things at

Starfleet Command, and one of them is surely in line to become commander-in-chief. Alongside these stars, I was content that I had shone to the very best of my ability. I had done my father and my grandfather proud; most of all, I had done myself proud. There could be no question now that I had not earned my place at the Academy. Now I had to prove myself worthy of Starfleet—and worthy of command.

The powers that be stage these last couple of weeks very well. After the officially unsanctioned prank came the exam results, and then there were a couple of days to enjoy the feeling of elation (or come to terms with the disappointment) before the graduation ceremony itself. We partied hard that year, I have to say; that's the kind of class we were. Everything got our full attention and our best effort. Besides, we knew that we weren't in for an easy ride. The Cardassian border conflicts dragged on, and our graduating class knew that it was going to see active service straight out of the door in a way that previous years had not. Exploration would have to wait.

Graduation came and went, with my whole family present (Phoebe decided not to steal my thunder this time around), and then came the serious business as we learned our first postings. This is a major rite of passage for every newly graduated cadet. We all gather in our brand-new dress uniforms, and our new assignments are formally announced. This is tough if you didn't get the grades; it's even tougher if you did well but you've not got the posting your heart was set on. I saw a few brave faces being put on that day, when assignments turned out to be station personnel or desk jobs. But I wasn't disappointed. I had been assigned a junior science officer's post on the *U.S.S. Al-Batani*, serving under one of the most respected men in Starfleet: Captain Owen Paris. He was going to be a significant presence in my life from here on, in ways I hadn't entirely anticipated.

But I'm getting ahead of myself! What about my other friends, my gang? We all ended up where we wanted to be. My copilot on the glider got a test-pilot placing out at Utopia Planitia: he was beside himself with delight. And my dear friend Nexa took up the analyst's posting she wanted with Starfleet Intelligence. We were a happy band of brothers and sisters, and the party lasted the rest of the week. After that, we all departed, with promises to stay in touch and meet again. And those of us who could—we've kept that promise, and we've never forgotten the ones who couldn't keep it.

Some of you might be wondering how that ex-boyfriend did. I didn't ask and I'm glad to say that nobody took the time or trouble to tell. I guess he graduated; I didn't hear that anyone had failed or been asked to repeat the year. I must have heard them read out his first posting, but I've forgotten what it was. Strange though; his name cropped up last year, fourth in the list of authors on a report I was reading. So I do know one thing: he never did make captain.

CHAPTER FOUR

CHILDHOOD'S END—2357-2358

"ENSIGN KATHRYN JANEWAY, REPORTING FOR DUTY, MA'AM!"

It was my first day of my first posting, and I was shaking in my shiny boots, and tugging away at the cuffs of my stiff uniform. My new direct superior, Lieutenant Commander Flora Kristopher, the *Al-Batani*'s chief science officer, was waiting in the transporter room to welcome me on board, leaning against the console. She looked at me steadily, and—bless her—did not smile at my overseriousness and formality, but simply said, "Welcome aboard, Ensign. Please don't call me 'ma'am.' Makes me sound fifty years older."

I blushed bright red. "Sorry… Commander!" (He won't thank me for this, but I can't help but recall a certain Ensign Harry Kim, so keen to make a good impression on his new captain in our first meeting that I thought he was going to strain something. Don't worry, Harry. We've all been there.)

Kristopher gave me a lopsided smile, pushed herself up from the console and nodded to me that I should follow her. I snapped to it. I was desperate to make a good impression. I trotted at her heels as she gave me a rapid tour of the ship, introducing me to various other officers, senior and junior. They were all friendly; one or two invited me to the mess hall for a drink once I was off shift. I gratefully accepted, muttering their names, ranks, and specialisms under my breath as we went on so that I wouldn't forget them. After about an hour of this, Kristopher said, "Relax, Janeway. This is home now. Keep up this level of intensity much longer and I'm going to have to go for a lie-down."

I blushed again. "Sorry, Commander. I'll try and take it a little easier."

"Good. Don't worry, Janeway. You're going to do fine."

Kristopher was a supremely talented officer, who gave the appearance of being very laid back, but who never missed a thing. She had an enviable gift for being able to come up to speed rapidly in hugely technical subjects, ideal for a chief science officer, who frequently finds herself having to offer expert advice in fields well beyond her specialisms. Kristopher's own area of study was sustainable xenoagronomy. She had grown up on Mars, on one of the terraformed colonies, and so had early experience of experimenting with crops growing under less than propitious circumstances. By this stage in her career, numerous colony worlds had benefited from various technical advances she had made in soil science. My mother, learning that I would be serving under her, was incredibly excited. I had been instructed to get advice on a new rose hybrid she was trying to grow. Kristopher, in her turn, was delighted to discover that my mother was *that* Gretchen Williams: she had, so she told me, been inspired toward her field by an early encounter with her stories for *The Adventures of Flotter*. (I have to say that I thought it would be my father's name that went before me on my first Starfleet posting, not my mother's.)

Flora Kristopher was a fine mentor to have at this stage of my career. She was patient with mistakes born from inexperience, tough on mistakes born from sloppiness, and more than usually able to spot the difference. The only way to get on her bad side was to point out the nominative determinism of her first name. My word, she hated that. She must have heard it almost every day of her adult life. I am eternally grateful that another new ensign made this mistake before I did. I've never seen a young man so thoroughly cut down to size. Under Kristopher's guidance, I flourished, and I started to gain confidence—which is, after all, exactly what a newly minted officer needs at this stage of her career. I thought about her constantly when I had junior staff of my own, when I tried to instill this same kind of confidence: trusting their judgement but always having a backup plan in case their inexperience let them down.

I was lucky too that I got on well with my commanding officer. Captain Owen Paris had a reputation for rigidity within the service, but he and I hit it off immediately. We both came from families that had been in Starfleet for generations, and this shared culture eased our relationship from the outset. I too can be rigid in my own way, and the discipline of his ship suited my nature. I know that my father respected him greatly and I took my cue from this. He lacked much of a sense of humor, but he got things done. It was a pleasure to serve under him, and I have been personally grateful to him for his many kindnesses over the years, not least in the roadblock I hit during my second year, but also in his championing of the Pathfinder Project that allowed *Voyager* to establish contact with Starfleet.

My first six months on the *Al-Batani* were, broadly speaking, a success. Half a dozen new staff had come on board at the same time, and we formed a close-knit group. One of our number—a Vulcan named T'Nat—had been captain of the Velocity team at the Academy and persuaded us to form a junior league with some of the junior lieutenants. I had not played the game at the Academy, but I was always ready for a new physical challenge, so I agreed to try it out. I took to it immediately; it filled a tennis-shaped gap in my life. The game became popular across the whole ship, leading some of the more senior officers to form their own league. Flora Kristopher was instrumental in this, and the first officer, Commander Shulie Weiss, joined too. The captain kept his lofty distance. The inevitable challenge was offered, which we junior officers accepted with alacrity: surely we would have no trouble defeating what we gleefully referred to as our "elders." Well, this is where I learned that Velocity is as much about wits and guile as it is about speed and agility. I won't say that we were trounced, but… all right, we were trounced. I have never seen a more triumphant set of senior officers. Paris came and awarded a trophy he'd organized for the occasion, and we junior officers swore to get our revenge. We never did while I was on the team.

Between this and our survey mission, which expanded my scientific knowledge and my practical skill immensely, I had a good and challenging life. I count myself lucky to have entered Starfleet during this period. The border skirmishes with the Cardassians rumbled on, but there was still time and space for us to enjoy something of the old Starfleet, when ships were dedicated chiefly to exploration, and we were able to pursue our primary purpose as individuals, devoting our energies as much to our own personal advancement as to protecting the Federation. I knew that at the back of our minds we all feared that a larger conflict was coming—even outright war—and we were intent on seizing the day. Speaking to officers younger than me, who came of age just before and during the Dominion War, I know that they had a very different experience during their first postings. They were straight into the thick of it. Even after the Dominion War was over, there was the hard work of reconstruction, and not as much time to play. I am fortunate to have been on a ship like this. I enjoyed my work; I enjoyed my downtime; I was making good friendships and I was earning praise from my superiors not only for my work, but for my handling of various situations that were intended to prepare me for command. I was pleased with my performance. The only risk was that I was starting, perhaps, to get a little cocky, but Starfleet has its own corrective measures for this kind of thing, as I was going to find out.

About six months after I joined the crew of the *Al-Batani*, I had a first meeting with an individual who was later to become extremely important in my life—and who made his presence felt from the first moment that we laid eyes upon each other. It's testament to his quality—and his judgement—that this first encounter did not put me off him for life. The *Al-Batani* had come back to Earth to allow Captain Paris to participate in a conference about the ongoing crisis on Bajor. The Occupation was now decades old, and the Cardassians showed no signs of ever intending to leave (they were gone, I'm glad to say, within the next eleven years). The situation was increasingly desperate: not only the increasing numbers of refugees, but a growing sense that Bajoran culture was in danger, and also the ecosystem of that beautiful world. The Cardassians were stripping the place of resources, and an environmental tipping point would surely soon be reached. Starfleet was constrained in what it could directly do, both by its policy of nonintervention, but also from the natural concern of embroiling the Federation in a war with a highly militarized and aggressive neighbor.

"It will take a major alliance to defeat the Cardassians," my father used to say. He was right—a bigger alliance than perhaps he had realized, but, then, he hadn't known about the Dominion, and he hadn't expected the scale of that defeat.

This conference on Earth that Captain Paris was attending was very significant, with representatives not only from Starfleet and the Federation Council, but various relief organizations (my mother ran a panel about efforts by artists and writers to raise awareness), and, of course, displaced Bajorans, coming to speak out on behalf of their people, and ask for whatever aid Starfleet and the Federation could offer. The whole event lasted a week, during which time we junior officers were left in charge of a skeleton ship. Kristopher, who was taking some shore leave, said to me, on departing, "Don't mess this one up, Janeway."

By the end of the week, we had perhaps got a little slapdash, and I'm sorry to say that I didn't pull it back together in time. On the day that the senior crew was due to return, I received an unexpected message from Captain Paris that the *Al-Batani* would be carrying three admirals from Earth to Betazed, and that since they would be arriving before the senior crew was able to return, I should receive them on board with all due ceremony and protocol. I therefore arrived in the transporter room at the right time and watched as the three admirals and their security team arrived on board. I put on my most welcoming smile and stepped forward, intending to make a good impression.

"Sirs, I'd like to welcome you aboard the *Al-Batani*—"

I was stopped midflow when the senior officer in charge of their security team, a humorless-looking Vulcan, said, "Ensign, you have not performed a weapons sweep upon us."

I turned to look at him. "Sir?"

"We gave you only four hours' notice of our intention to travel on the *Al-Batani*. Are you not aware of the regulation that requires that any passengers travelling upon a starship who are brought on board without twelve hours' notice should be subject to a weapons sweep?"

"I am, sir."

"And yet you have not conducted the sweep. Can you explain your reason, Ensign?"

There *was* a reason. The reason was that I had forgotten. (I didn't say it was a good reason.) And… Well, we were within the solar system, after all. What threat could there be? (It's not a mistake anyone entering Starfleet during the Dominion War would have made, is it? The threat of a Changeling on board ship seriously changed security procedures. But these were simpler times.) Anyway the protocol existed, and I had not followed it. I had made a mistake, and I was being dressed down—and in front of three admirals.

I raised my chin and looked squarely at the Vulcan officer. "No, sir," I said. "I cannot."

"May I ask how you intend to remedy this situation?"

It's possible that I have never loathed someone as much as I loathed this lieutenant right at that moment. By far the worst thing about it was that he was of course completely right. I'd been sloppy, and I'd been called out, and there was nothing I could do but suck it up.

"Sir," I said, "I should conduct the weapons sweep immediately."

"That's correct, Ensign."

I conducted the sweep. As expected, nobody was carrying any unauthorized weapons, these three admirals clearly having decided not to hijack Captain Paris's ship that day.

"Is everything satisfactory, Ensign?" said the officer.

"It is, sir."

"Are we cleared to board, Ensign?"

"Yes, sir, you're cleared to board."

"Anything else, Ensign?"

I sighed to myself. He really wasn't going to let this one pass without drawing blood or, possibly, while leaving me standing. "My apologies, sir. It won't happen again."

"See that it doesn't, Ensign."

He gestured toward his charges and led them out of the transporter room. One of the admirals, on his way past, winked, and said, "Don't take it too hard, Ensign. But don't do it again, huh?"

They left the room. I fell back against the transporter console. My colleague, Ensign Chang, who had been operating the transporter, said, "Wow. Kathryn. Are you okay?"

I made a show of checking myself over. "No limbs lost," I said. "Just fatal damage to my dignity."

Chang shook her head and whistled. "There's a reason I didn't go for the command track," she said. "That was *brutal.*"

And I was sure that wasn't going to be the last of it, either. That security officer was bound to submit a report to my superior officers. When the summons from Captain Paris came, as was inevitable, I took a deep breath, made sure I looked as faultlessly smart as I did on my first day, and reported to his ready room, steeling myself for the dressing-down that I was sure was coming.

Bizarrely, it did not come. Captain Paris let me stand there and sweat for a while as he sat and studied me, and then said, "I hear you met Lieutenant Tuvok."

So that was the damned security officer's name. I filed that one away for future reference. I'd been keeping an eye out for it—to keep well away. "Yes, sir."

"I hear he had a few things to say to you."

"Yes, sir."

"And I hear you took them on the chin."

Cautiously, I said, "I'd like to think so, sir."

"Which suggests to me that you thought you deserved it, Ensign."

I swallowed. "Yes, sir," I said.

"Yes," he said. "I think you deserved it too."

"My apologies, sir."

"Accepted, Ensign."

"If it's any consolation, I'll have cold sweats about this for the rest of my life, sir."

"As you should, Janeway. Don't let it happen again."

"No, sir," I said, fervently, and then I was dismissed. Outside his ready room, I took a deep breath and thanked my lucky stars. I'd been expecting much worse. Had I really got off this lightly? Possibly, but just recounting this story I felt my stomach sinking, and, yes, those cold sweats breaking out. I think I got exactly what I deserved.

✦

That, thankfully, was my worst experience during my first year on the *Al-Batani,* and once Kristopher was back from leave, up to date on the whole sorry episode, and gave me a scolding for letting her down, that was the last I heard of it. I'd made a mistake, I'd got told off, and I'd made it clear that it would never happen again. I put the experience behind me and concentrated on making my time on board a success, learning as much as I could from example and from practice. The Academy can teach you the principles of being a Starfleet officer, and it can even present you with holo-training simulations covering as many different scenarios as you can think of—but there is no substitute for learning on the job. Nothing knocks the corners off a cocky young ensign like finding yourself floundering and having your more experienced colleagues move in smoothly to help you out. Every day brought a new practical challenge; every day, I found myself muttering, "They didn't cover *that* at the Academy."

(After I managed to delete a morning's worth of data analysis from readings we had taken from a nebula, Kristopher got this legend printed on a t-shirt for me, and ordered me to wear it each time I used the gym.) But I started to find my feet, and most of all, I started to enjoy myself.

Without doubt, my favorite experiences on board the *Al-Batani* at this time were when I had the privilege to observe first-contact scenarios. Surely this, at heart, is why we all joined Starfleet: to seek out not only new worlds, but new life; to learn from these encounters and thereby enrich ourselves and our own civilization, by ever increasing our knowledge and our diversity of experience. Let me note that, as such a junior officer, I was only ever allowed to observe, and then in circumstances in which we were plainly dealing with a friendly species. There were other, more complicated situations at which a probationary officer was not allowed even to be present, and these were tantalizing, since they were the cases which posed the most interesting questions of intercultural and interspecies communication. I longed to participate more actively in these meetings, and I envied my superiors their direct involvement, but protocol demanded that such delicate encounters were handled by experienced officers. (And I certainly wasn't intending to breach protocol again in a hurry.) But I read every single report of these encounters several times over, and I must have annoyed the hell out of my superior officers, demanding they recount every contact down to the very last detail. I looked forward desperately to the day when, as a captain, the privilege would be mine. And when that day finally came it was indeed my privilege to participate in these encounters (though I might wish I hadn't had to go so damn far to have them).

It strikes me as ironic that I ended up giving many junior officers on *Voyager* their first experience of first contact well before they would have ever been permitted involvement back in the Alpha Quadrant. But if material resources were thin on the ground in the Delta Quadrant, then so too were human resources. All we had was what we brought with us. Tacit knowledge, experience: these things were at a premium, and to bring my ship home again, I had to accelerate my junior officers, ask them to take on challenges well ahead of schedule. It remains a great source of pride that these young people invariably stepped up to the challenge. I surely could not have asked for a better crew.

✦

At the end of my first year on the *Al-Batani*, I joined Lieutenant Commander Kristopher and Captain Paris for my end-of-probation meeting. We had a full and frank discussion of my year on board ship (I even managed to laugh about my encounter with Tuvok). They commented on my tendency to take on slightly too much (although they had to admit they hadn't seen any effect on my performance so far), and encouraged me to consider strategies for conserving my emotional and physical resources as I took on more duties and seniority. Overall, I had to be pleased with my first appraisal:

> *"Practical and solution-orientated, hard-working and personable, Ensign Janeway's doggedness gets the job done, and only sometimes translates into stubbornness. A highly committed junior officer, who inspires trust and respect from both peers and senior officers, she is well on track for command."*

Not the flashiest of reports, I'll grant you, but who wants to burn out in a flash? I was working hard to curb my stubborn streak and turn it into something productive, and I was remembering that hard work could be overdone, and downtime was necessary. The report duly went back to Starfleet Command, and I got a holomessage from Dad the next day. He sent me an image of a glider soaring over the Grand Canyon: *That's my girl, Katy. Keep flying.*

The *Al-Batani* had taken on half a dozen new ensigns at the time I joined, and Captain Paris held a cocktail party to celebrate the end of our probation. This was the occasion where I met a young man who was going to feature significantly in later years. At twelve years old, Thomas Eugene Paris was energetic, full of mischief—and clearly already a source of some exasperation for his more straight-down-the-line father. I often wonder where Tom got his high spirits from: Owen was so steady, so upright, and his wife, Julia, very grand and sophisticated. It might simply be that Tom had found getting into scrapes was a good way of attracting his father's attention… although it was invariably not the kind of attention he might have preferred. At this party, I noticed how bored Tom was looking, and I had a sense that some trouble was about to ensue. I had a word in Kristopher's ear, and we marched him off down to the holodeck where we ran flight simulations for him for an hour, and got him back to the party in time for the speeches—none of us missed, and the youngest of us in a very good mood from getting to play pilot all afternoon. I don't know if Tom remembers this—there must have been a lot of tedious cocktail parties over the years—but I've been keeping a close eye on you from an early age, Tom, and I didn't miss a trick.

✦

Altogether, I decided to count my first year in Starfleet a success. But events were about to hit me that I hadn't prepared for and couldn't have predicted. I was about to suffer the first serious blow of my life.

Around the time that I entered the Academy, my father had been assigned to oversee a number of projects which were aimed at designing new flight technologies for use against Cardassian warships. He had, after all, been a test pilot at the start of his Starfleet career, only retiring from this role when he married and had young children. The details were hush-hush, of course, and I am not sure of the extent to which my mother and sister were aware of the details of his work during this period, but I had an inkling of the kind of thing that he was doing. Nevertheless, he and I never discussed it. Perhaps if we had, I would have known that his involvement was more hands-on than I would ever have guessed. I knew that by this stage he was spending substantial periods of time at the Utopia Planitia shipyards; what I did not know—what none of us in the family knew—was how often he went along on test flights, and that in fact he had started flying again.

I don't know my father's reasoning behind this. Perhaps he was unwilling to ask pilots to take risks that he himself wasn't willing to take. Perhaps now that Phoebe and I were grown-ups and established, he wanted to get back to what he always thought was his real work, the work that he had given up when Phoebe was born. I don't know what was in his mind, and of course I never had the chance to ask. It's the question I most want to ask him: Dad, what the *hell* were you thinking?

I remember receiving the news of his death vividly. I'll never forget it. Traumatic experiences burn themselves into your neurons, don't they? I was on duty on the bridge. The XO, Shulie Weiss, was in the captain's chair, and we were all surprised when the captain appeared and went to have a quiet word with her. Then Weiss called over to me and asked me to go with the captain. I followed Captain Paris into his ready room, wondering what the hell I'd done wrong and whether I was about to get in trouble for a late-night gambling session with the other ensigns... I was already preparing my defense: we hadn't made any noise and we hadn't stayed up *that* late... Everyone had been bright-eyed and bushy-tailed the following morning... But of course, this was nothing to do with that.

"Please sit down, Kathryn," the captain said.

I knew from the use of my first name that this was something else, something truly serious and not simply a quiet word about the high spirits of some of his junior officers.

"Is something the matter, sir?"

For a moment, I saw that he was lost for words. He pressed his fingertips against his temple. "It's about your father. It's about Ted. Kathryn, I am so sorry to have to tell you this—"

"Injured?" I think I already knew this wasn't the case.

"I'm so sorry, Kathryn. He's been killed."

A whooshing sound rushed through my head; there was a ringing in my ears. My eyes went strange: black patches in front of my field of vision.

"Kathryn! Kathryn!"

I became aware of Captain Paris's voice, somewhat distant and muffled.

"Here, drink this."

He had found some whisky (we can always lay our hands on it from somewhere in dire need—and my need was dire), and he put the glass up to my mouth and made me drink. That helped restore me to some kind of equilibrium; sufficient to be able to ask a few questions and listen to what he was saying to me. There had been an accident, it transpired, out on Tau Ceti Prime... At first, I struggled to understand: An accident? What in God's name had he been doing all the way out there? What had taken him from the shipyards on Mars? I listened to the captain, talking clearly, and began to piece things together. Here's what happened.

Cardassian activity along the border had, in recent months, been focused on Etaris IV, a disputed world that had great strategic significance in securing supply lines between two Cardassian border systems. Starfleet had no intention of letting that happen. These barren rocks that we fight over! Etaris IV was a dead piece of ice in the middle of nowhere! Still, that was the battleground that the Cardassians had chosen, and Starfleet had no choice but to meet them there. As a result, Starfleet had been testing a ship that could operate under lower-than-average temperatures without giving off heat signatures that would allow the Cardassians to trace it. The ship needed to be able to fly not only in orbit above Etaris IV, but also within the atmosphere and, ideally, be able to dip below water. This meant it needed to be able to work beneath the ice that covered most of the planet's surface. A prototype had come off the production line at Utopia Planitia, and now was being tested under the polar ice cap on Tau Ceti Prime, where conditions came closest to the surface of Etaris IV. They had six successful runs, shifting from orbit, to atmosphere, then under the ice for over an hour, then back again. On the seventh run, my father decided to see for himself how well it was operating. That was when the damn thing broke down. Full systems failure. After a hellish couple of days, they got the ship back up again, but by that time the three-person crew was dead. Including my dad.

I had nightmares about his final moments for many years after. I have still not read the full report, in case the reality was worse than what I could imagine. Had they died on impact? Or had they lasted a while, as their air ran out? Had they escaped the ship, only to drown beneath the ice? Had they faced fire? I did not want to know. But all these images were burned into my brain; no wonder, when I was traveling home on *Voyager*, that an alien found that these were a potent means to convince me that I too had died. More than anything in life— more even, perhaps, than wanting to get home to the Alpha Quadrant—I longed to see my father again. No wonder I was nearly persuaded of the truth that I was dead and had joined him in the afterlife. No wonder I was so nearly fooled.

✦

I went directly home. Captain Paris told me to take as long as it took. By this, I assumed that he meant for as long as my family needed me. As it turned out, I was the one who needed the break.

The funeral was hard. Not just because Mom was so grief-stricken, and yet being so brave, but because there were so many *people*… Our quiet little home in the country, our haven, suddenly became the focal point for hundreds of people, all of whom wanted to pay their respects, many of whom were Starfleet top brass… I honestly don't know how Mom kept on going throughout that day. I know how much I was struggling; I know how much Phoebe was struggling. To have to listen to people tell you, over and over again, how brave he was, how well respected, how many people he had served with and supported and encouraged… Trying to find a "thank you" to everyone who took the time to come and speak to us… As the day went on, we came up with a system—the widow and the two daughters—one of us coming forward to be the point of first contact for well-wishers; another one moving in to take over when that person began to flag… All the grandparents were there too; Granny- and Granddad-in-town distraught at the death of their boy… God, it was hellish. I think what made it worst of all was that all this grief and sorrow had come to what had been such a happy home. The picture I have painted of my childhood may seem to make it too idyllic, but I was lucky and blessed in my early life. This was the first real tragedy I ever faced. I talked to more admirals and captains and councilors and ambassadors that day than I think I have in the whole time afterward. But do you know which conversations hit hardest? The ones with our neighbors. It turned out that whenever Dad was home, he never missed a meeting with the local astronomical society. I knew he was a member—he'd taken us there when we were small—but I didn't know how active he'd tried to be for a man so often away from home. They put out a newsletter every two months, and it turned out he always wrote something, however small; sometimes just a letter, sometimes as much as an article. That short but heartfelt conversation with the secretary and the president of that little society of enthusiasts was the closest that I came to breaking down completely that day. My father was a busy man, an important man, with lots of responsibilities as the border situation got worse, and still he had found the time to stay in touch with them. At heart, he remained the little boy who had looked up at the stars and wanted to fly among them.

As the afternoon wore on, and our guests began to leave, Parvati Pandey, who had known Dad well, came to speak to me. She took both my hands in hers and gave me a steady look. Remember that look? The commander's look? Checking out the reserves of her junior.

"How are you, Kathryn?" she said.

I was frank with her. "I'm... I'm not good, ma'am."

"This is going to take time, you know. Grief and shock—it can take a while to bounce back from that."

If only it had been grief... I think I would have understood that. Feeling bereft, feeling shocked... But what I couldn't understand was the *violence* of my emotions... Pandey must have seen something in my expression; she frowned and said, "What is it, Kathryn?"

"I... I don't feel sad, ma'am. I feel... *angry.*"

"That's natural," she said. "When someone dies suddenly, we often feel angry with them—"

"Not with him," I replied softly. "With the Cardassians."

She looked at me in surprise. "He was nowhere near the front, Kathryn—"

"But he was still fighting that war, wasn't he? Putting himself into danger because he wouldn't ask people to take risks that he wasn't ready to take. If they weren't pushing their luck, forcing us to respond, he wouldn't have been in that damn flyer—"

"Kathryn," she said firmly. "It was an accident. Nobody was to blame. This isn't productive; it won't help."

I nodded.

"Do you understand? This won't help, Kathryn."

I let her think she had persuaded me, but she didn't. I knew who was to blame. And I knew there wasn't a damn thing I could do about it.

✦

That helpless anger: that's what lays you low. In the days and weeks that followed, I just couldn't shake off this sense of deep rage that I had. Thoughts kept whirling around my head: angry, vengeful, vicious thoughts. I would lie in bed staring up at the darkness, thinking about what had happened, and how the Cardassians were to blame. I thought about how I could get reassigned, get to the front, start paying them back for all that they had taken from me. And then at the crack of dawn I would fall into a restless sleep, and I would not be able to drag myself out of bed until late the following day. Even when I was awake, I couldn't settle. I would wander around the house (I didn't want to be outside), or I would sit in one of the big old armchairs and stare into the garden. I knew my family was worried about me, Mom and Phoebe and all the grandparents. I received a message from Captain Paris, telling me that I'd been granted indefinite leave. I thought, *But I didn't request it…* and then fell back onto the bed and into a deep and exhausted sleep. Eventually, I stopped feeling angry. I stopped feeling anything at all.

Looking back on this gray, lifeless period, I think I understand now what was happening to me. Many people lose parents young—I was still only twenty-two, remember—and aren't hit so hard. I think my problem was that so far, I'd been able to achieve pretty much everything that I put my mind to. Tennis trophies: sure, I lost them one year, but the following year I came back and won them in style. Getting into the Academy a year early: I'd checked that one off. Graduating near the top of my class: I did that and proved to everyone I was more than just my father's daughter. But this—there was nothing I could do. No action of mine, not even if I had brought my revenge fantasies to reality, could have brought Dad back. He was dead, and there was nothing that Ensign Kathryn Janeway could do about that. And that realization—of my own incapacity—was too much to bear.

If I have ever wanted proof of how much my mother loved me, it was how she cared for me during this time, when her own grief must have been overwhelming. I guess people always thought my father was the strong one—the Starfleet officer, the hero—and perhaps thought my mother's artistic, homebody personality meant that she was sensitive or easily shaken. But she proved to be the toughest of us all. She must have thought that she and Dad were going to have a long and happy retirement together—like her parents, like his parents—and instead that future was lost. But she gathered herself up, and faced that changed future, and found some strength within her to prop me up as well. Phoebe too—I don't know what I would have done without her quiet patience. She took a term's absence from art school; stayed at home; made me get up and go for walks; made me sit with her and sort out photographs. And she faced my sudden outbursts of incoherent rage with equanimity.

One night, passing her bedroom door, I heard her crying to herself. I tapped on the door and walked in. She was lying on the bed. I went over to her—my baby sister—and wrapped my arms around her and let her cry. That's when I knew I was coming through the other side of this. I felt something else again, beyond the pendulum swing of dull ache and bitter anger. I felt compassion, the need to look after my sister, the desire to care. Phoebe, you got me through this. I hope I helped you too.

Four months went by, altogether, and then someone came to see me: Parvati Pandey, dressed in civvies. "Just passing by," she said, with a sly look. Whoever would be "just passing by" our place? We were at the end of our own damn lane.

We sat on the porch and drank iced tea. She said, "Still angry, Kathryn?"

I shook my head. "No. Just tired."

"Tired?" she said. "Or bored?"

The words seemed to break a spell. I looked across the land, and suddenly it was as if I could see in color again: the green trees and fields, the bright roses, the sparkle of sunlight. I felt something surge inside me, some upswell of energy that I had started to think I would never experience again. I felt... like I could do something.

I looked at Pandey. She was smiling at me, fondly.

"I think... I'm ready," I said.

"I think you are too," she replied. "I knew you'd get there, given time."

And I was ready. Ready to start over.

After Pandey left, I contacted the *Al-Batani* and asked to speak to Captain Paris.

"*Kathryn,*" he said. "*How are you?*"

"I'm much better, sir," I said.

"*I'm glad to hear that, Kathryn. It's good of you to check in—*"

"Sir," I said. "I'm ready to come back."

He gave me the commander's look, sizing me up. "*Are you sure?*"

I looked back, steely-eyed. "Surer than I've been of anything, sir. Permission to return to duty?"

I saw a gleam of pride in his eyes; perhaps I'm not going too far to say of paternal pride. "*Permission granted, Ensign. We're ready to welcome you home.*"

I learned later that Owen Paris had lost his own father young, a father killed while serving in Starfleet. No wonder he understood. No wonder he was so patient with me. Looking back now on my first year in Starfleet, with its great highs and its desperate lows, I see now how easily my career could have been derailed even before it started. And I recognize—and am beyond grateful for—the good luck that I have had in my mentors. Flora Kristopher, who took me from rookie cadet to capable ensign. Owen Paris, who gave me the space to bring myself back from the worst blow of my life. Parvati Pandey, who helped me understand my grief and anger. And of course, Tuvok, who has never allowed me to let my standards slip. I am grateful to them all, and I have tried to pay it forward.

CHAPTER FIVE

MISSION ACCOMPLISHED—2359-2364

IT WAS TIME TO SAY GOODBYE TO MOM AND PHOEBE, and the grandparents: a more tearful farewell than usual. Home would never be quite the same again, but it was still home, and always would be—the place of rest and restoration; the place where I could always go, whenever I was in need. Before I left, Phoebe and I had one last walk down the country lanes which we knew so well, stopping to look at the little schoolhouse where our journeys away from home had begun as little girls, all those years ago.

"I worry about Mom," I said.

"But I'll be here for a while yet," Phoebe said. "Don't let it stop you going back."

I felt bad. Phoebe had her own career to think of. She had a studio over in Portland, and I knew there was a romance back there, someone special that she surely wanted to be around. "Shall we give it a few months?" I said. "I could come back… Take over…?"

Phoebe shook her head. "I don't think so, Katy. Now you've got the nerve back, I think you should go for it. You know, I think Mom will surprise us all."

On my way back to Starfleet Command, I stopped for a day with the Grands-in-town. That was a sad visit. Granddad-in-town had lost some of his ebullience; Granny-in-town looked gaunt. They lived long lives—happy lives, too, to the end—with many grandchildren and great-grandchildren (Granny even saw a great-great-grandson), but that loss of their child was always there.

How could it not be? Feeling a decade older and wiser and sadder than I had been only a few months earlier, I made my way to San Francisco, to report, as instructed, to Starfleet Command, and my meeting with Captain Paris and Admiral Pandey.

Before the meeting, I took a little time to wander around the grounds of the Academy. How young the cadets looked! How green! The last eighteen months had changed me more than any other period in my life: not just my time on board the *Al-Batani*, but the fundamental shock of my father's death. There was no one ahead of me now, nobody clearing the path for me. We have such an expectation these days about how long our parents, and our grandparents, will live, but it isn't always the case that they survive to old age, especially if you're Starfleet. I felt strangely exposed. I know from speaking to other friends who have lost parents relatively young that they felt something similar: that some significant barrier had fallen too soon. It was both terrifying and yet, at the same time, strangely exhilarating, as if I had been initiated fully into the adult world. Still, I would have done anything—gone anywhere—if I thought it would bring Dad back home to us. But some journeys have no return.

I wandered through the garden, sitting on a bench among the roses, breathing in the deep rich scent. With that preternatural skill by which he always seems to appear when needed, I saw Boothby walking slowly down the path toward me. He seemed no different. Did he ever age? My father said he had looked exactly the same when he was a cadet. I wouldn't be surprised if he'd looked this way when Grandad-in-town was at the Academy. I wouldn't have been surprised to learn he was here when the foundations had been laid. He stopped beside me and pushed back his hat.

"Good to see you, Ensign Janeway." He sat down beside me, his face saddening. "I was sorry to hear about your father. Poor Ted."

"Thank you, Boothby."

"It's worse when they're so young."

It was strange to me to think of Dad as young, but of course Boothby was right. He had been no age at all. "I know."

"How's your mother?"

"She's amazing."

"Roses flourishing?"

"Always."

We smiled at each other. He said, "Have you got some time to help me today, or are you too busy?"

I breathed in deeply. Suddenly, more than anything, I wanted to stay in this peaceful place, quietly pottering around after Boothby, tending the garden, watching the weather and the seasons change. How strange, for one who had always wanted to get out of these chores and get back to flight. Suddenly, my mother's way of life made perfect sense. But it wasn't my way. I wanted to be out there. I wanted to be among the stars.

"I wish I could…"

"But the admiral and the captain await you." He stood up, surprisingly agile for such an old man, and offered his hand courteously to me to help me to my feet. "The garden will always be here, Kathryn. Home from home. Come back whenever you need us."

We parted company: I went to my meeting; he went back to his garden. Later that day, I found fresh roses had been sent to my quarters.

✦

Captain Paris and Admiral Pandey welcomed me into her office and put me at my ease. Tea was poured, and we took seats around her desk. She had a fine view over the harbor, the kind of view that, when the weather was fine, as it was today, lifted the heart. Looking out over that big blue sky I could feel my spirits rise. I was ready to take flight again.

Pandey eased herself into her chair. "Kathryn. Good to see you looking more like yourself again."

"Thank you, Admiral. I won't deny it's been a tough time, but the worst is definitely past. I'm ready to resume my duties." I glanced at my captain, sitting in the chair beside me. "If you're still willing to take me back on board, sir."

I saw the two senior officers exchange a look and felt worried. Was something the matter? Had they decided against my return? Had they decided I wasn't fit for duty? But I felt so well, so capable…

"Well, Kathryn," said Paris. "That's partly why we asked you here today. We want to hear from you *exactly* how you are. We want to know what you're ready for."

I spread my hands out across my knees. "Like I said, it's been a rough ride. I wasn't prepared for him to…" It was time to say it loud, way past time to speak the truth. I took a deep breath and said, "I wasn't prepared for Dad to die. And it knocked me miles off course. Like I'd been…" I searched for the right words. "Picked up by a tornado and swept into a world that didn't make sense." Like Dorothy, I thought, whisked off to Oz. I was glad that some of her nerve, her grit and determination, had come back to me.

Pandey leaned forward, chin resting on her hands, and studied me carefully. That commander's look. *Are you fit? Are you ready? Are you able?* "And now, Kathryn?"

"I'm better. Things make sense again. It was a horrible accident, and it wasn't fair. But I can't do anything about that, so I need to concentrate on the things that I *can* do, and let…" I gave a sad smile. "Let grief take its course. I want to get back to work, and I'm ready to get back to work."

Again, she and Captain Paris glanced at each other. "All right," said Paris, relaxing back in his chair. "I'm glad to hear that. Because we do have a posting for you—although we want to hear first whether you want it."

My ears pricked up. "I'm grateful for the opportunity, sir."

"You might not have heard," he said, "but Flora Kristopher is moving on."

I hadn't heard. "Oh, that's a big loss to the ship, sir!"

"I know!" he said. "But it's a fine opportunity for her, and one that will take her back to her real work."

"Where's she going?"

"Over to the *U.S.S. Cúchulainn*," Paris said. "They're heading across to some of the worlds being settled by Bajoran refugees to work there on soil reclamation projects."

I'd heard from my mother about these projects. Bajorans fleeing the Occupation hadn't had much choice about where to settle, and some of the places where they'd landed were largely barren worlds. This was a good and practical way in which Starfleet and the Federation could help them, and I was not surprised to learn that Flora had been persuaded to become involved. It was a chance for her to use her technical expertise to achieve genuine good.

"That's a great move for her, sir," I said.

"It's where her heart is," he agreed. "But, unfortunately, it does leave me without a chief science officer."

"Who do you have in mind, sir?" I said. I started running through a list of names of likely candidates, but nobody on the *Al-Batani* came to mind. Kristopher had been young for the job and had been building up a young team. I'd been part of that cohort of new cadets, serving under Paris as their first posting.

"Well, Kathryn," said Paris, "the job's yours if you want it."

I stared at him. "Me?"

"It will mean promotion, of course. To lieutenant, junior grade," he said. "But it will also mean being away from Earth for a long period of time. We have a new mission."

"Sir, I don't know what to say..." I was deeply touched by this offer. For him to show this much faith in me, after the difficult time I had been through.

"Perhaps," said Pandey, "you'd like to hear about the mission before you make your decision."

I was still reeling from the offer. "Yes please, Admiral."

Paris passed over a padd and began his briefing. "The *Al-Batani* is being sent out to the Arias system."

I had heard about the system. About a year ago, some interesting massive compact halo objects had been identified out there which required closer analysis. The problem was that the system was extremely close to the Cardassian border, and the class of ship that was generally assigned these kinds of exploratory and analysis missions was not sufficiently well equipped to defend itself against attack. I listened to Paris describe the scientific objectives of the mission for a while, but he said nothing about the proximity of the system to the border. He wrapped up his briefing.

"Any questions, Kathryn?"

"Yes, sir," I said. "Is this only a scientific mission?"

He began to laugh. "No fooling you, is there? Our other purpose is to gather intelligence about Cardassian fleet movements along the border. That part of the mission is of course classified, and you'll not discuss that outside of this room, please."

"Absolutely not, sir."

Pandey said, "There's also a strong chance of encountering hostile forces, and of direct combat. What I want to know—and what Owen here also wants to know—is, are you ready?"

I thought about this. Was I ready? "Can anyone really be ready for combat, Admiral? I'm trained for it."

"Good answer," she said. "The other thing that I want you to be clear about is that this is going to be a lengthy mission, Kathryn. Several years. Are you ready for that too? Do you need to remain near home for a while longer?"

I could see why she would ask. But throughout that day, something had been lifting from me, some burden of grief. I felt as if I had been pushing against a door that suddenly opened and I was stepping out into the light of morning.

"I know why you're asking, Admiral. I've had a serious downswing. But I'm through. It's done. I'm ready for this mission—more than that, I'm *eager* for this mission. I want to get back to work."

A third time they looked at each other. This time they were smiling.

"Told you so," said Paris.

"I didn't doubt for a second," replied Pandey. She rose from her seat, and therefore so did we, and she came around the desk and stood before me. Reaching into her pockets, she brought out my new insignia. "Congratulations, Lieutenant Janeway."

"Thank you, Admiral. Thank you, sir."

We saluted each other. I felt marvelous—buoyed up, lifted up. It was a feeling as good as flying. I'd come back from the edge, and now two of the senior officers I most respected were signaling their trust in me. I'd be damned if I would let them down.

Paris reached out to shake my hand. "I wish Ted could be here to see this," he said. His voice was surprisingly hoarse.

"Me too, sir," I said.

"He would be damn proud of you, Kathryn."

I clasped his hand more tightly. I felt the need to console him, rather than to receive consolation. "Thank you, sir."

He cleared his throat. "Well. A good morning's work. Get your gear together, Lieutenant; I expect you back on board the *Al-Batani* in thirty-six hours."

"I'll be there, sir."

Suddenly his eyes twinkled with mischief. I knew that look, and I didn't trust it.

"Something the matter, sir?"

"Only that I've saved the best surprise till last," said Paris.

"Surprise, sir?"

"I have a new chief of security."

"Oh yes, sir?" I said blithely. "Anyone I know?"

✦

"Lieutenant Janeway," said Lieutenant Commander Tuvok.

"Sir," I replied, as calmly as I could manage. *Of all the damn dirty tricks, Owen Paris*, I thought. It's not as if I would have refused the mission or the promotion, but he hadn't needed to be so gleeful about revealing the identity of his new security chief, and he didn't need to send me to the transporter room to welcome him aboard. People who said that Owen Paris didn't have a sense of humor didn't know him. He did have a sense of humor, and it was damn twisted.

"I'm delighted to report that you are clear of weapons, sir," I said, dryly. "Welcome aboard the *Al-Batani*."

Tuvok raised a puzzled eyebrow. "Lieutenant Janeway, thank you for the welcome. The regulations with regard to weapons only apply when less than twelve hours' notice has been given of arrival. I was assigned to the *Al-Batani* two months ago and confirmed my day and time of arrival immediately. The regulation therefore is not relevant in this instance. Nevertheless, I commend your diligence." He stepped off the transporter pad. "I believe I am expected in the captain's ready room. I would be grateful if you could direct me there."

Paris had asked me to bring him along. "This way, Commander Tuvok," I said with a sigh. I'd learned my first lesson of dealing with him: sarcasm would be taken at face value, and completely miss the mark. Either that, or he had forgotten me completely. Just another cocky ensign who needed teaching a lesson. Well, I could work with that. I certainly wasn't that ensign any longer. We walked along the corridors toward the bridge, Tuvok's hands clasped behind his back. I gave the usual spiel, although I was sure that he would have familiarized himself completely with the ship's specifications within twenty-four hours of receiving the assignment. Nevertheless, he listened gravely and attentively, and asked questions which showed he was taking on board everything that I said.

I delivered him to the door of the ready room in one piece. Paris was sitting behind his desk, smirking at me. I risked a small glare back. "Nice to see you two making friends," he said. "Always good to have senior staff who get along."

Tuvok turned to me. "Lieutenant Janeway," he said, "allow me to thank you for your attention this morning. I have followed your career with interest since our first meeting, and I have heard only excellent reports. I am looking forward to serving alongside you."

That took the wind out of my sails. "I... Well. Thank you, Commander. I... look forward to serving alongside you too." I nodded to Paris, who was looking too damned pleased with himself. "Dismissed, sir?"

"Yes, thank you, Janeway."

I left, and the door closed behind me. "Well," I said. Looked like Tuvok wasn't going to be such a pain in the damn neck after all.

✦

"That man," I said to Laurie Fitzgerald, the CMO on the *Al-Batani* and my closest friend on board, "is a damn pain in the neck."

He laughed. "Commander Tuvok does have a knack of rubbing you up the wrong way, Kate."

"You know what the worst thing is, Fitz? It's not reciprocated. Nothing I do annoys him. He just... always seems to find it lacking somehow."

"Kate, you run on intuition so much of the time," said Fitz. "I bet he finds you damn irritating."

"Thanks, I think." We were making light of the situation, but the truth was that my working relationship with Tuvok was troubling me. It seemed to me that he shot down every suggestion that I made—and, worse, he shot it down with logic. At heart, I am a scientist—I understand how to hypothesize, gather evidence, analyze that data, and provide measured conclusions or reasonable conjectures. But there was the other side to my personality; the side that I guessed Tuvok saw as irrational, but which I called instinct, hunch, gut feeling. Fitz was right: some of my best decisions have come from following my intuition. But Tuvok could see no place for this, and clearly seemed to think it was a fault. I knew that Paris was keeping an eye on things; for this reason, among others, I wanted to make this relationship work. But, most importantly, our mission was likely to take us into dangerous situations. We needed to function as a team. We needed to trust each other implicitly—and I wasn't sure that Tuvok entirely trusted me.

"Show him what you can do, Kate," said Fitz.

"You know, I think I will."

We had been out in the Arias system for a little over nine months. Our scientific mission was progressing well, although since this involved shifting in and out of the system regularly to examine other similar phenomena, our intelligence mission was, as a result, proving less successful. We knew there was Cardassian activity around here: we kept on picking up odd transmissions; nothing we could trace, but hint after hint that something was going on. The Cardassians denied everything, of course; any activity in this area would be a violation of agreements made about territorial expansion, but we didn't believe them. We just couldn't pin them down. At this point, however, we were all getting tired, and restive, and ready to head back to Starbase 22 for a break. But I just couldn't let the matter go, and I kept turning it over in my mind.

At the senior staff meeting before we were due to return to Starbase 22, Paris heard our reports, and then said with a sigh, "And are we any closer to working out what the Cardassians are doing out here?"

All around the table heads were shaking. I raised my hand, and said, "I have a suggestion, sir."

His interest piqued, he said, "Go on, Janeway."

"I think we should take a look at the ninth moon of the ninth world."

Now everyone around the table was looking at me as if I'd jumped up on the table to show them my Charleston. The ninth world was a barren chunk of rock that would make Pluto feel overdressed. It was something of a joke on board. As for its ninth moon...

"Another trip," Paris said, doubtfully.

I saw my colleagues agreeing. Everyone just wanted to get back to base.

"He makes a good point, Janeway," said Paris. "Any good reason we should drag all the way over there?"

"I can give a reason, sir, but I'm not sure you'll think it's a good reason."

I saw a twinge of something—Amusement? Irritation?—pass across the captain's face. "Try me," he said.

"It's the ninth moon, sir. Of the ninth world."

"How's that relevant?"

"Cardassians like to do things in threes."

There was a pause. Fitz, sitting beside me, muttered something about me dropping by later for a checkup.

"All right, Janeway," said Paris. "Explain your thinking."

"Cardassians have a tendency to do things in threes. Look at how their government is organized: Central Command, Obsidian Order, Detapa Council. Look at the design of their insignia; damn it, even the architecture of places like Terok Nor. Their music: triple harmonies. Their art: all around a principle of triples—"

"Are you a student of their culture, Lieutenant?" said Tuvok. Damn the man, I could never tell when he was sassing me.

"No, but it does no harm to understand something about your..." I hesitated at saying the word *enemy*, and ended up with "your rivals for space and resources."

"*They do things in threes...*" Paris was shaking his head. "Tuvok. What do you think?"

Tuvok shook his head. "This is not a logical reason to investigate, sir. Nor is it a logical reason to locate a base upon so remote a location—"

"That's part of my point!" I said. I was starting to enjoy myself. "It *isn't* logical. It's intuitive. It's possibly superstitious. It might even be a kind of joke. These aren't Vulcans we're dealing with. They're Cardassians! Whatever we might think of their ethics, they have a strong sense of *aesthetics*. The ninth moon of the ninth planet. We've been looking for a base. I bet it's on that moon. It can't be any moon of the third planet—because it's got no moons."

Paris had been observing our exchange with great interest. "Well," he said.

"Sir," said Tuvok. "I must advise against wasting time and effort on this. The crew is tired, we have been out here for some time, and everyone is ready for rest and relaxation."

"I know that what you're saying makes sense," said Paris. "But... *they do things in threes*. I can't pass that up. We'll set a course for that moon, and if we're wrong..." His eyes gleamed. "I'll send anyone who complains about the delay to their holiday over to you, Janeway."

"Sounds fair to me, sir," I said.

The meeting ended. "Follow me," murmured Fitz. "You need your head examined."

✦

It was nearly six weeks before we were able to return to Starbase 22, but nobody was complaining. As we drew nearer to the ninth moon, we were able to pick up a steady stream of Cardassian transmissions. It turned out that this ninth moon of the ninth world in the Arias system was home to a Cardassian communications array and deep-space freighter repair station. The existence of this outpost was directly contrary to the terms of a nonexpansion agreement signed between the Federation and the Cardassian Union the previous year, the purpose of which was precisely to prevent the militarization of this part of the border. Well, of course the Cardassians were violating that agreement with this outpost, and of course this hidden outpost was on the ninth moon.

We kept the *Al-Batani* out of reach of the outpost's sensors, but close enough to be able to monitor transmissions. The Cardassians on that outpost were arrogant, and that made them sloppy. It took me and Tuvok no time to crack their encryption codes. It wasn't long before we assembled the evidence that proved that the intention was to establish a larger base here, an outpost that would serve as spearhead for a larger Cardassian military presence to threaten Federation supply lines along this section of the border. We slipped away and were back on route to Starbase 22 just as the president was summoning the ambassador from the Cardassian Union to explain himself and his government.

I was sitting in the rec room enjoying a drink with Fitz and some of my team when Tuvok appeared.

"Lieutenant Janeway," he said.

"Commander Tuvok," I replied. "Can I help you?"

"No," he said. "I wished simply to acknowledge that you were correct in your assessment of the situation, and that I was wrong. Your analysis was... impressive."

Well, he didn't have to say this in front of other people, and that was impressive in its turn.

"Not analysis," said Fitz. "Intuition."

Tuvok tilted his head in acknowledgement. "So it seems."

"I'm just very relieved we didn't have a wasted journey," I said warmly.

"So are the rest of the crew," said Fitz.

"Sit down and join us, Tuvok," I said. "We'll be breaking out the kadis-kot board in a little while. I'd like to see your game."

"I am not familiar with the game," he said.

I stood up and pushed out a chair. "You soon will be."

He did sit down with us, if a little stiffly, and watched us play the game for a while, whereupon he proceeded to defeat us all in multiple rounds. As we talked that evening, it turned out that we were both great admirers of Parvati Pandey.

"I attended the admiral's classes," he said. "On—"

"The Ethics of Command," I finished up. "I attended those classes too."

He looked at me with interest. "Only the very best cadets were invited to those classes."

"I wasn't such a bad cadet," I said. "And I was only very briefly an arrogant ensign."

"You are neither a bad nor an arrogant officer," he said.

"Why, Tuvok!" I said. "That's almost a compliment!"

"Merely a statement of fact," he said, and proceeded to win another game.

I'm glad to say that after this, not only did we establish a cordial professional relationship, but we began to establish to a genuine rapport, a real friendship, and one that has stood me in good stead over the years. Tuvok would say, I think, that I changed his opinion of humans—although I do have a regrettable tendency to rely on intuition and insist on making decisions based on emotion and gut feeling. I take that, too, as a compliment.

✦

That mission brought us several close encounters with Cardassians. I must admit that, however irrational this was, I still bore considerable anger toward their species as a result of the circumstances of my father's death. I'd like to say that this was aimed specifically toward their government, but in all honesty at this time my antipathy had a more general focus. It was very easy to find oneself slipping into generalizations: that Cardassians were bloodthirsty, that they were duplicitous, that they were not to be trusted. Captain Paris came down hard on these sentiments whenever he heard them; such speciesism, he would say, should never be heard in the mouth of a Starfleet officer. But border wars are dirty fights: not outright hostilities, but sniping at each other, month after month, until respect is whittled away. My mother's work with Bajoran refugees, to my mind, lent support to my sense that there was something fundamentally wrong with Cardassian society. It has been a long journey away from this prejudice, which I know was shared by many of my peers after the Setlik massacre and reinforced during the Dominion War.

I did not experience the war, spending that time with my own business in another quadrant, and saw only the plight of the Cardassian Union after the murderous rampages of the Jem'Hadar. But my attitude had already undergone a substantial sea change during my time on the border on the *Al-Batani*. Strangely enough, this was during an actual firsthand encounter with the Cardassians at Outpost 936. Tuvok, myself, the second officer, Luis Martinez, and another officer had been sent down to a small outpost in the Retik system. There were only a dozen personnel there, at most, and we were providing technical assistance to upgrade their communications system. Nevertheless, we found ourselves under attack from the Cardassian Militia 29, part of the Sixth Order under the command of Gul Pa'Nak. (The Cardassians later claimed that we were the first to open fire; I will deny this until my dying day.)

Communications with the outside world were cut off within the first few minutes of the attack (one reason to assume that this was planned rather than in response to any action of ours). We were under bombardment for the next three days, struggling to reopen communications and call for backup. We made good use of our resources, our defensible position, and our knowledge of the local terrain, and, after three days, struck back hard against the Cardassian unit attacking us. After a very long twelve hours, the Cardassians fell back. We sat and listened to the sounds of the brush around us—and then we heard the unmistakable sound of someone in pain. It wasn't one of ours; it could only be one of theirs.

We listened for a while. He was in agony.

One of our ensigns was trying not to weep.

Martinez said, "I can't listen to this any longer. Janeway, take Ensign Sinclair and go get him. Bring him back."

"Luis," I said, "that's crazy! They're waiting for us to go and get him! He's *bait*!"

"Whatever else he is, he's someone in pain. Go and get him."

Well, I wasn't quite tired enough to disobey a direct order, so Sinclair and

I slipped out under cover of darkness, made our way to where our enemy lay shivering and dying, and gave him a sedative. I remember his eyes—bright and feverish, staring up at me. He was very young. Younger than one of our first-year cadets, and already in battle. I took his hand.

"You'll be all right," I said. "We're here to help you."

He passed out, mercifully. Sinclair and I got him on the stretcher and carted him back. While we'd been out there, they'd got the comms link working again. Reinforcements from the *Al-Batani* were on their way. Fitz transported down and took our prisoner back up to the ship to treat him, although he wasn't in time to save the young man's left arm. Later, once the outpost was secured, we went out into the brush again, looking for the dead. We found half a dozen bodies; none of them much older than the one we had saved. Back on the *Al-Batani*, I went to see our prisoner. His name was Tret Rekheny. He was an ordinary foot soldier, not even an ensign (or a *glinn*, as the Cardassians would say), and this was his first action. He was scared of us, and scared of what his commanding officers would do once we returned him to them. "They'll think I gave them away," he said. "The Order will want to see me. I don't want to see them…" I realized that he was shaking with real terror at the thought of falling into the hands the Obsidian Order.

There was little that we could do for him: there was a long-standing agreement that we returned theirs if they returned ours, even though poor Rekheny was not much to bargain with. He was with us for no more than a few days before he was well enough to send home. I saw him most days he was on board the *Al-Batani*. I remember hearing him chanting names, three times each. It was part of the Cardassian funeral rite, he said: naming the dead to remember them. I said, didn't I, that they did things in threes. I found myself wondering about his friends, too, the lives behind those dead names. Who they were; where they'd come from; who would learn of their deaths, and whether they would be struck down by grief, the way that I had been when I heard about my father. I knew that I would never see Cardassians in the same way again. They felt pain, they grieved, they were afraid. For the first time ever, I felt compassion for the Cardassian people.

I have often wondered what happened to our prisoner after he went back, and whether the Obsidian Order did indeed finish what the Central Command had started when they sent him out there to fight us in the first place. I doubt that he survived the Dominion War or the Jem'Hadar's mass slaughter: very few of his rank did. Perhaps it was better if he did not live to see all the pain that followed. When it was time for him to leave the *Al-Batani*, an Order operative came over to collect him: a slick, supercilious man who put a possessive hand upon the young soldier's arm, and said, "We'll take care of you now." I have never loathed anyone so much in my life. They beamed back across to their freighter, and that was the last that I saw of Tret Rekheny.

The four of us—Luis Martinez, Tuvok, Anna Sinclair, and myself—were all decorated for our part in this operation. I suppose that I am proud of what I did, even though at the time I thought the order that Shulie had given us was madness. But what I took mostly from these events was what I tried to tell Seven of Nine later, that a single act of compassion can transform us. Having met Tret Rekheny, however briefly, it was not so easy, in future, for me to think of all Cardassians as cruel, as murderous, as vicious. Some of them, it seemed to me now, were as much victims of their government as the peoples they oppressed.

✦

Altogether, I served as chief science officer under Owen Paris on the *Al-Batani* for eight years. Much of that time I spent out near the Cardassian border, trying to combine scientific observation with intelligence gathering. To some degree these purposes could be made to work together; in other respects, they were completely at odds. For one thing, science does not care for borders. It does not care that the place where you need to be to make necessary observations would violate a treaty or test diplomatic sensitivities to the limit. Sometimes we found ourselves tantalizingly close to a breakthrough, an expansion in our knowledge, and we would have to pull back, away from territory we had agreed not to enter. I would have found this less frustrating, had I not known how flagrantly the Cardassians would break their word when the situation was reversed.

Altogether, I found it increasingly difficult to resolve the tension between these two objectives, and, privately, I was coming to believe that further and more serious conflict with the Cardassians was inevitable. I often found myself thinking back to a conversation I'd had with my father, when I was first making my decision to join Starfleet. He'd said: *It takes two sides to make peace. And*

I'm not sure that both sides want it. The Arias expedition had taught me two things: that not all Cardassians were bloodthirsty warmongers, but that the bloodthirsty warmongers were the ones calling the shots on Cardassia Prime these days. War was coming—the question was, what could I get done before it came to me?

I knew that the *Al-Batani* would be continuing in this dual role for the foreseeable future. But I wanted my chance to experience the old Starfleet: the Starfleet of exploration and scientific study. I decided to put in for a transfer. When I told Owen Paris my decision, he did me the kindness of saying how far I had come in the years that I had served under him, and that he now considered me one of the best rising officers within Starfleet. "Whoever gets you next is a lucky captain, Kathryn," he said, and sighed. "Three requests for transfer on the same day! I must be losing my touch."

"Three, sir?"

It turned out several of his senior staff had made similar decisions. My friend Fitz was heading off to Caldik Prime, to take up a surgeon's post at the medical facility there. It was one of the leading hospitals in the Federation, with a specialty in biosynthetic prosthetics. I think Fitz's mind was on the forthcoming war too. I knew that he felt he had been ill-equipped for some of the field surgery he had been required to perform during our time on the border. And Tuvok was moving on as well, to take on a senior security role on Jupiter Station. That evening, the three of us met for supper and a game of kadis-kot, for old time's sake. We discussed our future plans, and they asked me where I was heading.

"The *U.S.S. Billings*," I said. "Captain Melita Vas. It's a big survey of the Glass Horse Nebula, and I'll be heading up a pretty large team. Which means a promotion!" I was now Lieutenant Commander Janeway, having been promoted to full lieutenant during the Arias mission.

"Overdue," said Fitz.

"I note that scientific study has won out in your affections after all," Tuvok said. "I am glad that your rational side is moving to the fore."

"I think I'm just tired of looking over my shoulder for Cardassians," I said.

"You and me both," said Fitz.

"I want to do some science, some real science! I want to feel as if I've had the chance to explore, before... Well."

"I understand that contrary to all expectations, there is hope that a treaty may well be signed between the Federation and the Cardassian Union within the next five years," said Tuvok.

"I don't see that happening," said Fitz. "Even if they did sign it—they don't keep their word, do they?"

Fitz really was very bitter about some of what he'd seen over the last few years.

"I guess we have to hope," I said.

"Hope has nothing to do with it," said Tuvok. "Peace is the rational choice."

Fitz and I glanced at each other but held our tongues. I knew what he was thinking. If only the Cardassians were as rational as our Vulcan friend.

"Well," I said, raising my glass. "Until we meet again."

Tuvok and Fitz raised their glasses in turn. And we did meet again: as captain, chief of security, and CMO of the *U.S.S. Voyager*—but only for the briefest of times.

✦

There's one last meeting I should record before bringing my account of my time on the *Al-Batani* to a close. Before we all left, Captain Paris held a lavish party for his crew at his home in Oregon. And there I met young Tom again; seventeen years old now, but not, I thought, a happy young man. Observing the interactions between father and son, I sensed a lot of regret on one side, a lot of sullen resentment on the other. He clearly didn't like having all these young officers around, the apples of his father's eye.

"I hear you're heading to Starfleet," I said.

He shrugged. "What else is there to do?"

I hid my surprise. "Plenty of things—"

"Not if I want to fly."

"Is that what you like doing, Tom?"

That shrug again. "I guess."

It wasn't the most promising of encounters, but I couldn't put young Tom Paris out of my mind. I suppose on some level, I sympathized with him. It's not easy, having a Starfleet officer as your father. It's not easy proving yourself. I often found myself wondering about him, over the next years, what he was doing, and where he was going to end up.

CHAPTER SIX
NEW CHALLENGES—2365-2370

BEFORE HEADING TO MY NEW POSTING ON THE *BILLINGS*, I was due a few weeks' leave. Naturally, I went home, back to Indiana, on from Bloomington, into the country and back to the farm. As ever, the place restored me to myself. Gone now was the sense that everything was smaller, that I was returning to a coop in which I no longer fit. Instead, I found peace and quiet, the chance to rest, the familiar places and patterns of childhood—although, inevitably, there was a great sense of sadness that one of our number was missing.

My mother, as brave and beautiful as ever, had made great strides in coming to terms with her widowhood. As many women do who lose their partners young, and who cannot ever imagine themselves marrying again, she had thrown herself into tasks that turned her focus outward. She was now deeply involved in the Bajoran relief effort, and it was notable that she spent a great deal of time away from the farm. My father's absence was of course a significant element in this change: even though he had spent so much time away from home, there had always been the promise of his return. Throughout their marriage, my mother had been content to wait, living the life that she loved best, waiting for the person that she loved best. It was not as if she was running away, but the house must surely have felt lonely at times. I had left; Phoebe had left; and, while her parents were still living nearby and in good health, it was not the family life that she had been used to.

This time when I came home, my mother was still coming back from a long trip to the headquarters of the Federation Bajoran relief effort in Geneva. That must have been a poignant visit for her, bringing back the time when she and my father had met, all those years ago. When I arrived at the house, late one evening, the place was dark. I believe that may well have been the first time that I had ever seen it that way: lights off, blinds up, nobody there. I went inside, listening to the unusual quiet, and then I wandered around, asking for lights, making tea, slowly bringing the place to life. Phoebe arrived about an hour later, apologizing that she hadn't made it in time to meet me, smothering me with hugs and kisses. My mother was not back until well into the evening. There was a touch more silver in her hair these days, a few more lines upon her face, but when she saw us, she threw out her arms to embrace us both.

"My girls," she said. "My two darling girls."

That was a fine vacation, one of the best. Chief among my pleasures was getting to know Phoebe's wife and children, who joined us a day or two later. Just before I set out on the Arias expedition, Phoebe had taken an artist's residency on Trill, where she had been exploring the effects of longevity upon their creative practice. How did joined Trills relate to the art produced when joined to a previous host? Where did their artistry lie? Fascinating ideas, posing fundamental questions about identity and personhood, questions that I found myself wrestling with over and over again on my voyage home. During the fourth month of Phoebe's year-long residency, she met a painter, a joined Trill named Yianem Lox. They fell deeply in love and were married by the end of the year. Yianem, always ready for adventure, had agreed to come back to Earth with Phoebe. They were currently living on the West Coast, near Portland, part of a writers' and artists' community. They also had three small daughters—one of whom, the eldest, I had met before, but as a baby. The younger two, still small, I was planning to get acquainted with during this break.

What a busy, fun, joyous leave that was! Three little girls under the age of four, full of curiosity and mischief. Their moods were ever changing: sudden laughing sunshine followed by rapid squalls of tears, then rainbow smiles. With one aunt, one grandmother, and four great-grandparents in attendance, they now had roughly the attention which they thought was their due, and both Phoebe and Yianem could take some well-earned rest. Two grown-ups with three children are outnumbered, and not even the guile of a long-lived joined

Trill is necessarily the match for the wits and speed of a toddler who has just learned to walk and is intent on wreaking havoc. These three children filled the gaps in the house. Sitting on the porch with my mother one afternoon, watching them tumbling over the grass, I said, "It's like the place has been given a second life, Mom, don't you think?"

She smiled and nodded. "I know what you mean. There were some days when I couldn't seem to bring the place alive. Some of the rooms stood empty for days on end. Nobody there. It was hard, after having you two here…" She breathed in deeply. "But these three—aren't they marvelous? I think they cause more mayhem than you and Phoebe ever did. As it should be."

I watched her, watching her grandchildren. She looked vibrant, happy, alive; and I knew then that she would be fine. Her relief work had given her purpose, but her grandchildren had given her heart. I knew that I could take up my next posting and not have to worry about her without Dad. She was strong and brave, with a huge capacity for love, and although my father's death left a hole that could never be filled, she had found a way through. I knew that when my leave was over, I could return to Starfleet with my mind at rest.

✦

After two months back at home, it was time to say goodbye again to my family, and head off to near-Earth orbit, where the *U.S.S. Billings* was waiting to take on its new crew. I could only be pleased with the ship itself: a prototype *Nova*-class exploration vessel, one of the very first of its kind, kitted out with excellent facilities for our mission. The science and data analysis team, of which I was now in charge, was well established, but made their new senior officer very welcome. Taking over a team like this can be a huge challenge, particularly when you join one that works well together, and who must be concerned about a change at the top. None of them had requested my position, I was glad to realize, so there were no resentments about my appointment. They were a grand set of people, the best of Starfleet, competent and intelligent, and well able to train a new commander overseeing her first big team. They made a huge difference to my time on the *Billings*.

Rather than their new senior officer, they were more concerned about the fact that the ship had a new captain. I too was somewhat worried about this change: I had requested this posting in part so that I could serve under Captain Melita Vas, who had such a good reputation. Unfortunately, Vas, after a sudden period of bad health, had accepted a long overdue promotion to admiral and was, in effect, retiring to teach at the Academy. I was most disappointed by this news, and sorry that I had not had the chance ever to wish her well: she had left the *Billings* a day or two before my own arrival. A new captain had been assigned: Neil Ward, who was taking up his first captaincy, and was on his way from Mars when I arrived on the *Billings*.

The captain sets the tone of any starship, and there was a great deal of anxiety about the new man. I'm sorry to say that it was not misplaced. Serving under Neil Ward was one of the most difficult periods of my life (just edged out by being flung seventy thousand light-years from home), and I came very close to leaving Starfleet as a result on several occasions. What can I say about Ward? Certainly, he had a way with admirals, all of whom seemed to like him, and spoke well of him. He was certainly ambitious, and plainly did not intend to remain captain of a comparatively small research vessel like the *Billings*. His facility with the egos of the top brass meant that he did have a knack of getting resources and equipment, but the benefits were not equally shared. Provided you were one of his favorites, you didn't struggle to get whatever you required. If you were not one of his favorites, the situation was much different—and I'm sad to report that it rapidly became clear to me that I was not one of the chosen ones. I sat through several meetings of the senior staff having my opinions passed over, taken apart, or simply ignored, while others were encouraged to speak. After one very difficult meeting, I decided that I had to say something. This situation simply could not continue; I was finding it increasingly difficult to be able to function.

"Captain," I said, as the other team heads were leaving, "may I have a word with you?"

He gave a sigh. "Is it urgent, Janeway? I'm pretty busy."

"It's not urgent, sir, but I do think it needs to be addressed."

"All right," he said, but he opened his companel and began to look at messages there. I remained standing; he hadn't invited me to sit again. Nor did he attempt to lead the conversation.

"Sir," I said, at last. "I have the distinct impression that you don't like me, and I want to understand what it is that I've done wrong, so that I can rectify that."

He closed the companel. "What makes you say that, Commander?"

"I just… It seems to me that I haven't been able to make a suggestion that you like, sir."

"Maybe you haven't made any good suggestions yet, Commander."

I was beginning to feel angry. I knew my weaknesses—but I also knew my strengths. "With respect, sir, I don't think that's true."

"*With respect…*" He eyed me thoughtfully. "You're blessed with confidence, aren't you, Janeway?"

"I beg your pardon, sir?"

"I meant—you don't often doubt your judgement, do you?"

Well, what on earth could he mean by that? I was well trained, experienced, smart, and hard-working. I'd learned good lessons early in my career about arrogance. I liked working in teams, and I tried my best to mentor junior colleagues. I was, on the whole, pleased with my performance, and a captain as good as Owen Paris had agreed. Had we all been missing something? I wasn't entirely sure what to say in response to this. Carefully, I said, "I try to give my best, sir."

"I envy that kind of confidence," he said. "Your father was a vice admiral, wasn't he?"

"Yes," I said. "Sir, I don't see how that's relevant to this conversation. My grandfather was Starfleet too. I imagine you could find a few Janeways here and there over the last century or so."

"That wouldn't surprise me in the least," he said. "I've often observed this kind of confidence in officers with a long family history with Starfleet. Like Starfleet is an extension of their family. It's not, of course."

Now, I thought, I was beginning to understand some of his antipathy toward me. He thought my success was down to me being my father's daughter. Well, it was a while since I'd come across this prejudice! There had been a few asides at the Academy, swiftly quashed when my first semester's grades arrived. Since then—a few comments here and there in my early days, but nothing much since. My work, my dedication, and my experience spoke for themselves. By this point in the conversation, I was pretty angry, as you can imagine. I had served in Starfleet for nearly a decade; I'd seen active service along the Cardassian border; I'd worked hard, and I'd earned every damn one of my promotions. I had not expected to hear this kind of thing again, and I was alarmed to hear it coming from my new commanding officer. I had committed to this mission. Had it been a mistake?

As calmly as I could manage, I said, "I'm sorry to hear that, sir, and I'm certainly sorry if I've given that impression."

"You had a leave of absence, didn't you, a few years back? And came straight back to a promotion."

Now I was furious. "It has been my good fortune, sir," I said, "that I have been shown various acts of kindness since my father's death. But I'd like to think that I didn't take any of this for granted."

He did have the good grace to look embarrassed at that. "Yes, well, just so we're all aware—everyone is equal on board this ship, Commander."

"You're the captain, sir," I said. "You set the rules."

"That's right." He turned back to his companel. "Is there anything else, Janeway?"

"Not right now, sir."

"Dismissed."

I left feeling very downhearted at this whole exchange. I'd signed on for a long trip, and it seemed that the captain, for reasons best known to himself, did not like me. Worse, it was difficult to know who to broach this with. Had I been back on the *Al-Batani*, among colleagues with whom I had served for a long time, then I would have someone to talk to. I'd have talked to Tuvok, and received good counsel; or to Fitz, if I'd wanted some cheerleading; or even to Captain Paris himself, if I thought the matter was serious enough to warrant his advice. These were people who knew me well. But here on the *Billings* I was new, trying to establish myself. I did not want to get a reputation of being someone who arrived only to complain. This was a very tricky period, and also rather lonely. Increasingly, as Ward's antipathy showed no sign of abating, I found that I was starting to second-guess myself. I started questioning whether my opinions were justified, grounded in data and good reasoning, or whether I was being overconfident. I withdrew slightly from crew activities, not realizing that I was starting to get a reputation for being standoffish. I'm not ashamed to admit that I spent some evenings alone in my quarters, shedding a few tears.

(Years later, talking to a colleague about this time, she shook her head, and said, "There's a word for this, Kate. It's called gaslighting. Make someone doubt themselves. It's a rotten, stinking trick." And I think she was right. But I do wonder now, looking back, whether I was little too sure of myself, a little too certain about my career path and its upward trajectory. In other words, I have tried to see it from Ward's perspective—although I do wonder whether he ever tried to see it from mine.)

At the time, however, all I knew was that this was the reality of serving on board the *Billings*, and that I was stuck for the foreseeable future. As I approached the end of my first year, I began to contemplate putting in for a transfer. It would mean a sideways move, perhaps even losing my seniority (I was indeed young to be in charge of such a big team), but I was wondering whether it would be worth it. I went along to an appraisal meeting with Ward and, bizarrely, he was all smiles. Pleased with my performance; pleased with the team; seemingly pleased with everything. The next day, sitting in the ready room with the other team heads, he ignored my contributions entirely. I knew I couldn't carry on like this. I needed advice, good, level-headed advice. I naturally turned to Tuvok.

I sent my old friend a long, rather rambling message, in which I outlined the events of my first year on board; minor exchanges that seemed almost ridiculous and inconsequential as I detailed them. But as I spoke, and they accumulated, I began to realize how much of a toll this was taking on me. I wrapped up the message: "I know that you of all people will look at this with a cool eye. I know you'll be able to tell me whether this is all in my imagination, or whether what I hear and see is true. I hope to hear from you soon, Tuvok."

It was a week or so before he replied. How glad I was to see his cool and sensible face upon my screen—and how far we'd come since that first meeting! As ever, his advice brought me fresh perspective.

"*As you know, Kathryn, I have been able to study you across the whole of your career so far. I saw you at the very start, making elementary mistakes, and I saw you the day before you left to take up this posting. I am pleased to say that by that time you had evolved into a capable young officer. It is not possible for you to control your captain's emotions, nor is it your responsibility. I see no reason why this should have changed in the short months since we have been serving together. Therefore, I must conclude that the problem does not lie with you, but with your commanding officer. And a commanding officer who squanders such as resource as an officer like you is not acting rationally.*

"*Whatever irrational impulses motivate Captain Ward are his responsibility.*

What you are able to do is control your own response. Therefore, I would say that it is for you to determine whether this situation is tolerable for you, or whether it has become intolerable. There are clear benefits to you in remaining on the Billings. You are young to be put in command of a large team. To ask to be transferred would, in some quarters, be seen as an admission of failure. This may affect your route to captaincy, which I suspect is not something you are prepared to sacrifice simply for the sake of avoiding Ward. One alternative, then, is to treat your relationship quite logically—as a kind of transaction. A means to an end. Do your duty to the best of your ability. Act in good faith. Take all that you require from this posting in terms of experience, and, when the time is propitious, move on."

I took his advice to heart. When I was dealing with the captain, I thought of myself as Vulcan. I responded logically, accurately, precisely, and unemotionally. I stuck to data and evidence and kept away from conjecture. It's hard to fault someone when their facts are straight. He tried to find fault (after all, not everyone wants to act in good faith), but he was rarely able to do it, and that brought a little job satisfaction, even if it never brought much in the way of thanks or praise.

But I am not Vulcan, and I could not cut my emotions out entirely. I was too sociable to be able to sit alone in my quarters every night for another four years, and I was damned if I was going to do so. Screwing up my courage, I decided to make some friends. I started tentatively, inviting two of my lieutenants over to my quarters for dinner, then, as my confidence returned (and they began to realize I wasn't so standoffish after all), I began to get the whole team to socialize together. Soon I began to find my feet again. Invitations from people began to arrive. I joined the Velocity team—there's nothing like helping your team win a few games to make your colleagues fonder of you! I began to find my way again. I began to feel more like Kathryn Janeway.

And I began to find out that it wasn't just me with reservations about Ward. Quite a few of my team didn't like their new captain very much either. The ship had changed since Vas had left, they said. Ward's an empire builder, one said. He's only using this ship as a stepping-stone to something else, said another. He plays people against each other, said yet another. No, they didn't like him at all, and they missed their old captain immensely. We were well into my second year, and when I asked my colleagues why nobody had brought this up before, they looked embarrassed. I'd arrived at the same time, they said, and I'd got associated with him in their minds. And I'd been so damn serious! No fun at all! They thought I was part of the new regime. They weren't sure I was on their side.

Well, there's a lesson about isolating yourself. I saw that I had been failing my team in a significant way: part of my role as their commander was to act as a buffer between them and the captain, to make sure that his irrationalities didn't affect them. It wasn't an easy situation but knowing that I was actively improving my team's day-to-day life went a long way to making me feel better about being on board ship. We all wanted to see this mission through, and, part of my role, I realized now, was to make sure that my team were not affected by the maelstrom of difficult emotions swirling around and the unhappy environment in which we found ourselves. I wish things had been different on the *Billings* (not least that I had served under the previous captain), but I learned valuable lessons there which stood me in good stead on board *Voyager*. You can learn as much from a bad captain as you can from a good captain: how not to motivate people; how not to get a team to come together; how not to build trust and loyalty. If I'm ever in doubt, I think, "What would Ward do?" and I do the opposite.

✦

The irony of all this is that Cardassian–Federation relations were the best they had been in decades. An armistice had been signed in 2367, considerably easing tensions between us, and, while there were still numerous incidents around the border, the feeling was that peace was now a real possibility, and the word was that the top brass and the diplomats were hard at work on a treaty. This became even more likely when the Cardassians announced that they were withdrawing from Bajor. I remember being in the mess hall with my team when this news came through: the sense of elation, and relief, was enormous. There were one or two Bajoran crew members, and they were in tears. I don't believe any of us had ever thought we would see that day. It gave us real hope that things had changed for the better, and for good, which seemed to be borne out with the signing, in 2370, of the Federation–Cardassian Treaty, which established the border between our territories, and created the Demilitarized

Zone, a buffer zone between us. With the treaty, we all felt that peace was on its way. (Although there were complications that none of us had foreseen, when some of the colony worlds within the DMZ began to realize what the treaty meant for them.)

In general, however, the mood was positive, and this brought home how petty the situation on the *Billings* was. It was around this time I received some information from Tuvok that clarified my difficulties with Ward. Tuvok reported to me that the *U.S.S. Rotorua* had recently stopped off for refitting at Jupiter Station. Tuvok, entering a turbolift, overheard a conversation involving the ship's chief science officer. It seemed that this person had been expecting a posting on the *Billings* by the new captain, but it had gone to somebody else.

"A vice admiral's daughter," they said. "You know how it works! And it was promised to me!"

Several things clicked into place when I heard this. Ward, I guessed, knowing that he was taking on the captaincy of the *Billings,* must have known that the post of chief science officer had also become vacant, and promised it to his friend. But he was behind on the news: Vas had already assigned me, in more or less one of her last acts before taking ill. Ward arrived on the *Billings* expecting to be able to promote his crony—only to find Kathryn Janeway, the vice admiral's daughter, firmly in place, and raring to go.

This was more or less what I'd come to expect from Ward, but finally having an explanation for his behavior went a long way toward relieving any lingering sense I had that things going wrong was my fault. A further experience I had with him that year reduced any respect I had for my captain to rock bottom: not a happy situation. We had detoured into the Katexa system for a brief survey mission, where we detected some unusual volcanic activity on one of the moons of the fourth world in the system. We all agreed that this was worth closer analysis and consequently took the ship toward the moon. Around this point, having seen some preliminary analysis of the magma flows, I began to have serious misgivings about the whole idea, which I expressed in a meeting of the senior staff.

"We can get some fine readings from on board ship," I said. "Not to mention it'll be a chance to find out whether the adjustments we've been making on the forward sensors have been worth the effort."

I don't know whether it was because I was the one who had made the suggestion, but Ward wasn't having it. He insisted sending down an away team.

"Where's your sense of adventure, Janeway?" he said.

Well, my sense of adventure was fine, thank you very much; my sense of whether it was right to risk an away team in a shuttle on a volcanic moon was simply much stronger. And I'm sad to say that I was proved right: the away team's shuttle had barely entered the atmosphere when there was a massive magma eruption, badly damaging the craft. There were a couple of hours when we thought that the three crew members were lost. I was furious with Ward. He had ignored my advice—my *considered* advice, my *expert* advice—and he had, so far as I could make out, done it for no other reason than spite, risking the lives of three members of his crew. I kept these feelings bottled up while we were trying to find out what the hell had happened to my team, but I was enraged. I knew it; he knew it; and the whole damn ship knew it.

Eventually, I am glad to report, we were able to retrieve the three members of the away team, but they had some pretty serious injuries. One of them was out of action for a couple of months. The shuttle was a write-off. After everyone was safely back on board, the captain called his senior staff together for a debriefing. I imagine everyone was expecting that I was going to explode in much the same way as that volcano had, but I kept my cool, even as I watched Ward make excuse after excuse. I could see that he wanted to blame this debacle on me in some way. But he couldn't. The decision to send the away team had been his, and he had made it against the advice of his chief science officer, and in front of the whole senior staff. I let him talk, and I watched as the respect leached away from almost every single person in that room.

Eventually, he dismissed us all. I waited until the room was empty.

"Sir," I said. "Permission to speak freely?"

"Go ahead, Janeway."

"I know that you didn't want me for this post, but I'm here now, and there's nothing either of us can do about that. But I sincerely hope, sir, that you won't ignore my expert advice again. We're just lucky that nobody was killed today." I headed for the door. "One more thing," I said, before I left. "You want those damn readings? You'll get those damn readings. I'll go and get them myself— but I'll go when it's safe. And I'll be the one who decides that—based on sound scientific judgement."

He got his readings. I was able to go down the next day, by myself, and get them. And the *Billings* moved on.

✦

As well as Tuvok, I had remained in contact with my old friend Laurie Fitzgerald, CMO on the *Al-Batani*, who had taken up a surgeon's post on Caldik Prime. In one of his messages, he passed on some worrying news about our old captain, or, more accurately, his son Tom. It turned out Tom's career in Starfleet had come to an unpleasant conclusion: he had, it seemed, been the cause of an accident which had led to the tragic death of three officers. Worse, he had tried to cover up his responsibility for the accident but had been found out. He had been cashiered out of Starfleet.

"I know you liked that kid, Kathryn, but he never impressed me. Careless, cocky—the worst. Owen Paris must be heartbroken."

I imagined he was. I sent my old captain a message, saying how sorry I was to hear about his troubles, and I received a kind note back. But I couldn't help feeling sorry for young Tom, who had always struck me as a young man who was floundering, and never felt quite good enough. This was a tragic end to his career, before it had even had a chance to start. I could only hope that this was not the start of a downward spiral for him, and that he found his way somehow.

I, meanwhile, was still considering my next move. I had found a way to work on the *Billings*, and I had earned the respect of my team, and of many of my direct colleagues. But I was never going to earn Ward's favor. and he was never going to earn my respect. I was never going to be one of his cronies and I didn't want to be. There was a wider universe out there, as my correspondence with Tuvok reminded me—but I did feel constantly on high alert, ready for the next putdown, or the next sharp word.

This made my trips back to Earth even more blissful. And one of these occasions, during my fourth year serving on the *Billings,* just after I'd been promoted to full commander, changed my life. I was visiting Phoebe and Yianem and their tribe, out in Portland, and they invited a friend of Yianem's over for dinner. "It's a sad story," Phoebe said, as we stood together in the kitchen, she busy dressing the salad and me drinking wine. "His wife was killed in a shuttle accident on Mars eighteen months ago. He's only really started to come out again. He's still very fragile. We just want him to have some cheerful evenings."

Well, I was happy to switch on my charm, such as it is, and I'm pleased to report that their friend, a handsome man of about my age named Mark Johnson, was not immune. He certainly laughed a great deal that evening, more so as my stories about my appalling captain became less and less discreet and more and more pointed. (It did me a world of good to talk about Ward like that too: all of a sudden, he felt ridiculous, rather than powerful.) While Phoebe and Yianem were busy in the kitchen organizing dessert, Mark said, "Are you back on Earth for a while yet, Kathryn?"

"A couple of months."

"That's good. Are you around Portland for most of that time?"

"A week or so. Then I'll visit my mother near Bloomington for a while. I don't intend to travel much, though. Just take it easy."

"And what does 'take it easy' mean to Kathryn Janeway? From what your sister says, I imagine you're planning to climb Everest, or hike across Mongolia—"

I laughed. "Not this time! I was thinking of getting a dog."

"A *dog*?"

I looked at him in alarm. "Do you not like dogs?" I don't trust people who don't like dogs.

"I've… I've never owned a dog. Aren't they a lot of hard work? Don't they need a lot of walking?"

"That's the general idea," I said.

"You're going to spend your leave walking the dog?"

"Precisely that. Sounds blissful, doesn't it?"

He smiled at me. "Depends on the company, I'd say."

"You can't go wrong with a dog, Mark."

"And is the dog sufficient for your purposes, company-wise?"

"What are you asking, exactly?"

"I'm asking whether you'd like some company. When you go and walk your dog."

"Depends on the company," I said, with a smile.

"How about mine?" he said.

"Then the answer's yes."

After that night, we saw a great deal of each other. He helped me choose my new dog—a very affectionate Irish setter named Mollie, whom I'd seen listed in a pound on Taris Seti IV (she was the runt of the litter, but I sensed a little fighter there, and I'd found a fine kennel for her for when I was away). As promised, he joined me on our walks. I was embarrassed at first—I'd come all this way to see my sister and her family—but she and her wife were warmly encouraging. "I've never seen you so serious about someone since the Academy, Kate," Phoebe said. "I think we all want to know where this is heading."

"Oh, Phoebe! We've only met half a dozen times!"

I saw my sister and her wife exchange knowing looks. Is there anything more annoying to a single person than their partnered family and friends? Always so very smug about the whole business, always in a hurry to pair you off! It was hardly as if I'd been living as a nun. I'd had various dalliances during my time on both the *Al-Batani* and the *Billings* (no, I won't say who). It was true, though, that this was the most serious relationship since my near-miss at the Academy.

"He's very nice though," said Phoebe.

"If he wasn't nice," I said, "I wouldn't be spending time with him."

Yianem said, "Remember to be gentle with him, Kathryn, please. He… he's had a bad time."

I hastened to reassure her. "Oh, of course I'll be gentle! That's all either of us want. A little tender loving care."

Our walks together became a daily fixture, Mollie bounding between us. And the more we walked, the more we opened our hearts to each other. I talked about the trials of serving on the *Billings*; how much my confidence had been knocked by that first year; how hard I'd worked to earn the trust of my colleagues and to make a few friends. He talked about his wife. How terrible a blow it had been; how sudden (I knew how that might feel); how he'd thought he would never get through some of the long and empty days. "I think because she was away from home when she died, when the shuttle went down," he said. "I kept expecting her to walk back through the door, complaining about missed flight connections or something… Of course, she never did."

He had moved house in the end. Tried to draw a line underneath those years. "They had been so happy—we had been so happy. But eventually you have to admit that they're finished. That you have to move on."

"Like my mother," I said. "Finding a new way to live. I think it's about the bravest thing I have ever seen."

"Brave!" He shook his head. "Surely what you do is brave!"

"What do you mean?"

"Fight Cardassians—"

"You make it sound like I'm in single combat!"

"I wouldn't put it past you, Kate!"

I laughed. Mark always made me laugh. "Well, it's all a lot less exciting than people think. Mostly I'm on board ship, tracking transmissions, analyzing data—"

"Ah, you're spoiling the magic!"

I looked into his eyes. "I hope not."

We stood there for a moment, looking steadily at each other, and then we both moved forward, and shared a kiss. "I think you're something special, Kathryn Janeway," he said.

"I second that emotion, Mark Johnson," I replied.

Later that night, when I quietly slipped back into my sister's house, Mollie asleep in my arms, Phoebe was sitting up waiting for me. She took one look at me, and said, "It's serious, then."

My head was spinning; my heart was dancing. I felt like a girl again. "Phoebe," I said, "I really think it is."

✦

I had another two weeks of leave, and I did spend most of it with Mark. (My mother was not in the least put out that I didn't come home: it seemed that Phoebe had let her know what was going on.) On the last day before I was due to head back, we went out into the woods together, and walked arm in arm under the huge trees.

"You know," he said, "I was going to suggest we go somewhere for this last day. Rome, or Paris... But then I realized I just wanted to be here."

I smiled. I'd had the same thought.

And then he said, "Kate, you do realize, don't you, that I want to marry you?"

I stopped dead in my tracks. Mollie was snuffling around my boots. "I beg your pardon?"

He smiled at me. "You must have worked that out by now!"

"Mark, we've known each other… What? Two months? Not even that! Seven weeks!"

"Long enough for me to know."

"But… You don't mean it, do you? Surely you don't mean it."

He took my hand. "Kate," he said, "I mean it absolutely. I think you're great. I haven't laughed this much… Well, you've made me feel happy again."

I felt a deep wave of affection toward him. "Oh, Mark, I'm so glad about that! But *marriage*?"

"Listen," he said. "Losing Lisa…" For a moment, his face took on a haunted look. He went on, "It brought home to me how fragile life is. How easily we can lose everything. And that if another chance comes our way, we should have the good sense to seize it. I mean it, Kate. I want to marry you."

For a moment, I wavered. He really did make me feel so special. He made me feel loved. But I was leaving on the *Billings* the next morning. "Oh, Mark, it's much too soon!"

He lifted my hand to kiss it. "All right," he said, and began to laugh. "I'm hardly going to force you, am I?"

"Can we still see each other?"

"When you're back home, you mean?"

"There is that," I admitted. "Please?"

"Oh, Kate," he said. "I'll be waiting at the docking bay to welcome you home."

So that's where we left it, for the moment. Agreeing to see each other whenever I was home… And I found that whenever I was with him, that's how it felt—like coming home. The *Billings* was close to Earth during this period, and so we saw a fair amount of each other. We found, yet again, that what made us most happy was simply being together. Lots of long walks, with Mollie, of course, but also just time at home. He was a great cook (I am not), and he would make me stop and take time away from messages and reports (once you reach a certain level at Starfleet, you're never totally on leave). Left to my own devices, I would lose myself completely in my work. But Mark made me look up from my desk, made me relax and enjoy the world around us. And did I mention how handsome he was?

I thought long and hard about his offer of marriage. I was trying to see a way through, but I couldn't yet. I didn't want to be an absentee wife—he had lost one wife already, lost the home they had together. And I guess, too, that I had been frightened by my experience with my former lover. In my mind, perhaps, I had conflated an offer of marriage with the need to give up some essential part of myself. A year after his first proposal, tucked up at home with my big silly dog snoozing between us, he asked again, "Is it still too soon, Kate?"

"It's still too soon, Mark."

"That's okay," he said. "I'm still prepared to wait."

Further discussion was interrupted as a message arrived for me.

"Damn," I said. "The kennels have cancelled—"

Mark sighed. "I'm even prepared," he said, "to take care of your dog."

And he did take very good care of my dog.

CHAPTER SEVEN
IN THE CAPTAIN'S SEAT—2371

EACH TIME THAT I SAID GOODBYE TO MARK (AND MOLLIE) WAS A WRENCH. Whenever I came home, we fell so easily back into step with each other. We picked up conversations again as if one of us had only been away for five minutes. We liked to do the same things. We liked to spend time with friends and family. We liked to sit in front of the fire, reading, sometimes sharing some piece of information that we knew the other would find interesting. We liked to be outdoors (his work, as an industrial designer, kept him at the drawing board; mine, of course, often kept me from the outdoors completely). And Mollie, of course, was growing and needed her exercise. We were often out together for hours, the three of us, walking through the woods or along the coast, Mollie running ahead. It was good just to be together. If this all sounds very sedate—I guess it was. My job brought enough in the way of adrenalin rushes. Home life I wanted to be steady and reliable.

We were fortunate that we both got on with each other's friends, and we liked each other's family members. Mark loved my nieces: partly for Yianem's sake (their friendship went back a long way) and partly because he clearly liked children. He was good with kids too. He had a great deal of patience (he needed that, given my stubborn streak). But I often wondered why he was not a father already. I wouldn't have minded if kids had been part of the package. One evening, back at his home in Portland, curled up before the fire with mugs of hot chocolate (with a good dash of brandy), and some Debussy whirling gently around us, I decided to ask. It's one of those conversations that most partners have to have at some point. I knew how serious he was.

"Mark," I said. "You don't have to answer this if you don't want to, but was there a reason that you and Lisa didn't have children?"

He looked at me in surprise, and with a little shock. I didn't very often bring up Lisa—that was his prerogative—although I by no means minded if he wanted to talk about her. I never felt that I was in competition with a dead woman. Mark had loved her immensely, that was clear from the way he talked about her, and they had been very happy. She was a huge part of him, a part that I would never want to change or deny. And his relationship with Lisa proved to me how deeply and carefully he loved.

"That's an interesting question, Kate."

His face was turning sad. I reached over to take his hand. "Hey," I said. "I don't want to upset you. We don't have to talk about this."

"It's okay," he said. "No, it's a fair question. It's just… another one of those regrets. I guess we thought there would always be time. We were busy; we were enjoying life. We'd only been married three years, you know."

I nodded. Another late starter.

"We knew it would be a huge commitment, a huge change," he said. "We'd both seen what happened when friends had children. You have to hunker down, don't you? Focus on building a home."

I had observed this too, with my childhood friends. Knowing this was something of a weight on my mind: How did I square that with my desire to be on board ship? With my desire to be a captain? How would I be able to make this work: ship life and home life? Would I want to be away so much, like Dad had been? In my heart I knew I couldn't give up ship life. But was it fair to ask this of Mark, who had lost one home already? I started to feel very sad that I couldn't square this circle.

"But it just never happened?" I said.

"Pretty much. I guess we thought, let's store up a little more time together as just the two of us before we brought someone else into the mix. But we were nearly there. I guess there would have been a baby within eighteen months."

My heart went out to him. This was another part of his future that had been lost: a child of his and Lisa's that could only ever now remain imagined.

I reached out to hold him and he accepted my embrace. We sat like that for a while, simply being together. Talking about this had made him sad, but I wasn't sorry that I had asked. I understood him better now.

"Do you not want children, Kate?"

I sighed. "I like the *idea*… You know how I love the nieces."

"Well, they're very lovable. But?"

"But it doesn't seem very practical, does it?" I said. "It's like you said, you have to hunker down. Turn inward. Build… I don't know, a nest, or something!"

"That's Phoebe and Yia, isn't it? Two momma birds running around, and three chicks, beaks upturned and squawking!"

I laughed. "That's exactly it!"

"And you don't want to build a nest, Kate?"

"I want to be a starship captain." I flushed. I sounded like a kid, saying what job they wanted when they grew up, blurting out a dream. But I was a Starfleet commander, chief science officer on a large ship, overseeing a big team. It wasn't a dream. It was within my grasp. "And I guess I struggle to see how I can do both."

He thought about that for a while. "Your father did it," he said.

"He did, didn't he." I looked Mark straight in the eye. "He also died young."

"I understand," he said. "But, you know, Kate—life is risk—"

"You need to visit my workplace, mister! Far too many Cardassians, these days!"

"But there's a treaty now, isn't there? I thought we were at peace."

And we were, more or less. Some rumbles on the border, and some very unhappy colonists.

"Anyway," he said, "I don't mean that kind of risk. I mean, risking connection. Risking what being with someone might mean. You know, don't you, that I'm ready to take that risk again."

After all he had lost. "Oh, Mark…"

He smiled at me. "I'm ready to wait, you know. And, Kate, one more word on this—if I've learned anything over the years, it's that we shouldn't meet trouble halfway. Life has a way of taking us by surprise, and we should take our chances of happiness while we can."

✦

Going back to the *Billings* that time was very hard. My conversation with Mark filled my mind, as if he had offered a glimpse to me of how I might have it all; how there needn't be this divide between ship life and home. He was right about Dad: he had kept on within Starfleet, and he would have carried on indefinitely—if it hadn't been for the Cardassians. I guess that this was what had always held me back: the thought that I might at any moment be called to action, and that this was not fair to someone outside of Starfleet. I knew how hard Dad's death had hit us all. I realized now that at the back of my mind I had always assumed that there was going to be open war with the Cardassians, and that when that happened, I would have duties to perform. But Mark was right: the treaty with the Cardassians had been signed, and the Demilitarized Zone established, and, at that time, it really did seem that war was no longer going to happen. Perhaps it really would be possible for me to combine my two loves.

Yes, I was most certainly in love with Mark, and it was like nothing I had ever experienced before. My affair at the Academy, my only other comparator, had been a children's game in comparison to this: two people who were barely adults playing at having a serious relationship. As for the affairs I'd had since, all of which had been with other officers—well, they had most certainly been a lot of fun, good company and great sex, but they had not been intended by any of the participants to be anything more than brief encounters while between postings. Being with Mark was nothing like that. With Mark, I had felt straight away that I was coming home. We had skipped the whole dating period completely; we had never felt the need to dress up and go out or spend time away in exotic and romantic locations. It was as if we didn't need these set dressings: we got the hang of each other very quickly. We were happy puttering around his home or my home; walking Mollie; reading and listening to music; cooking, talking, or even just being together. We were happy looking inward.

When I was back on the *Billings*, but still in near-Earth orbit, we spoke again briefly via the comm. "I've been thinking a lot about our conversation," I said.

"Have you changed you mind? About my offer, I mean."

"Not yet… I guess, I'm trying to see how we can make it work. When I'm on board ship so much. Away so much…"

"If that's all that's stopping you, Kate, then let's think about it. Because I don't think it needs to. What we have—it's great. It already works. We can keep on

making it work. We're grown-ups." He smiled. *"Aren't you Starfleet command types meant to be tactical geniuses?"*

"We have our moments."

"Then, like the song says—we can work it out." I heard a whining noise in the background. Mollie jumped up into view and barked. Mark sighed. *"You'll have to excuse me. Your damn dog needs walking."*

✦

The treaty with the Cardassians was in place, but during the following year we were seeing how fragile it might prove to be. During this year, a new complication arose which threatened the hard-won peace with the Cardassians, and which certainly tried the consciences of everyone in Starfleet. There were numerous Federation worlds that now found themselves within the new Demilitarized Zone. Other worlds found that, with the new border that the treaty established, their worlds were suddenly transferred to Cardassian jurisdiction. Naturally, these people did not want to become subjects of the Cardassian Union. Everyone was offered the chance of resettlement—and the resources were put there to assist them—but who willingly abandons their home? How would I have felt, if I had been told that our old farm was now the property of the Cardassians, and that I could either live with it, or move on? I had a great deal of sympathy with their plight, but there were broader concerns, and a larger peace to maintain. When colonists on these worlds began to arm themselves, my sympathies lessened considerably. Terrorism is never the answer, and, ultimately, that's what the Maquis were. Suddenly, that peace we had all expected had become more precarious.

It's remarkable, looking back, to realize how many Starfleet personnel went over to the Maquis. Some went out of principle—this was why Chakotay joined them, and I respect that decision, although I do not agree with it. But some were just looking for adventure, a chance to live outside the confines of the Federation. Laurie Fitz informed me that Owen Paris's son, Tom, had gone out there. I guess I wasn't surprised—Tom's decisions now seemed to be entirely guided by what would most cause embarrassment for his father—and my heart went out to Owen. All of this, as well as my conversation with Mark, whirled around my head. What was my duty? Was there anything that I could contribute to this? I had believed that I had a duty to stay in Starfleet as long as war was coming, and although war seemed no longer imminent, the peace was still not secure. The next few years would surely see me back in combat, even if this time I was fighting people who had once been colleagues.

Life on the *Billings* had not improved. After a couple of months back on board, playing Ward's pointless games, I began to give serious consideration to resigning my commission. I was missing Mark terribly, and I was starting to think I had made a bad decision coming back. I felt that I was not being reasonable asking him to wait. I knew he wanted to marry me, and I knew he wanted children. He had lost so much when Lisa died, and I felt that maybe this delay wasn't fair on him. I felt as if I should make a decision, either way. I should commit, or I should let him move on. Increasingly, however, I was struggling to think of how I could be happy without him, and I was struggling to see how I could combine this with fighting the Maquis. This wasn't a decision to take lightly, so I turned to my mentor for advice.

Parvati Pandey was semiretired now, but was still teaching her Ethics of Command classes at the Academy. She smiled when she saw my face.

"Kathryn. Always good to see you. How's life on the Billings*?"*

"That's part of what I want to talk to you about."

"I think I can guess. Ward being his usual self?"

"It does baffle me, Parvati, how he's gotten this far."

"I've seen him in action. He knows how to flatter people."

I guess it was indiscreet of an admiral to talk this way to a commander about her captain, but I've observed that as people move closer to retirement, they start to care less and less about workplace diplomacy. I suppose they're halfway out of the game, and this is their last chance to shape how it's played after their departure. These days I sometimes find myself doing the same.

"I never did quite work out how to flatter people."

"Oh, you have your own charms, Kathryn. I've watched senior officers fall over themselves to raise a smile from you. But you said in your message that you wanted some advice?"

I took a deep breath. "I'm thinking of resigning my commission."

She looked at me in horror. *"What? Kathryn! That's a terrible idea!"*

I laughed. "Well, I guess I don't need to force you to tell me your opinion!"

"Why on Earth would you do that? Not over Neil Ward, surely!"

KATHRYN M. JANEWAY VS-982-429

STARFLEET ACADEMY
CLASS OF 2357

▲
Kathryn Janeway's graduation photo
Image courtesy Starfleet Archives

LCARS-161.95

342371 334 232342388 • 334 432371 24 3734 • 232342368 334500 231 34853 • 231 87334500 31 4431 • 85534853
124633 124 34235078 • 124 396124833 24 1524 • 34208578 • 222 45353458278 • 222 • 22 007 • 8569078

SFA SURVEILLANCE DD.11.06.2354

SEA.SECURITY
ONLINE

PZ: 214500.3/11.22/4

LEVEL IV

MONITOR
D#: 1701

+ ▼

MODE SELECT

PZ: 35500.3/11.22/4

FILE ID: SFASP4412688
LCARS-161895 STARFLEET ACADEMY SURVEILLANCE TAU16D

44002.3 ▶

△ Cadet Janeway piloting the *Colditz Cock II*
Image courtesy Starfleet Archives

Starfleet Notice of Death for Edward Janeway
Image courtesy Starfleet Archives ▽

STRFLT. SEC.CD 331154989WSV ▶

CLASSIFIED

SECURITY LEVEL 770
STARFLEET SB-SPC
FREQUENCY:
6G112224P

STARFLEET COMMAND
UNITED FEDERATION OF PLANETS

U.S.S. AL-BATANI   6611.2333
CAPT. OWEN PARIS, COMMANDING   TAU CETI PRIME FED. O.P. 1138.0966
ENSIGN KATHRYN JANEWAY: 0907 16 JUNE 2358

DEEPLY REGRET TO INFORM YOU THAT VICE-ADMIRAL EDWARD JANEWAY
IS OFFICIALLY REPORTED AS KILLED IN THE LINE OF DUTY, 15 JUNE.
IMMEDIATE COMPASSIONATE LEAVE APPROVED.
DETAILS TO FOLLOW.

LT. DONALD DAVIS, T.C.P. ADJUTANT

2359: Newly promoted Lieutenant Janeway with her friend/mentor, Boothby
Image courtesy K. Janeway

USS VOYAGER NCC-74656 MAKES
HEROIC RETURN FROM DELTA
QUADRANT AFTER 7 YEARS

STARFLEET COMMAND REPORTS SHIP'S
COMPLIMENT INCLUDES NEW ARRIVALS

IMMEDIATE
RELEASE

FREQUENCY:
001122224P

STRFLT. PRESS 331154889WSV

United Federation of Planets press-release announcing *Voyager's* return.
Image courtesy N. Wildman

Admiral Janeway with her daughter, Ensign Amelia Janeway, at Starfleet Academy Commencement, 2395
Photo credit: Yianem Lox Image courtesy K. Janeway

"No, no, it's not just that, although—damn the man, he sure does make life miserable! It infuriates me! It doesn't have to be this way! It shouldn't be this way!"

"It's not how you'd run your ship?"

"Damned right."

"So at least you've learned something from him."

"I guess…"

"And you've made sure you've got command opportunities?"

"Yes, night-shift command, all the usual boxes checked."

"So tell me the whole story."

I explained about Mark; how much I missed him and wanted to be with him. How he wanted me to marry him. How I felt I was being unfair to make him wait.

"Is he asking you to resign, Kate? To choose between him and your commission?"

"What? No! Quite the opposite—"

"I'm glad to hear that."

"I made that mistake before, Parvati. Marriage isn't sacrificing yourself, is it? It's… about each of you letting the other flourish."

"But you don't think that's possible?"

"I think it's hard."

"You never struck me as someone who would back away from a challenge. Do you think you can flourish outside of Starfleet?"

I thought about that. Haltingly, I said, "Starfleet isn't everything."

"I think it is for you, Kate. All right. Let's say you leave. What would you do instead?"

"Maybe… teach at the Academy?"

"You could, I guess… But what would you do? I guess Boothby's always in need of an extra pair of hands."

She was right, and I knew it already. What would I teach? I couldn't teach her class. I hadn't yet commanded a ship. I'd be teaching freshman science, and I'd always be looking up to the stars and wondering what kind of captain I would have been.

"I'm doubting myself, Parvati. I'm doubting that I can do it all, or, maybe, doubting I can do it all as well as I would want to."

"You don't know that," said my wise mentor, "until you've tried."

That was true.

"Then my advice, Kathryn, is to seize the day."

I didn't mention this conversation with Pandey to Mark. I felt oddly embarrassed, as if I'd been doing something clandestine. I simply knew that he would be upset that I was thinking of leaving Starfleet on his account. Next time we talked, it was about our usual, comfortable topics: the exploits of the redoubtable Mollie; our families and our friends; about what we planned to do next time I was back. In the meantime, my work with my team kept me busy, but I felt increasingly detached, as if I was halfway out of the door. I just didn't know where that door was leading yet… One interesting effect of this was that the captain seemed to sense that I had moved on in some way and, as a result, our working relationship was the best it was throughout the whole time I was on board ship. Well, he did already have my replacement lined up, didn't he?

About six weeks after my conversation with Pandey, she contacted me again, on a secure channel. *"Time to talk, Kathryn."*

"Go ahead."

"You have a ship—if you still want one."

Her words took a moment to sink in, and then I felt myself begin to tremble. Calmly, I said, "I'm listening, Admiral."

"It's called Voyager."

What a name! A name to make the heart soar!

"Intrepid class, brand new, just about to leave Utopia Planitia for McKinley Station. It's got everything, Kathryn—bioneural circuitry, variable geometry warp nacelles… It's even got a mission. What it doesn't have yet is a captain."

I didn't want to get ahead of myself. "What's the mission?"

"A trip out to the Badlands. We've got a few simple missions in the area— perfect for a new captain. They all have one thing in common though."

"Maquis," I said, grimly.

"Tracking one ship in particular—the Val Jean."

Named for the hero of *Les Misérables*, an underdog unfairly hounded by the authorities. That was revealing, to say the least.

"It's captained by a former Starfleet officer—a man named Chakotay. We want it infiltrated, and ideally stopped. Our plan is to put an undercover on board."

"You got someone in mind?"

"An old friend of yours—Tuvok. He's already out in the DMZ."

An old friend indeed. I was wondering why I hadn't heard from him for a while. He'd been undergoing briefing and training, presumably, and now his mission was underway.

"What do you say, Kathryn?"

"You mean—"

"The ship's yours if you want it. If you still want to be a captain, that is." She smiled at me. *"Or have you decided to quit after all?"*

Well, I could see now how ridiculous that idea had been. Pandey had known too, and I imagine Mark would have known, if I'd broached the subject with him. The little girl inside me—the one who had always wanted to fly—was leaping for joy.

"Admiral," I said, "it would be my privilege."

"Congratulations, Captain Janeway." She smiled. *"I'm so pleased for you, Kathryn. You've earned this. Now—do you want to tell your captain, or shall I?"*

"Oh, I'll tell him," I breathed. But the conversation that I wanted to have right now was with Mark.

✦

It took most of the morning to persuade Ward to fit me into his hectic schedule. I guess he thought I wanted to complain about something or other. Eventually, I finally tracked him down to his ready room. He didn't offer me a seat, so I stood to attention by the door.

"What is it, Janeway?"

"I've been offered a new post, sir," I said.

"Oh yes? What's the ship?"

"The *U.S.S. Voyager.*"

"I haven't heard of that one," he said. As ever, he was looking at his companel, rather than directly at me. I was glad I wasn't going to have to put up with this nonsense for much longer.

"It's new, sir. Just out of the shipyard. *Intrepid* class."

"Very nice. You always land on your feet, Janeway, don't you? I wish I had that… knack. Who's the lucky captain?"

"I beg your pardon, sir?"

"Who are you going to be serving under?"

He was making this extremely easy for me. I smiled. "The captain? That'll be me, sir."

That got his attention. I saw his hands quickly flex into fists, and then relax again. He looked up at me. "You're going to be a captain?"

"It was always the plan."

"Of the *Voyager*?"

"That's the name of the ship."

"A brand-new, state-of-the-art starship, and you're going straight in as captain."

"That's correct."

He sat back in his seat, lost for words. For a man who liked to flatter his immediate colleagues and his superiors, he had not been bright enough to remember that sometimes juniors get promoted. We were equals now, and my first captaincy was a significant step up from his. I saw it cross his mind that he might, one day, find himself saluting me. I was watching some of his house of cards tumble, and I'm not ashamed to say that it was quite a pleasant sight.

"With your permission, I'll take a shuttle to Starbase 39. I can travel on from there to Mars. *Voyager* is waiting for me there. I've checked the duty rosters, and Lieutenant Crossman is available to pilot the shuttle to the starbase and bring it back again. I'll be off the ship within twelve hours." I saw him starting to come up with some reason to disagree, and quickly added, "Unless there's any reason my expertise is required any longer?"

"I suppose that's acceptable…" He collected himself. "Well," he said. "I guess that'll be all—Kathryn."

"I guess so." We looked at each other coldly. "I'm sorry we couldn't get this to work, Neil. Perhaps we can both learn something from this."

✦

On board the shuttle, I sent a message to Mark. His face appeared on-screen, rumpled and sleepy. "Hell," I said. "What time is it there?"

He peered at the chronometer. *"There's a four in that number. That can't be right. That's not a real time."*

"I'm so sorry!"

I watched him start to focus on me. *"Is everything all right, Kate?"*

"I have some news," I said.

"*Oh yes. You know, I have some too.*"

We gazed at each other.

"*You go first,*" he said.

"I've been offered the captaincy of a ship," I said. "The *Voyager*. I'm on my way there now."

Bless his heart, his face lit up in sheer delight. He was happy for me. "*Oh, Kate! I'm so glad! After all your hard work! Sweetheart, I am so proud of you!*"

"The bad news is… We have our first mission. It's not a long trip, but it's going to be risky. I can't say more."

He nodded his understanding. Good man. There would be more of this lack of detail in our future, I suspected.

"What's your news, Mark?"

He looked sheepish. "*It's not news, not really. You know, I think it can wait…*"

"No, tell me! I've no idea when I'll get a chance to speak again—I've got a crew to get together, and a mission to get underway!"

"*I feel bad now,*" he said. "*The last thing I want to do is steal your thunder…*"

"You can't. I promise. Go on."

"*It's just that… Last week was the anniversary of me proposing for the first time, and I thought, well, third time lucky… And I was away for work, and I kind of bought a ring…*"

He reached into his pocket and brought it out. Even at this distance I could see it was one *hell* of a ring… I put my head in my hands. "Oh, Mark! I'm just about to go away!"

"*Look, Kate,*" he said quickly. "*It doesn't matter. I know what your being in Starfleet means. We've been living that life for nearly two years now—and it's a good life! I miss you, and I want to be with you—of course I do!—but while you're away I fiddle about, and I look forward to the times when you're back with me. I want to be your home, Kate, whenever you come home. Why would I want anything else?*"

I was beginning to waver. What had Parvati said? *Seize the day.* But was it fair to him?

"Mark," I said, my voice thick, "I love you, I truly do—"

"*Uh-oh…*" he said.

"I don't want to be the absentee wife. It's not fair on you, not after Lisa—"

His expression changed, as if something had suddenly become clear to him. *"Oh, Kate—is that's what's been on your mind? Sweetheart, you're not Lisa! You're Kathryn Janeway! That's whom I'm asking to marry me. Because she's brilliant and brave and the most incredible woman, and because even when she's not at home with me, she's changed my life so much for the better that waiting for her to come home is all I want to do. We can make it work, Kate—we already have, for two years! You can have everything you want, you know,"* he said. *"There's no reason why not. You of all people, Kathryn Janeway, can have everything. Let's give it a go."*

What can I say? He was so good, so kind, and I didn't ever want to be without him. He lifted up the ring. *"We'll make this work, Kate. Whatever it takes—we'll make this work."*

I held out my hand, and he mimicked setting the ring in place. I held up my hand and pretended to admire it. *"Hot damn!"* Mark yelled. *"I did it! The captain said yes!"*

In the background, I heard barking. We'd woken Mollie.

"Just so we're clear on one thing, Mark—love me, love my dog."

"Ain't that the truth," he muttered.

I believed then—and I still believe—that we would have made a success of things. If only life hadn't got in the way. We blew kisses and said goodbye. I sent quick messages to Mom and Phoebe, saying: *Here's my news—there's quite a lot of it.* Then I got back to work. As I drew ever closer to my new ship, I realized how happy I felt. All the burden and misery of being on the *Billings* had gone away. I was taking charge of my life once again. I had never had it so good.

✦

Now was my chance to assemble the team I had always wanted. Many of the junior staff were already in place, and a first officer had been assigned to me—John Cavit, who had been a couple of years behind me at the Academy. While we had never served together, we had many mutual friends and colleagues, and I knew he was a fine officer: dependable, with an easy manner but excellent discipline. We quickly established a rapport, and his loss is a source of great grief to me. I brought a couple of people over with me from the *Billings*, not just science officers, but a couple of others who had heard on the grapevine about my new command and wanted to serve under someone else. I was happy to offer them a lifeboat. Tuvok was already in place as my chief of security, and I sent a message to my old friend from the *Al-Batani*, Laurie Fitzgerald, asking him if he was ready to leave the Caldik Prime medical facility, and come with me. As luck would have it (or so I thought at the time), Fitz was on Earth. He got back to me within twelve hours, saying his transfer request had been put through, and he was already heading out to McKinley.

"It'll be good to have the old team together again, Kate," he said. *"Owen Paris will be delighted—he's been having a bad time over Tom, and he could do with hearing some good news."*

Ah, yes, the problem of Tom Paris. His career with the Maquis had been about as successful as his time in Starfleet. He had been with them for no more than a few weeks before being captured. The last I'd heard of him he had been sent to a penal colony in New Zealand for eighteen months. My heart went out to my old captain, but I couldn't help still feeling sorry for Tom. All of that promise, and he had been reduced to this. It was a damn waste. Surely there was still potential there? He had been, by all accounts, a fine pilot. My mind started working overtime. Perhaps he might come in useful. He had knowledge of the Badlands, knowledge of the Maquis, he could certainly fly a ship… I sent a message off to Starfleet Command, asking about a special assignment. Well, if you don't ask, you don't get. I knew I'd have a hard time selling this to Fitz, though. He loved the old man, as he called Owen Paris, but had very little time for his son.

My crew was coming together, and I was approaching McKinley Station, where my new ship was waiting for me. I was already fielding a vastly increased number of communications—plus messages were starting to flood in from family and friends, delighted at all my news. Phoebe had said, *"Damn, Kate—a ship and a fiancé in one day?! This time you've stolen your own thunder!"* My mother said, *"I am so proud of you, Katy. Dad's heart would be bursting for joy. And Mark is a treasure. I'm so glad. You're going to be so happy. Mark deserves it, you deserve it."* My dear family. They said everything I needed to hear, as I embarked on this new stage of my life. There was a little parcel waiting for me too; a present from Mark, beautifully wrapped. When I opened it, I found a fine copy of Dante's *The Divine Comedy*. There was a note from Mark, which said:

For my Beatrice—my love, my redemption, may we share a long life's journey.

Just as I was arriving at McKinley, I received news that the Maquis ship on which Tuvok was undercover, the *Val Jean*, had gone missing in the Badlands. That accelerated our plans somewhat: there would be no time to take a day to catch up with Mark and my family and celebrate our news. A huge disappointment, but this was the way it had to be. Everything was coming at me all at once (to top it all, it turned out the damn dog was pregnant…). I took the time, however, to speak to Tuvok's wife, T'Pel, whom I had met on several occasions. This was not an easy conversation: I could not give her details of his mission, but of course she understood that he was in considerable danger. I assured her that I was going to do everything within my power to bring him home again, safely. I was his captain now. I had a duty of care, not just to my crew, but to their families. I kept that promise to T'Pel—even if it took a lot longer than any of us had anticipated, and led me to make decisions I had not expected.

At last I arrived at McKinley, and I beamed over to take command of my beautiful new ship. I was more than ready to fall in love, and *Voyager* did not displease. I was met on board by my old Academy instructor (and source of many a nightmare) Vice Admiral Theoderich Patterson, and he promptly set about quizzing me. I must have passed the test, since I got a bear hug and warm congratulations, and we went on a tour of my new ship. Fifteen decks, upper limit of warp 9.975, and of course the latest in bioneural circuitry: a brand-new captain, and I had been entrusted with a brand-new ship. I was planning to take good care of her. I caught up with Fitz in sickbay (he was talking about the new Emergency Medical Holographic program, which I hadn't had a chance to look at yet) and broke the news that we had an extra crew member joining us, and who it was. Fitz was not pleased.

"Tom Paris is a liability," he said. "On your own head be it, Kate."

Patterson had sent me a message to say that my unusual personnel request had been approved, and that I could proceed to New Zealand to speak to my man. I remember distinctly the moment I set eyes again on Thomas Eugene Paris. I hadn't seen him since my days serving under his father on the *Al-Batani*, when he had been something of a sullen teenager, but I still recalled that twelve-year-old boy that I'd taken to the holodeck. It was a tragedy to see all the youthful effervescence turned into bitter resentment. At the back of my mind, I was hoping that this mission might be something of a second chance for Tom; I couldn't have guessed to what extent. It wasn't going to be an easy ride for him. Fitz was not prepared to cut him any slack, and my XO, Cavit, had serious reservations about him too.

"People think he's getting an easy ride because you knew his father, Captain," Cavit admitted.

"Nobody on my ship will get an easy ride, Commander," I said. "Tom Paris will have to earn his keep. But I think he can, and I think he will."

Just before we were ready to go, I fielded a touching request from the mother of one of my new ensigns.

"Mrs. Kim," I said, "I am so sorry—but we are minutes away from setting out for Deep Space 9. I'm afraid Harry will have to manage for a little while without his clarinet."

With the news of the disappearance of the *Val Jean*, we were in such a hurry. I was so worried about Tuvok, and eager to get underway. How I wish now I had said yes.

✦

At Deep Space 9, I had time to exchange intelligence reports with the chief of station security, Odo, and spoke briefly to Commander Sisko about Maquis activity in the area. I was startled to learn that his former senior officer, Cal Hudson, had defected to the Maquis. Bearing in mind what I now knew about the crew of the *Val Jean* and its captain, Chakotay, I was starting to think that the Maquis was almost entirely run by former Starfleet officers. With the final members of the crew gathered, we proceeded toward the Badlands, and I began to ease myself into command. The Paris situation needed monitoring; otherwise I was content that my crew were well able for the mission assigned to us.

And then everything changed.

Has ever a captain had a first week on the job like mine? I was prepared for action so close to the border, whether it came from dealing with belligerent Maquis, treacherous Cardassians, or furious plasma storms. I was not prepared to be flung seventy thousand light-years away from home at the whim of an ancient and dying alien that was trying to make amends for ruining the world of a childlike species. Nor was I prepared to make enemies so quickly with the local Kazon warlords. And I was most certainly not prepared for Neelix, although I was damned grateful. Most of all, I had not been prepared to lose so many good people, so quickly. My first officer. My chief engineer. And, hell, my chief medical officer, Laurie Fitz, my dear old friend, who had come over specially to *Voyager*, because I had asked him. How I regretted that now; how I wished beyond measure that he was safe back on Caldik Prime. That was the hardest of all, and there were so many, many others, some of whom I had not even had a chance to meet properly, to hold even more than the briefest of conversations with...

But in the rush and chaos of the moment, I had to put this aside to be able to ensure the safety of my ship and crew, to work out what was happening, and to try to put a stop to it. In the end, it came down to listening to an ancient dying alien as he came to understand that he had to let his children go; that he had to accept that there was an end to all things, and that change and growth and evolution might be painful, but they are for the best. The Caretaker had done his job: now it was for the Ocampa to make their way. They were ready for it: we could see that from the ones who had been struggling to get their elders to accept the changing reality. But it was going to be hard—and without our help, their move toward self-determination would have been stopped before it had the chance. The Kazon were waiting to move in and seize the array, whatever it might cost the Ocampa. And I couldn't let that happen.

Let me lay down once and for all my reasoning behind making this choice, since I know that many have disagreed with the one that I made that day. Perhaps it would help to remember how much, throughout my career, I had longed to make first contact with an alien species, not as observer, or even as senior officer, but as captain of my own ship. Now that I had, I could see that this encounter cut both ways. Meeting the Ocampa, we acquired responsibilities toward each other. Not the suffocating love of the Caretaker, but the responsibilities that every sentient being has toward each other. The Ocampa, even after the Caretaker sealed them away, had continued to change, to develop. Despite their short lifespan, only nine years, they led full lives. They were natural telepaths. They had a rich culture, and religious beliefs. They were their own, unique species. Allowing the Kazon access to them would have been a monstrous act. I knew what they were capable of; they had brutalized Kes. But it was more than that. The Kazon would do to them and their world what the

Cardassians had done to Bajor. They would strip the planet for resources and enslave its people. The Ocampa would suffer every possible indignity that a species could suffer. I knew from what I had seen—and what my mother had seen through her work—what would happen. I could not allow that. I could not condemn a whole species so that the one hundred fifty members of *Voyager* could get home. I know that many on the ship—and many in the Alpha Quadrant, when at last I was able to speak to them—disagreed. Tuvok, at the time, warned me that this decision was even in violation of the Prime Directive, altering the balance of power in this region of space. But it was too late for that. We had been flung into the whole situation against our will; we were involved by others. We didn't involve ourselves. The Ocampa would not have survived without our helping hand. If I had done anything different, I might have brought *Voyager* home at once—but I would not have been any kind of Starfleet officer.

✦

The first night of our journey home, I sat in my ready room composing letters of condolence to the families of those crew members who had been lost. I had no idea how or when I would deliver them, but it was my duty, and I knew that I should write them now, as close to the event as I could. It was a grueling task, and I found myself writing letters about some whom I had barely spoken to. It had been my intention to meet each crew member one-to-one over the coming weeks. Now some of them were dead. I never got the chance, for example, to talk properly to my conn officer, Veronica Stadi. I looked up her record that night. Only out of the Academy three years. One of the best up-and-coming navigators around. I never got a chance to quiz her about the classic of Betazed poetry, *The Shared Heart*, on which she had written a short monograph. Instead, I had to write to her mother and father—Anissina and Gwendal—that their wonderful daughter was not coming home. I finished the letter and stopped. I was done. I was tired, and sad; I felt grief-stricken over Fitz, and I was missing Mark like hell. We were seventy thousand light-years from home, and all I could do was point the ship in the right direction, and hope.

Sometimes it's not as easy as clicking your heels together three times and saying, *"There's no place like home."*

I was captain at last, of a lost ship, battered and bruised, and in charge of a wounded and divided crew. Be careful what you wish for.

I gave up on my letters. I took down the book that Mark had given me as an engagement present and looked at the inscription: *For my Beatrice—my love, my redemption, may we share a long life's journey.* Beatrice, Dante's love. She died young. I turned to the start of *Inferno,* and I read:

Midway on life's journey,
I awoke to find myself in a dark wood,
I had wandered from the straight path…

CHAPTER EIGHT

SEEK OUT NEW LIFE—2371-2372

IN THAT FIRST WEEK, WE WERE REELING FROM THE EVENTS that had left us stranded, from the shock of the sudden deaths of so many of us. At the same time, we tried to fix some of the damage to our ship, though I think most of the crew barely had time or energy to take stock. It's the captain's job, however, to think ahead, and to consider above all the wellbeing of her crew. It seemed to me that some stability and certainty would help amid all the chaos. I know that my insistence on running *Voyager* so strictly as a Starfleet vessel has attracted criticism in some quarters: believe me, I've heard it all before, mainly from the ex-Maquis on board ship. I know that people think that this was rigidity—denial, even, a failure to come to terms with our changed circumstances. But it was crucial in those first few weeks. We all needed something upon which we could depend. The uniform, the formal relationships, and the protocols of Starfleet were the closest thing that we had to a shared culture or system of values. Many of the ex-Maquis had been in Starfleet—or, at least, the Academy—and knew how it functioned. Still, it was not an easy sell. They all had their reasons for leaving, or staying away in the first place.

Somehow, we pulled it off. Somehow, we persuaded everyone to pull together, under the shared banner of Starfleet and the Federation. None of this would have happened without the support that I got right away from Chakotay. I thank my stars that he was the one captaining the *Val Jean*, a rare stroke of good fortune for me in those days. Consider the alternatives. I could have had a fanatic, someone who would never work with Starfleet under any circumstances. I could have had a mercenary, spending the next seven years watching my back in case he took the ship and decided to make his fortune in the Delta Quadrant. Instead, I had a man of principle: dare I say it, a Starfleet officer through and through. I relied upon Chakotay completely, and, even when we had disagreements, he never let me down. Without him, the former Maquis crew members would not have integrated so successfully—and no doubt I would have had a mutiny on my hands. Handling the ex-Maquis crew was difficult enough: B'Elanna Torres seemed to be fueled entirely by fury, and only the complexities of engineering seemed to come close to soothing her, giving her a challenge that worked her intelligence without causing frustration. Still, she was what I needed right now in engineering, and I could only hope that something over the coming months and years would give her a much-needed sense of stability. I came to rely on many other former Maquis during those years: Lieutenant Ayala for one; Chell, too, more or less, despite various problems. Maybe I should have let him loose in the mess hall sooner.

But there were other members of the ex-Maquis crew who left me uneasy— the Betazoid Lon Suder, for one. Having said that, his former colleagues didn't like or trust him either and for good reason. Suder murdered Frank Darwin, and for his sake, I wish that I had taken greater heed of their concerns sooner. It seems a terrible tragedy to me that Frank died at the hands of a member of the crew. But there was so much happening in those first days, and while I had anticipated discord, possibly even mutiny, I had not anticipated having someone with such antisocial tendencies on board. As we struggled to deal with the ramifications of these events, I found myself recalling a line from the start of Hawthorne's *The Scarlet Letter*:

> The founders of a new colony, whatever Utopia of human virtue and
> happiness they might originally project, have invariably recognized it
> among their earliest practical necessities to allot a portion of the virgin
> soil as a cemetery, and another portion as the site of a prison.

We were a new colony, in a way; a little collection of people striving to pull together in order to make our way and survive. It saddens me beyond belief that I so quickly found myself conducting a funeral for a murdered man and ordering another man's quarters to be converted into a holding cell. Suder came good in the end, finding some kind of peace and developing a sense of right and wrong. Of course, then your previous acts become difficult to live with. I think he was always, given the chance, going to sacrifice himself in some way, and so he did, and as a result we were able to retake our ship from the Kazon who had captured it. Lon Suder saved himself. But I wish I had been able to save Frank Darwin.

Then there was Seska. In one of my earliest conversations with Chakotay, and thinking of the defection of Cal Hudson, I said to him what I had noticed before: that the Maquis seemed to be almost entirely made up of Starfleet officers, whether undercover or renegade.

"Perhaps that's something that Starfleet should start considering, Kathryn," he said gently. "Ask a few questions about why so many are choosing to leave."

"Right now," I said, "I don't care. I don't care who has been undercover or Maquis as long as you all do your job."

I wonder if he recalled this conversation later. None of us expected Seska's betrayal, and the whole series of events was a terrible shock to Chakotay, who had trusted her and loved her. The revelation that she was not Bajoran, but an undercover Cardassian agent planted on the *Val Jean* was shock enough. But that in itself would not have been enough for me to expel her from the ship. Indeed, had she revealed her identity to us, and then gone on to prove herself, I would have invited her to join the crew in her own right. We all wanted to get home to the Alpha Quadrant, and I needed experienced people to crew the ship. But it seemed that treachery was too ingrained. Almost from the beginning she had been working against us, joining forces with the Kazon, ultimately taking a Kazon warlord as a lover, and having his child. I wonder often about that child, and the life it must have led.

Seska's betrayals threw a long shadow. Almost three years into our journey, Tuvok's holodeck simulation of a Maquis insurrection was activated, causing all kinds of unexpected strife and grievances to reemerge. And Seska, long dead, turned out nonetheless to be the cause, having found the simulation and reprogrammed it to cause maximum disruption. I will never understand why, faced with the choice between carrying this distant war into the Delta Quadrant, or working alongside us to bring us all back home, Seska chose the former. But

Cardassian culture, at that time, was so pernicious, so harmful, that I guess it was always going to happen. Reflecting now upon these events, I see how they worked in my favor. Seska's treachery so shocked the ex-Maquis, that in many ways it drove them into my arms. There was an idealistic streak in the ex-Maquis crew members that was revolted by her actions, Chakotay and B'Elanna in particular. I knew that once I had won the hearts of Chakotay and B'Elanna, the rest of the former Maquis would follow. So it proved. But I wish we had known who and what Seska was before she betrayed us. We made a home for so many others: Maquis, holograms, even Borg. I wish we had been able to persuade a Cardassian to join us. But there it is—there's a utopian streak in every Starfleet captain. I wouldn't want to lose that—but I would wish, with all my heart, that it did not so often lead to a prison or a cemetery.

✦

As we began to find our feet, I tried to remember that I had been given a unique privilege as a Starfleet captain, to survey a part of space where nobody had gone before. Just the presence of Neelix and Kes on board ship required us to get to know two new species (and come to terms with their cuisine). I can't fault Neelix for his enthusiasm, however, and he was right to identify that someone needed to be keeping an eye on crew morale. Kes was a wonderful addition to our crew. She had a great calm about her, a real gentleness, that I found a great balm over the years that she spent on board. To look at her, an Ocampan, was a daily reminder that I had made the right choice stranding *Voyager* in the Delta Quadrant. Her people had been saved. And nobody was better suited to handle our Emergency Medical Hologram. Did any member of the crew come on as great a journey as our ineffable Doctor? In those very early days, it was difficult to think of him as anything other than a poor replacement for my dear Fitz, and quite an arrogant one at that. His bedside manner was terrible. But life—and personality—have a way of not just surviving but thriving. And our Doctor, so it was to turn out, had *plenty* of personality. I might have wished that Fitz had survived, but I could not wish the Doctor out of existence. His presence—his capacity for growth and change—made us truly wrestle with the nature of identity and selfhood. The Doctor, at every turn, exceeded the parameters of his programming. Our voyage created a new form of life.

And, it turned out, we had brought new life with us. I cannot begin to imagine the swirl of emotions that Samantha Wildman must have gone through, realizing that she was having a baby, and so far from family. In the case of Phoebe and Yianem, both of whom have been pregnant, I observed a great need for the familiar people and places. Much as I tried to make *Voyager* seem a haven for us all in the Delta Quadrant, it was, ultimately, not home. She missed her spouse, Greskrendtregk, too, very much. I knew how much I ached for Mark; to be the mother of a new child so far away from her spouse must have made the separation acutely painful for Samantha.

And then there were the practical realities of having a baby on board ship. I had not given much thought to how we might raise a child on board *Voyager*. It had never exactly been the plan! But you have to respond to the realities of the situation. I had a new mother, more in need of support than ever before, who was also a valued crew member in a situation where everyone was needed. We had to do all that we could to support her. It takes a village to raise a child, they say, and this was a ready-made village, one which now had another incentive to return home. We all wanted to see this little family reunited, so we all pitched in. With only one child, there was no need to establish a formal day-care center, although I would have done if it had been necessary. I see the provision of excellent childcare as a marker of civilization. I have had no personal need for it over the years, but I'm capable of empathy, and capable of seeing how crucial it is for others. Samantha was one of us: we loved her as a person, and valued her contribution as a xenobiologist, and we were behind her all the way.

I had no worries about medical care—for all his (how shall I put this?) *foibles*, our EMH was a faultless medical practitioner—and Kes, our new nurse, proved a wonderful support in the early days when Samantha was establishing a routine of work and caring for her daughter. But it was Neelix who proved to be the hero. Patient, good-humored, fun, and completely reliable—he was an ideal companion and playmate for that little girl. It was one of the quiet but constant joys of life on *Voyager*, watching Naomi Wildman grow and thrive. She was quick-witted, sensible, intelligent, curious, and a gift to our ship. I hope we did well by her. I think that we did. We never expected to find ourselves taking care of children (and there were more to come). I would like to think that we rose to the challenge. I would like to think that those children felt safe among us and able to flourish.

✦

What about myself? In those early days, and, in fact, throughout our voyage home, I struggled intensely with loneliness. I was the captain: I had to give a convincing show of being in command of myself and not on the verge of cracking, but sometimes it was hard. There was no way to contact a colleague or a mentor to sound out decisions, or confirm that I had done something right, or advise about what I might have done differently. Chakotay understood, I knew, and that quiet support got me through many tough times, but not only was I alone as captain, I was alone as Kathryn Janeway. The simple fact was that I missed Mark dreadfully. I played over and over again the messages from him that I had stored. I wrote to him twice a week. I told him how much I missed him, how much I wanted to be back walking in the woods with him and Mollie, enjoying the quiet calm of his solid presence beside me. I confided all my hopes and my fears, but ridiculously, I only shed tears once: three months into our voyage, I realized that Mollie must have had her pups, and that not only had I not been there, I hadn't even been conscious of the date. I felt dreadful, as if I'd let her down. It's strange what hits you. I haven't told anyone this before. I cried my heart out for a good hour. Then I washed my face, brushed my hair, pulled on my uniform, and went down to engineering to wrestle with a recalcitrant warp coil. Later, I challenged B'Elanna to a game of Velocity, and we both burned off some excess emotion. Turned out she was pretty damn good at the game too.

Throughout those early years, the thought of eventually being reunited with Mark was what kept me going. At the same time, I went through agonies thinking about what he must be experiencing. For him to have lost Lisa was terrible enough. For him to have taken the risk of loving someone again; pinning his hopes of a future on me (and children; I do believe we would have had children together someday) only to have this chance snatched away for a second time… It was truly, awfully painful; a double anguish of my own loss compounded by imagining what he must be going through. I had no way of knowing if we were assumed to have died in the Badlands; our own initial assumption had been that the *Val Jean* had been destroyed in the plasma storms. Would that same assumption be made about us? Even as we strove to come home by the quickest way possible, were others already grieving us, believing us dead, trying to carry on with their lives? The uncertainty was terrible. I wanted to be able to get back *now*, yesterday, a week ago! I wanted to click my heels together, say the magic words, and be whisked immediately home. Instead, we had to travel home the long way.

Chief among my concerns throughout the voyage was to find ways to shorten our journey, and I set this as one of engineering's main goals. I sure as hell didn't want to be arriving back in the Alpha Quadrant in time to celebrate my centenary, and neither did anyone else. Projects like this served a multiple purpose: they kept the crew busy; they kept us focused on our main goal and kept alive hope and belief that we might achieve it; and, damn it, there was also the possibility that they might even work! Just like that glider I had built, all those years ago, from pieces of string and globs of porridge. Those prisoners of war held in the castle who had built the first one had been given hope by this project. (And I never forgot that, although they never got to try it, that damn glider *flew*.)

We integrated all kinds of tech during this period and worked on all kinds of projects. I'd say the *Delta Flyer* was by far our most successful (although I often thought sadly about how such a flyer, with its capacity to operate in multiple environments, was the kind of ship on which my father had died). I know that the subject of the technological advances we made in flight technology is one that often came up on my return, with questions about Borg tech and wormholes and time travel and even breaking the maximum warp barrier. Sounds unbelievable, doesn't it? Breaking the warp barrier. Nobody could possibly believe it. You know, a lot of what we did here is classified, and so for all of your asking questions about that, let me fall back on official secrets. I guess you'll know—in a hundred years' time. As for some of the other rumors flying around: there are a lot of crazy stories about what we encountered on our way home, or things that happened to us. I'd say you shouldn't believe everything you hear. Hell, I was *there*, and I can't believe some of it.

As well as Mark, I missed my family dreadfully. I wrote many letters to them over the years. I wrote to Mom, and I went through agonies on her account too. Having already lost her husband, what must she be feeling now, having to come to terms with the loss of a daughter? I tried to comfort her, tell her that I was doing just fine, and that I was coming home as quickly as I could. I wrote to Phoebe and Yianem, my sisters old and new. I confided in them how often I felt despair at the vastness of the distance between us and home, and how often I felt that I wasn't up to this task: an experienced officer, yes, but a new captain, learning on the job. I wrote about how much I feared that Mark would give up and move on. I hoped they were looking out for him; taking care of him—I knew they would. These were perhaps my most honest letters. I could never keep secrets from my sister. I wrote to my nieces too (and tried to imagine how they were changing): chatty stories about the curious things we had seen; an adventure tale for children that I hoped my mother might appreciate too. I wrote to the grandparents, of course, and, every new year, I wrote a big newsy letter to the whole family. I tried to focus on the positive aspects of our journey home: the strange encounters; the camaraderie of the crew, as we pulled together; the various exploits of Neelix, the Doctor, Naomi Wildman. (Let's leave aside the time I had to break the news about Shannon O'Donnel to poor Aunt Martha. At least I got to practice in this letter before dealing with the real thing.)

One letter that I wrote from the early days I recall very well, imagining how my family would have laughed and groaned on reading it, recalling, as it did, the infamous "Year of Amelia," and my childhood obsession with her. I made this letter fun, lighthearted, imagining the family reading it together and laughing that Katy's stubborn streak proved so strong that she went all that way just to stalk her childhood heroine. I started with the mystery of the ancient SOS signal, and then the amazement of discovering—of all things—a Lockheed Model 10 Electra… Then realizing we had solved one of the greatest mysteries in human aviation history, and that I was about to meet my idol… They say that you shouldn't meet your heroes, but to my relief Amelia Earhart was willing to trust us, ordering her navigator to cooperate with us. She proved willing to believe the tall tale that we told her: that she had been taken by aliens, and was now living a long way from home, and many centuries in the future. I was not disappointed at how open-minded she proved to me. I was not disappointed in her at all. What an honor, to be able to show her my ship! To let her see that a woman in command was no longer considered an exception, but how the future would be.

I may have devoted more than a few pages of this letter to my encounter with her before remembering to finish up the story: of how humans, back in the 1930s, had been abducted by aliens, and brought to this world, only to establish what was now a human colony. More than a hundred thousand of them, across three cities, all thriving. Humans can be resilient in this way. Since I was writing this letter with the nieces in mind, I glossed over some of the less pleasant aspects of the tale: how the Briori had used these kidnapped humans as slave labor, and how brutal their later rebellion must have been. You don't lightly win freedom from slavery, as human history attests over and over again. But here was this human civilization, light-years away from home, flourishing, and ready to welcome us with open arms.

That offer brought about a tough decision, not just for me, but for all of the crew. Here was an established human colony in the Delta Quadrant. Here we could end our journey; we could settle, put down roots, lead what would clearly be happy lives among our own kind. I won't deny that the temptation to remain was strong: hell, I could have been Amelia Earhart's next-door neighbor! But the truth is, I never did waver. I was committed to going home. But while that was my decision, I had to let each member of the crew choose for themselves. I had, in effect, forced them into the Delta Quadrant when I made the choice to destroy the Caretaker's array, and it seemed only fair to give each person a chance to make this decision. This was a worrying time: I simply had no idea what each person might decide. Remember that we had been traveling for over a year by this point, only a tiny fraction of the voyage that still lay ahead of us. I would not have blamed anyone for wanting to stay behind, particularly those crew members who had been part of the Maquis, and could not be sure of the reception they would get back in the Alpha Quadrant. The problem was that if enough of them decided to cut their losses and stay, I would no longer be able to crew *Voyager*. The decision would be made for us.

I don't know whether there were behind-the-scenes discussions between the ex-Maquis crew members, and I've never asked. If there were, I suspect Chakotay of having a hand in them, and persuading people that they should trust me to look after them in the event of our return to the Alpha Quadrant. In any case, nobody opted to stay. This was a deeply significant moment for me: my first confirmation that all the work we had done to bind our crew together into a coherent, supportive community, bent toward a common goal, was working. I was hugely heartened by the fact that everyone was committed to our voyage home. I felt that I could enter the next stage of our journey with renewed confidence that we could make it; that we could hold together, and travel together, and one day come home together. I did want Amelia Earhart to come with us, though; boy, did I ever! Can you imagine? The wonders she would have seen on *Voyager* alone, never mind on the journey! I remember that conversation vividly, the note of yearning in her voice at the thought of flying in our ship. But the pull of the settlement was too strong. In my letter to my family, I jokily described my failure to persuade her to come along as the greatest disappointment of my life. Surely, I wrote, we would have been the best of friends! I am still convinced of this. But it remains a source of great joy to me that I met her—my great childhood heroine. What an honor to be the one to solve this great mystery. For me to be the one to learn the fate of Amelia Earhart!

This temptation to give up, to simply accept that we were now denizens of the Delta Quadrant and to make a home there, was very strong in the early years. On one occasion, it seemed to have been forced upon me and my first officer. On an away trip, we both caught a virus that would kill us if we left the environment in which we had contracted it. We suspected from our encounters with the Vidiians, a species in the Delta Quadrant who had advanced medical technologies, that they would most likely have a cure. However, the reason for the Vidiians' expertise in this respect was that the species suffered from a pandemic, the Phage. This horrible disease, which was slowly destroying their species, had led the Vidiians to take terrible actions against other species with whom they came into contact, harvesting their organs to save their own people. I forbade contact with them. As ever, I weighed the balance of the needs of the many against the needs of the few, and it was plain to me that the danger to the rest of the crew from a species of organ harvesters took precedence over the needs of myself and Chakotay. It seemed that, for a while, at least, my journey home was at a standstill. I put Tuvok in command of *Voyager*, and, in my final order as captain, instructed him to continue the journey home to the Alpha Quadrant. Under no circumstances, I said, was he to contact the Vidiians on our behalf.

Then Chakotay and I got on with taking stock of our situation. We were both experienced at living in the wild; we both had many years of camping and hiking behind us, as well as our Starfleet survival training, and his time in the Maquis had made him used to rough conditions. We built a shelter; we built, dare I say it, a home. I knew from the outset that Chakotay would have been happy to remain here: there was a stoicism about him that made him capable of accepting his fate, and he is also, at heart, a solitary man happy to spend time in his own company. But I was set on finding a cure. I didn't care how long it would take. Ten years, twenty: I'd find it, and then we could both leave this world and continue our own journey home. I know that this part of me—always looking ahead to the next adventure—has made me miss a great deal during my life. I sometimes forget to see the gifts and the blessings that are right in front of me. But I can't change this about myself— and I don't think I want to. That sense of curiosity, of longing to push myself onward and outward, is so crucial a part of my personality that without it I simply wouldn't be myself. I knew I wouldn't be content with the pastoral harmony this world offered me; I guess, like Eve, I would always want to taste the fruit of the tree of knowledge. Then a plasma storm came and destroyed all my work. It looked like I was going to have to be content with staying in the garden of paradise.

As it turned out, I wasn't allowed to. *Voyager* returned with a cure. As Tuvok described it to me later, my crew were not happy with the replacement that I had provided for them, and had insisted on approaching Dr. Danara Pel, with whom we had a good relationship, in order to find a cure for us.

"It seems," Tuvok said, rather dryly, "that only Captain Janeway and Commander Chakotay are acceptable."

Well, that was certainly gratifying, although once I was back on board, I had more than a few things to say to my senior staff about disobeying orders. I had expressly instructed them not to contact the Vidiians, and they had ended up fending off a Vidiian attack. This was one of my least effective group rebukes. The whole time I was talking, Tom Paris had a big self-satisfied grin plastered over his face, and even Tuvok looked about as unrepentant as it's possible for a Vulcan to be (I have a sneaking suspicion he didn't enjoy the captain's seat). I could see B'Elanna beginning to bristle; the words *"You could always say 'thank you'!"* were clearly forming on her lips.

"Nevertheless," I said, "I would like to *thank you* for your initiative, and most of all for your loyalty. If I couldn't spend the next seventy years living in the wild on a paradise planet, then there's nowhere else I'd rather be than on board *Voyager*."

"Seconded," said Chakotay, although I wasn't so sure about that.

✦

The letter writing was a crucial part of how I dealt with the realities of my unusual command. I had the best support that I could hope for from Chakotay and Tuvok, but a captain needs someone outside of her own crew. These letters, together with the occasional ones I wrote to Parvati Pandey and to Owen Paris, reflecting on some decision I had made and imagining their advice, provided me with a version of this external reality check. Of course, I couldn't send them, never mind expect a response, but I filed them all away, and I treated them as if they had been sent, and I didn't go back to them at all; I made a point of that. I have only reread them now, writing this memoir, and my heart goes out to Captain Kathryn Janeway in those very early days, thrown into these circumstances on her very first mission. I wish I could go and tell her that everything would turn out all right. I wish I could go and give her some comfort. She had a tough job. It would be good to let her know that all would be well.

Reading them back now, I see plenty of other encounters that I have long since forgotten. I recall species that we met in those early days that we left behind as we moved on through the Delta Quadrant. As well as the Vidiians, there were the Kazon—I wasn't sorry to say goodbye to either of those. And then I had my first encounter with the Q Continuum: you can be sure that I raided *Voyager*'s data banks, but nothing could truly have prepared me for the tragicomedy that unfolded. The Q we encountered—he took the name Quinn—was trapped, imprisoned, inside a comet. We released him, whereupon he immediately tried to end his own life. It transpired that Quinn was a being that had thought deeply about the nature of immortality—and wanted it to end. He was not the trickster figure, the fool, that we had assumed, or that we associated with his species. When the other, more familiar Q appeared, wanting to return Quinn to his imprisoned state, Quinn requested Federation asylum. I was duty bound to take it seriously and decided to hold a hearing to consider Quinn's request.

Well, this being the Q Continuum, a variety of most interesting witnesses were called to support Q's case that Quinn should not be allowed to die. It seems that Quinn had been pivotal at all kinds of moments in human history. But Quinn had his own argument to make, and he showed us what it was like to live as part of the Continuum. What a bleak vision that was. A dusty country road, that only came back to the place where it had started: a run-down gas station and store, a dead end where the inhabitants sat around, almost comatose from boredom. Everything done; everything said. Nobody talking to each other; nobody had in millennia. It truly was a vision of hell. I couldn't think of anything more dreadful: at least my own road was leading somewhere, took me past marvels and wonders. At least my life still held *novelty*. But living in the Q Continuum was a road to nowhere—for eternity. Quinn, having shown us this, argued that to condemn him to this unchanging life was cruelty. I was moved by this argument—and, ultimately, it was his life, and he should have the chance to choose what to do with it. I granted his request for asylum. (This was the moment when, poignantly, he chose his name.)

I had hoped, of course, that the transition to mortality might provide Quinn with sufficient novelty to persuade him that he might explore this new condition, and that this would keep him alive for at least a while longer. This was not to be the case. Q, respecting the other man's wishes, had given Quinn access to Nogatch hemlock, and he took his own life. I wish this could have turned out differently. There was still so much for Quinn to see and do. But it was not to be.

These encounters form some of the most memorable aspects of our journey home—and it was part of our mission, to seek out new life. I tried not to forget that in many ways I was lucky to be the captain of the Starfleet ship that had traveled furthest, and that I might, one day, bring information about these places and new species home. But I was fascinated at least as much by watching how my crew responded to our unique challenge. Harry Kim, struggling with homesickness and a first assignment that nobody should receive, not even the Academy's finest. B'Elanna Torres, trying to put aside her anger and find a way of life that used her passion and her intellect constructively. Tom Paris, who, with seventy thousand light-years between them, was finally able to live outside of his father's shadow and become his own man. Our Doctor, evolving every day beyond what his programming had ever anticipated. Chakotay, day by day coming back to his old life as a dedicated Starfleet officer. Even Tuvok, perhaps the most collected and stable of us all, had to find a way of living with the exigencies and irrationalities of our situation.

Damn, though—I wish Amelia had come on board.

✦

There is one series of events that preys on my mind after all these years. I still am not sure that I made the right decision: I'm not sure that there was a right decision to be made. The whole affair started in a most straightforward way: Tuvok and Neelix went down together to investigate an M-class planet which we had encountered and to collect botanical samples which we hoped to be able to use. When they—and the samples—were beamed aboard, we were confronted with a single individual. Investigations showed that the samples they had collected, when demolecularized through the transporter, acted as a symbiogenetic catalyst, merging the DNA of my two crew members into a single being. We had lost two people and replaced them with one.

Tuvix. He made his presence felt from the outset. He combined the knowledge and capabilities of both men—I had lost neither a chief security officer nor a head chef and morale officer—but I had lost Tuvok, my old friend and mentor, and Kes had lost her Neelix. I know how difficult this time was for her—Tuvix was so like Neelix in many ways, and yet so unlike. I recall the conversation that I had at this time with Kes, who was going through a kind of loss that we had all faced when we were stranded in the Delta Quadrant, not least myself, with the loss of Mark. She had been shocked that Tuvix still retained Neelix's feelings for her—while, at the same time, still loving T'Pel in the way that Tuvok had. I sympathized: this must have been deeply disconcerting. Tuvix was not Neelix. To his credit—there were many things to his credit—he did not press himself on Kes and gave her the space and the room to deal with what was, to all intents and purposes, a bereavement. And he was, in himself, a good and kind man. He had fine instincts on the bridge. He even cooked well! However, the Doctor found a way to reverse the process, enabling the transporter to separate the DNA of the two men. Most of us wanted this resolution—with one notable exception, Tuvix himself, who wanted to live.

I will not dwell on the decision that I made. I am, to this day, unsure about it. The Doctor would not perform the procedure, and therefore I took it upon myself. Tuvix died, and Tuvok and Neelix lived. Later that evening, Tuvok came to my quarters.

"An interesting decision, Captain," he said.

"What can I say, Tuvok? You know, just before we set out to look for the *Val Jean*, I told T'Pel that I would do everything in my power to bring you home."

"But at the cost of another man's life?"

"Tuvok," I said, "remember Pandey's classes at the Academy?"

"The Ethics of Command. Of course."

"Do you remember the session on the trolley problem?"

"The clash between utilitarian and deontological ethics," he said.

"Only you would phrase it that way," I replied, with a wry smile. "Yes, whether an action should be judged by its consequences, or according to a set of moral principles."

Pandey set us this thought problem, a well-known one in moral philosophy. A runaway trolley is heading toward five incapacitated people, and you are left with a choice: reroute the trolley, which will save those five people, but kill one other person, or else let the trolley take its course, and save that one life at the cost of those five. What is the ethical action? You know, we argued that problem back and forth for a couple of hours. I guess I never thought that I would have to answer it so directly.

"On the one hand, I had Tuvix, a single life," I said. "On the other, I had you and Neelix—two lives, established, with people who loved them and who were grieving for them. You know, Tuvix had your tactical skills, and he was at least as good a chef as Neelix. But you had families, Tuvok. People that I knew, people that I had met. Could I have faced them, knowing that I could have saved your life, and not done it?"

He sat for a while before replying. "The logical choice, certainly," he said. "Although I myself would have hesitated."

Maybe there is no answer. I made my choice. Can I live with it?

I will learn to live with it.

CHAPTER NINE
YEARS OF HELL—2373-2374

WE ENTERED OUR THIRD YEAR IN THE DELTA QUADRANT acclimatizing to our situation, but with the growing and sinking thought that we were indeed out here for the long haul. Day by day, week by week, our life seemed to alternate between shipboard routines and sudden, explosive encounters with the worlds and species that we met. Starfleet protocols went a long way to stabilizing our life on board ship, and my decision to enforce these was vindicated when even a few former Maquis confessed to me that these routines helped them along the way. I could see that B'Elanna, for example, for all her frustrations, was flourishing on *Voyager*: her technical expertise and creativity were vastly appreciated, and by no means taken for granted. Those of us who watched the crew carefully—by which I mean myself and Chakotay—did not miss the growing closeness of B'Elanna and Tom Paris. Chakotay explained how the attraction had been clear to him when the two had met during their time in the Maquis, although Tom's capture had prevented it progressing further. Still, it was a situation worth watching. Close relationships gave comfort to the crew but, if there were breakups, then there was the potential for resentment, which could cause excessive disruption within a crew so small. Either Tom would persuade B'Elanna that he was a good bet, or she would decide to eat him alive. Neither Chakotay nor I could call it.

I began to give serious thought to what it might mean, if we did indeed take seventy years to reach home. The crew would age; we would need people to look after us, never mind continue the ship on its journey. How would families work on board ship? How would we teach the children, care for them, bring them up? I watched Samantha Wildman closely, and how the crew supported her, and wondered how we might scale this up, when the time came. I know that others were thinking the same: we had been en route for two years now and were likely to be in the same condition for the foreseeable future. Perhaps this was how the rest of our lives would be. The urge to create stability in this transitory situation seemed catching: many of the crew, in this third year, seemed to commit to longer-standing relationships. Besides, we all knew each other very well. We were used to each other and, perhaps, more forgiving of each other. Even the Doctor experimented with a home life: an exploration of his humanity that became a tragedy when his simulated daughter died. I would not wish this on anyone, not even someone made of photons. The Doctor loved his little girl, Belle, as much as any person had loved their child, and he grieved her loss. A first, true encounter with the vicissitudes of life. It is to our Doctor's credit that he did not abandon his experiment at this point but continued to risk change and growth.

Some of us, however, were not prepared to leave the past behind, or could not. For Harry Kim, as an example, giving up on his beloved Libby would clearly be an admission that he would not get home, and Harry was never going to do this. He coped with life on *Voyager* by insisting that it was a temporary interruption to his real life, that one day he would go home, and see his parents, and pick up with Libby where they had left off. I know that Tom Paris tried to make him accept some of the realities of our situation and consider at least going on a few dates. Not the most tactful advice, but Tom Paris was proving to have a kind streak that had not been allowed to flourish in the past. You saw it with how he looked after Harry; in how he tried to take care of B'Elanna. Chakotay too frequently expressed surprise at how Tom was maturing. I had always thought that all he needed was a chance: to get out and prove himself. The Maquis must have seemed like this to him; of course, it went disastrously wrong. But now another chance had come, and Tom seemed to be pulling himself together.

For myself, I was not prepared to give up on my old life. Men like Mark Johnson don't come along every day. My chief regret was that I had not accepted that first proposal when it was made. We could have had a few years of married life behind us. I have wondered, sometimes, whether that might have made a difference to how things worked out, but some things can't be changed, and you can't live in the past. For now, I wrote my letters to him, confided in him as if he were there, and hoped beyond hope that I would see him again. There was no question of my starting a relationship with a member of my crew: as captain, I could not risk this and hope to keep the necessary distance upon which rank and, thus, authority depend. Yes, it was lonely; sometimes it was extremely lonely. Chakotay was my rock when it came to my fears about our journey home, or my worries about individual crew members. We established a long-standing routine of a weekly supper together, a time when we could both relax and put aside, if only for a few hours, the burden of our senior rank.

But it was Kes who came closest to becoming a confidante for Kate, rather than Captain, Janeway. The conversation that we had when she thought that Neelix was lost had created a closeness and warmth between us that I found a great consolation. Even if I rarely discussed with her how I felt, I knew that someone on board *Voyager* had seen this side of me and understood. Her growing psionic powers no doubt gave her increased sensitivity, and, of course, the fact that she was not Starfleet helped. But besides her gifts, there was an inherent gentleness and wisdom to Kes, a calmness about her, that inspired trust. I was grateful for her quiet and steady support. We were always conscious, with Kes, of her abbreviated life span in comparison to the rest of us, and that every moment was precious. As it turned out, we lost her sooner even than we anticipated, but not in the way that we expected.

Triggered by our encounter with Species 8472, her psionic abilities began to outstrip what her body could bear, and even began to threaten the ship itself. Kes made the decision to leave. I begged her to stay with us, to hold out until the Doctor had a cure for her condition, but she wanted to go, to find out where her powers could take her. Before she left, she sent us forward through space more than nine thousand light-years, past Borg territory, taking nearly ten years off our journey. A gift indeed. Her departure was a great blow for Neelix, even if their relationship had already concluded. It was noticeable how from this point on he began to spend more time with the Wildmans. Naomi, with her accelerated growth from her Ktarian heritage, was starting to want playmates rather than carers, and Neelix was ready and willing to fill this need. I imagine it gave him solace too. (Kes warned us, in her last days, about a species named the Krenim: one reason why we elected to avoid entering their space. I often wonder what might have happened had we chosen to go there.)

The urge to create a family seemed to be endemic, as I learned when we once again encountered the Q Continuum. Motherhood had certainly not been on my agenda at that moment in my life, and even more certainly I had not contemplated that Q would father any child of mine. Nor is there any timeline in which I would ever contemplate this. I was more interested—if alarmed—to learn that our previous encounter with the Continuum had brought about significant changes (there's a reason the Prime Directive exists), although this had, after all, been Quinn's intention when he asked us to help him die. No longer a dead-end track, the Continuum was now on the verge of civil war, which Q was trying to prevent by bringing a child into existence. I sympathized with his purposes, having seen the plight of his faction; but it's his damn methods, as ever, that I take exception to. Never has a woman been so wretchedly wooed. Fortunately, he moved on quickly enough—and I acquired a godson. I guess I've mentored all kinds of people across the years.

✦

No person has challenged me on such a fundamental level as Seven of Nine. Nobody has made me reflect so deeply upon the nature of selfhood, on our responsibilities to ourselves and to each other, as she has over the years. Living alongside Seven of Nine was not always comfortable, particularly in the early days, but I must surely count coming to know her, watching her grow and change, as one of the most rewarding experience of my life. For this all to emerge from an encounter with the Borg is all the more satisfying. No other species, in their cruelty and conformity, in their pursuit of uniform collectivity over infinite diversity in infinite combinations, stands so much in opposition to my own culture and mores. As we approached Borg space, we identified a narrow band through which we hoped we might pass without being detected. We dubbed this the Northwest Passage, and, as we drew closer, we detected fifteen Borg cubes heading our way. I am sure we all believed this was the end... and the cubes went past us, and then registered as destroyed. What the hell could destroy fifteen Borg cubes? This, we learned, after sending an away team to one of the cubes, was Species 8472, which, as we discovered from the Borg logs, had defeated them many times before. Before we beamed back, Harry Kim was struck and infected by one of the aliens, and rushed back to sickbay, where the Doctor was able to modify a Borg nanoprobe and cure him.

My enemy's enemy is my friend. Perhaps, I thought, we could strike up an alliance with the Borg, using the Doctor's cure for the infection as bargaining power. My crew were not convinced of the wisdom of this—but we came up with no other alternatives, and took *Voyager* to a Borg world, offering an alliance. An attack by Species 8472 persuaded the Borg to take my offer seriously and sent a representative drone to communicate with us. This was my first encounter with Seven of Nine.

My account, from hereon, necessarily relies on others, since I was badly injured when Species 8472's bioships attacked us. Before I was sedated, I made Chakotay promise to continue working with the Borg. I gather that what happened next was that Seven of Nine, learning that millions of Borg had been killed in the middle of the sector, asked Chakotay to take *Voyager* to help, and he refused, on the grounds that this would take us too far off our course home. His intention was to leave the Borg behind for others to collect them, but Seven circumvented this plan by opening a spatial rift. When I was able to take back command, it was to learn that all the drones apart from Seven of Nine were dead, and that *Voyager* was stranded in fluidic space. I resumed work with Seven of Nine to develop a weapon to defeat the bioships, and she returned *Voyager* from fluidic space. We defeated the alien fleet, only for Seven of Nine to turn on us and attempt to assimilate *Voyager*. We knocked her out using a neural relay and resumed our course. When she awoke, she was severed from the Collective, and in our care.

Not the most auspicious introduction of a crew member, but we were responsible for her now, and began the process of restoring her individuality. The Doctor was initially unwilling to operate on her to remove her implants against her wishes, but as she was in no condition to make the decision for herself, I persuaded him that it was a necessary course of action. These operations saved Seven's life, but they left her in a condition which she did not want: severed irreparably from the Collective, and, not incidentally, hostile toward us. I presented her with information about her past—her name, Annika

Hansen, assimilated as a child— but this only enraged her.

Can you force freedom on someone? Of course not. I believed that Seven of Nine could return to some kind of humanity, but it was plain to us all that the journey was long and hard. She had to learn even the most basic of human actions, which we learn as babies: how to eat, how to chew food. She began to have hallucinations of a raven (it was the name of her parents' ship, which she was on when they were captured by the Borg). She experienced flashbacks. The Doctor diagnosed post-traumatic stress disorder. As we learned more about her experiences, that came as no surprise. A small child, captured by Borg, her parents assimilated, hiding away until she herself was taken. I would not willingly imagine such horrors. We could not bring that child back, but we could, I hoped, bring Seven forward, allow her to become fully individual once again. My relationship with Seven was, in these early days, often marked by hostility and tension. At other times, I saw her courage and determination. When we entered a region of space where subatomic radiation from a nearby nebula would have killed us, Seven agreed to remain out of stasis so that we could pass through the space in a matter of weeks, rather than adding a year to our journey to go around it. Who else could have survived this isolation? She risked not only her precarious mental state but her life to save us.

What can I say? Like a mother, I had given Seven of Nine her life as a human being; like a mother, I could not force her to live that life in the way I chose. Her life was hers to live, and she must make her own choices. But above all, I believed that she could find herself. She was—she remains—unique. She has never failed to exceed my expectations of what she could learn, of how she could come to terms with all that had been done to her, of how she might live beyond the horrors that marked her early years—transcend them, indeed—and become her fullest self.

There is one situation I recall where her desire for perfection, instilled in her by the Borg, was at odds with the fact of human imperfection. Still, she came the closest that any of us can. Much of this mission remains classified; suffice to say that there are good reasons for this. It is a situation, too, where I hope that I was able to reciprocate in some way the lessons that Seven taught us and warn her that her pursuit of knowledge was leading her into a disastrous mistake. But she did, for a moment—for 3.2 seconds, in fact—see perfection, the alpha and the omega. What can bring us to a more forceful realization of our own frail and finite humanity, than a glimpse of the numinous? I found her on the holodeck, running my Da Vinci simulation, contemplating religious imagery. Contemplating the divine.

✦

The Da Vinci simulation gave me many happy hours over the years, once in unexpected ways. I sometimes think that my time on *Voyager* made me draw on every single one of my Academy experiences. Under no circumstances, however, did I ever imagine that I would be called upon to build a glider from scratch, and certainly not in the company of the Grandfather of Flight himself. We had come under attack from an unknown species who used their transporter technology to steal weapons and equipment directly from the ship. After tracking our missing goods to a nearby world, Tuvok and I beamed down to discover that the Doctor's mobile emitter had been one of the items stolen—and that the Leonardo Da Vinci simulation had been taken too. It was up and running, and Da Vinci was hard at work under a new "patron"—a local trader named Tau, responsible for stealing from our ship. The Master and I escaped by virtue of his technical expertise (with a little guidance from me), and, of course, my ability to land a punch upon our guard. This was a minor incident, I suppose, in our journey home, but one that my adolescent self would have adored. Like meeting Amelia Earhart, I suppose. Our time in the Delta Quadrant was not all bad.

Other holodeck experiences were significantly bleaker. At this time, we had regular encounters with the Hirogen, a nomadic species whose culture was organized around notions of "the hunt." Other species, across their hunting grounds, were seen as prey, and we were no exception. A group of Hirogen hijacked *Voyager* and forced half of us to reenact hologram simulations of ever more violent and vicious hunts, and the rest to act as slave labor, treating their wounded colleagues and turning more and more of the ship over to these sickening games. Many of my memories of this experience are hazy: those of us forced into the simulations were fitted with neural interfaces that made us believe the parts we played were completely real. I still have shards of memory of my life as a Klingon warrior, of the day that Troy was set ablaze, of chasing Black and Tans down the back lanes of Ireland. Most of all I recall the simulation in which myself and others of *Voyager*'s crew became part of the French Resistance. This simulation expanded so rapidly that the integrity of the ship came under threat, and only the overloading of the hologrid brought the program to an end. It was plain, even to our Hirogen captors, that this was now a zero-sum game. Nobody could win. We had to make a truce. I gave them the ability to create holodeck technology on their own ships, a small price to pay to get them off *Voyager*.

I've talked to other crew members about this whole episode, and I know we were all shaken at the extent to which some of these memories still seem real to us. A huge shock to your sense of self, and one or two have reported that they sometimes still wonder whether or not they are inside a simulation. Well, that way lies madness, I think; you have to proceed as if what's going on around you is real. But the thought of how the ship was taken over this way gave me many sleepless nights. The holodeck was a great solace to us across the years, but also proved an Achilles heel on many occasions. Some people cannot tell the difference between fantasy and reality, and sometimes, our own daydreams worked against us. There was one occasion, however, where our encounter with a simulation led to genuine rapprochement, and this time with a species we had real reason to fear.

I cannot describe how uncanny it was to encounter, on a space station so far from home, a near perfect recreation of Starfleet Academy. Yet there it was—up to and including our beloved Boothby, friend and mentor to so many of us during our time as cadets. I sent Chakotay and Tuvok to investigate, and they learned that this was a simulation created by Species 8472. This added significantly to our alarm: what could a species so terrifying that even the Borg withdrew in the face of them, want with our Academy? I ordered Seven to prepare warheads using Borg nanoprobes; I hoped, too, for a diplomatic solution.

Chakotay's investigations were uncovered, and Species 8472 were alerted to the fact that at least some of the humans within their simulation were exactly what they appeared to be. Chakotay was captured and interrogated by an individual who appeared exactly like Boothby; he described to me later how disconcerting this was—to know that behind this familiar, beloved, trusted face lay an intelligence of which we knew so very little. He learned from this simulated Boothby that Species 8472, having encountered us, was now afraid that Starfleet intended to invade fluidic space. The simulation had been created to prepare them for further encounters with us. I, in turn, was terrified that this simulation was a prelude to invasion—a training ground for Species 8472 before they took on the Alpha Quadrant for real. For a while, this seemed a dangerous and unresolvable stalemate. I wondered, however, if there was something of the real Boothby in this simulation and tried to speak to it with some of the warmth and trust I would have extended to the real man. It seemed to work. We traded information on Borg nanoprobes for expertise that Species 8472 had on genetic modification. We moved on—the truce holding, and I for one slept a little easier in my bed that night, knowing that an understanding had been reached with a truly terrifying species.

But wishing, truly wishing, that the simulation had been real, and that somehow, we had transported all that long way back to the Academy. All that long way home. Absence makes the heart grow fonder, or so they say; I would say too that a moment of presence makes absence just a little harder to bear.

✦

As the fourth year of our time in the Delta Quadrant drew toward its end, I found myself taking stock of our situation. We had all, more or less, come to terms with our life here, even those of us, like Harry, who were still hoping that our return would be sooner rather than later. We had found ways to live with the distances and the absences; we had found solace and friendship in each other. And then, quite unexpectedly, this equilibrium was disrupted. Seven of Nine, working on our sensors, had expanded their range significantly, and discovered an extensive relay-station network. By tapping into this network, she'd been able to locate a Starfleet ship on the very edge of the Alpha Quadrant, the *U.S.S. Prometheus*. This was not a ship with which I was familiar, and no wonder: this was a secret experimental warship under development for the war against the Dominion. Who the hell were they? What the hell was this war? And what was the significance of Romulan noninvolvement? Given our position, these were hardly questions to which we could readily gain answers. What we could do—or the Doctor could do on our behalf—was send news of us to the Alpha Quadrant. We temporarily transferred the Doctor to the sickbay of the *Prometheus*, and, speaking directly to Starfleet Command, he told them that *Voyager* was still very much intact, and that her crew was trying to find their way home.

I won't forget that conversation with the Doctor in a hurry. So much news, all at once. Learning that we had been declared dead more than a year ago and thinking about how dreadful an experience that must have been for all of our friends and family. My poor Mark, thinking himself widowed a second time; my poor mother, the loss of her husband compounded by the news of the loss of their older child… No, soon they would both know. All of our families and friends would know. We were alive and well and trying our very best to come home. And more than that, we knew now that Starfleet was working on our behalf. They would be working to bring us home, however they could, as quickly as they could. Most of all, they had a message for us: *You're no longer alone.*

It was a great privilege of my life to be able to pass that message on to my crew: *You're no longer alone…* I watched as the ramifications of this sank into their faces. There were tears: of relief and joy, and a few tears at the thought of what families must have suffered, believing that we were dead. Harry was almost beside himself with worry: I think he spent much of the next week quizzing the Doctor about what he'd seen and what had been said. Poor Harry, he went through torments thinking about Libby and his parents having to come to terms with his death, and then the shock of learning we were still out there. "But will she know that I'm still on board?" he kept saying. "Will she know that I'm okay?"

I had a responsibility to keep spirits up, however, and I kept myself all smiles and laughter while I was among the crew. But I'll not deny that when I was back in my quarters that evening, I was close to shedding a few tears of my own at that message. The loneliness: that had been by far the worst thing for me. The fact that, ultimately, Kathryn Janeway was captain of *Voyager*, and that here in the Delta Quadrant the buck stopped with me. Nobody would arrive in the nick of time to pull us out of any desperate situation in which we found ourselves. But this small communication reminded me that I was part of something greater: I was part of Starfleet. Contact had been established. Whatever happened next, whatever trials they were undergoing back in the Alpha Quadrant, I knew that some small part of this fine organization, some of those brilliant minds, were now at work on behalf of me and my crew. Captain Kathryn Janeway was no longer alone. Knowing this made it truly possible for me to bring my crew and my ship back home. I took a moment to be proud of myself—to acknowledge how far we had come, how far we had brought us—and then it was back to work. Miles to go before we sleep.

✦

This contact was quickly followed by a transmission from Starfleet Command via the network, but after a tantalizing few words the transmission ended. Naturally this became our priority, although this was not without complications, given that the hostile Hirogen controlled the array via which the message was sent, and were intent on using this to hunt down our ship, and that our ship was shaken by gravimetric forces coming from the array. Nevertheless, we had to get closer, and were soon able to download the message from Starfleet Command. It was seriously degraded, but I set Seven of Nine to work to get what she could from it. Letters from home. What we had all been longing for. Oh, be careful what you wish for...

Shock after shock. The devastating news for Chakotay and B'Elanna and others that the Maquis had been wiped out, the Cardassians and their allies from the Gamma Quadrant (that shadowy Dominion of which we'd heard) triumphant, and their friends either dead or in prison. It's a measure of how far we had all come that, as far as I know, the reaction of all the non-Maquis crew was only shock and sympathy for our friends and colleagues. Whatever our thoughts about the rights and wrongs of the Maquis, we knew that those people who had chosen to resist the terms of the treaty and fight for their worlds had on the whole done so as a matter of conscience. Their resistance had not deserved to meet such a brutal end. And it was terrifying, also, to think that the Cardassians had made an alliance that was destabilizing the fragile peace that had been constructed along the border, and were, if we understood what we were reading, on the warpath, and in the ascendancy. I tried to put these thoughts aside: much as I would have liked to have been serving alongside my fellow officers in whatever conflict now threatened the Federation, I was too far from home to be able to make any difference whatsoever. But the news was troubling, the uncertainty unhappy.

For others, the news was only good: we were able to celebrate the new addition to Tuvok's family, and all of us were glad to see how happy Harry was to have some contact with his people at last. Harry's regret was these communications were hardly likely to be a regular occurrence. There wasn't going to be a weekly mailshot, bringing his family up to date on his news, hearing from them what they had been up to. Poor Harry. For Tom Paris, meanwhile, the lack of a message was its own relief. Tom still had a way to go before he could feel free of the burden of his father.

As for me… The good news was that Mollie was thriving, and so were her pups…

But Mark was lost to me, forever. My handsome fiancé, the first man that I had been able to imagine spending my life with… As I had on some level feared, a second widowhood had been too much for him, and he made the wise choice—the choice that he had been forced to make once before—and moved on. I think what was hardest to bear was how narrowly we had missed each other. He had remarried only four months ago… But that was not a useful way to think. It was more than a year since we had been declared dead, and he would have made himself move on at that time. I did not, and could not, begrudge him this. Perhaps even if we had made contact, I would have told him to move on. Seventy years is a long time to wait for someone to come home from a work trip… He wanted to marry; he wanted a home life, and he wanted children. I knew this. I would not have made him wait for me… but pretending that he was had been solace. Now this fantasy was no longer available for me. I was alone.

"You're hardly alone," Chakotay told me, echoing that message from Starfleet that only a little while before had given me such comfort. I didn't talk to anyone beyond Chakotay, although I found that I missed Kes all over again. I would have taken some time to sit with her, I thought, to tell her how I felt. But she was gone. How much we had gained, in those few short weeks. But how much we had lost already. How many others on my crew must have gone through the same experience? There's no place like home—but even home cannot stay the same. What would we find, should we ever get there?

CHAPTER TEN

A LONG WAY FROM HOME—2375–2376

I HAVE BEEN TOLD ON MANY OCCASIONS THAT I TAKE DECISIONS on behalf of my crew that they would not take on their own behalf, and I must confess that there is some truth in this. But the fact is that while we were in the Delta Quadrant, I could not afford to lose the expertise of a single person. If the crew fell below a certain number, then *Voyager* was no longer sustainable as a working ship. I would not be able to staff her; I would not be able to bring the people remaining to me home. There are occasions, therefore, where I put the well-being of the whole above individual wishes. I know B'Elanna has a few words to say on this subject; so might the Doctor, if asked. I shall leave others to judge.

In B'Elanna's case, I made a call about saving the life of a necessary member of my crew, someone vital to the continued operation of *Voyager* and therefore the likelihood of our reaching home, rather than respecting her own wishes. We had responded to a distress call and found a ship containing a single, nonhumanoid lifeform, which we beamed directly to sickbay. This creature—which was scorpion-like in appearance—attacked B'Elanna, wrapping itself around her body, and piercing her with its "sting." The effect was to create a biochemical bond between them—but the prognosis was not good for B'Elanna, and the Doctor was not able to find a way to separate them that would not result in her death. Searching the ship's data banks, he learned about work conducted in this area by a Cardassian exobiologist, Crell Moset, and he programmed the holodeck to recreate Moset. Together, they set to work to find a cure for B'Elanna.

Nothing is ever this simple, however, and word about the Doctor's simulation of Moset passed around the ship. You will recall that I had one or two Bajoran crew on board *Voyager*, and one of these, Ensign Tabor, learning about Moset, confronted the Doctor in sickbay. Moset was notorious on Bajor; his work had involved experiments on thousands of Bajoran prisoners. Tabor wanted the work to stop—and, unfortunately, B'Elanna, overhearing the conversation, and, as a former Maquis sympathetic to the plight of Bajor, agreed with him. She did not want to be cured by any procedure developed by Moset, simulation or not. I understood her scruples, but I could not let her die. But I deliberated hard. The historical comparisons from our own human history were hard to put out of my mind—Thomas Parran and the Tuskegee experiments, or Joseph Mengele's work. I understood both Tabor's distress, and B'Elanna's scruples. But I could not let her die. We removed the alien—and were able to send it back to its own kind—but B'Elanna was very angry with me. We deleted the Moset program, and I remain uneasy about the choice I made to use the procedure that the Moset simulation and the Doctor devised together—but I do not, and I cannot, regret saving the life of B'Elanna Torres.

There were other occasions where I had cause to reverse my initial decisions. One such situation arose when the shuttle of an away team comprised of Ensign Kim, Ensign Jetal, and the Doctor came under attack. The Doctor managed to force the alien out of their craft, and fled back to *Voyager*, but by this point the unknown weapon used on them had sent Kim and Jetal into synaptic shock. Back on *Voyager*, the condition of both ensigns became critical, and the Doctor had time only to operate on one (nobody else was capable of performing the surgery). He chose Kim, and Jetal died. Nobody blamed him for this; absolutely nobody. He made a choice, and he saved a life. But the Doctor began to blame himself. He became obsessed with his choice, trying to determine why he had picked one ensign over the other. He entered what we could only call a feedback loop, with his ethical and cognitive subroutines at odds with each other. It manifested as obsessional thoughts, over and over, as he tried and failed to reconcile the decision to treat one over the other. He was in danger of breaking down completely. I made the decision to erase his memories of the circumstances of Jetal's death, and, indeed, of the ensign herself.

What can I say? I needed a functioning medic. These events in and of themselves had shown how close to the wire we were: there was nobody else—not a living flesh-and-blood person—able to perform the surgery that the Doctor had performed to save Kim's life. That alone showed how vulnerable we were in some areas of expertise. I could not afford to have my only medic out of action.

Well, the repressed invariably returns, and, after several months, after we had put the whole unhappy series of events behind us, the Doctor, conducting routine checkups, learned that Kim had undergone surgery—surgery which only he could have performed. By this time, of course, we had taken on a new crew member, Seven of Nine, and, with her customary combination of doggedness and technical acuity, she uncovered the deleted files, confronting the Doctor with memories of an ensign whom he did not know. I tried once again to delete them… but the Doctor was ahead of me. I explained, in general terms, what had happened, and that the deletions had been necessary to prevent the Doctor from a complete breakdown. To his mind, however, he had been operated on without his consent. I was prepared to do the same again—until Seven of Nine came to speak to me.

It's humbling, to say the least, to have your ethics called out by a Borg drone. But it was hard to refute Seven's arguments. If the Doctor was primarily a machine, she said, then to some extent so was she. When would I decide that I had the right to operate on her? I grasped her point immediately. Seven *had* been operated on without her consent; that little girl Annika Hansen had been transformed into a drone. How did this differ? How did I differ from the Borg who had eradicated her personhood? She left me struggling to see how. This is how Seven of Nine changed us. I had made this decision to eradicate the Doctor's memories before her arrival; with her on board, there was no question of doing the same again. It would have made a mockery of our attempts to humanize her. Seven told me that despite all the pain she had undergone, both mentally and physically, in her attempt to regain her individuality, she would not change a thing.

What course could I take, after that? I had to let the Doctor find his own way and live with the consequences. We restored his memories, and for two weeks we sat with him, as he wrestled with the choice he had made. I took on the bulk of this: this was my responsibility, after all. I listened to him repeat himself, over and over, and I despaired that he would ever find a way through. What finally drew him back was when he saw that I was ill. The solution to his pain was to see the pain of someone else and make a move to alleviate it. I guess we could call it compassion. I was sent off to bed (I had a headache and a fever), and the Doctor... I suppose he upgraded. He transcended his programming, yet again. All thanks to Seven of Nine.

I reflect often upon this decision of mine. Nothing in my Ethics of Command classes had prepared me for a Borg who had a greater sense of individual needs than I did, or a hologram that was in every meaningful sense alive. Our mission: to seek out new life. I am grateful to Seven for giving me the chance to make amends, for giving me the chance to change my mind. Recognizing our mistakes is part of what makes us human too, I guess.

Seven of Nine herself had to confront the consequences of her own actions a little while later, when we were docked at the Markonian Outpost Space Station. This interlude started out as welcome respite from our voyage: we had, for once, been made welcome, and we extended hospitality of our own, inviting people to visit and explore the ship. Seven of Nine was approached and, subsequently, attacked by three visitors, while she was regenerating in her alcove. They were attempting to inject her with Borg nanoprobes, but Seven was able to call for backup, whereupon we subdued her assailants and restrained them in sickbay. There, the Doctor was able to identify them as former Borg drones, which, on waking, they were able to confirm. Furthermore, they had been part of Seven's unimatrix. They had approached her to learn about a series of events that occurred several years ago, when their ship crashed on an uninhabited planet. Seven, who at first had no memory of these events, found her memories gradually returning.

It was not a happy awakening. After the crash, and temporarily severed from the collective, the three other drones, who had been assimilated as adults, found their individuality beginning to reestablish. But Seven, who had of course been assimilated at six years old and had much less of an established identity, fought against this change. Worse, when the others attempted to flee, she followed them, reinjected each with nanoprobes, forcing their reassimilation. It was, frankly, a horror story, made worse as we got to know these people, their lives and histories, the families from which they had been forcibly taken, not once, but twice, the last time at Seven's hands.

There was not much of a happy ending to this story. Again, we were faced with a choice: these three could not survive for long without reassimilating. In the end, a short life as themselves rather than a long life as Borg was what they preferred, and the Doctor and Seven performed the procedure to sever them permanently from the link that existed between them, the last remnants of Borg technology. Lansor, Two of Nine, remained at the space station, while P'Chan, Four of Nine, traveled on alone, to experience peace and quiet and solitude before he died. But Marika, Three of Nine, stayed with us on *Voyager*. This was a tender, sad, interlude—a few brief weeks making her acquaintance, before she was lost to us. One of the most poignant encounters of our whole time in the Delta Quadrant, and one that profoundly affected Seven.

✦

Reflecting back now on these cases where I had to make ethical decisions, all I can say is that I did the best that I could under the circumstances. I had a clear goal: to bring the ship home with minimum loss of life. I did not always get it right—but I tried always to bear this in mind, and to balance our situation as far as possible with the principles of Starfleet. I was out on a limb—a Starfleet captain without Starfleet. I could not summon up help or stop off at a starbase for extra supplies. I could not, for most of the time, even ask for advice on the decisions I had to make. Some were sound; some were less sound. Those Ethics of Command seminars could only help so far. I'm aware that the situation could, however, have been much worse. I am lucky that I arrived in the Delta Quadrant with my ship more or less intact, and enough people so that—despite some grievous losses—I was able to crew that ship. I know that this was not the case for Rudy Ransom on the *Equinox*.

Our astonishment in receiving a distress hail from another Starfleet vessel was matched only with our delight at discovering that this was no trap, but indeed another ship of ours, sent into the Delta Quadrant by the same means, at approximately the same time. They'd had a much rougher ride than us: an encounter with a power called the Krowtonan Guard had, in the space of a week, caused the death of half of Ransom's crew, and caused serious damage to the ship. I began to thank my lucky stars that our encounters—even with the Borg—had not caused so much harm. And I was curious as to how the

Equinox, although a smaller and less powerful *Nova*-class ship, had managed to cross the same distance, and was excited to learn that Captain Ransom's people had made enhancements to their warp engines. I hoped this was a technique that we could adapt.

Alas, this was not to prove the case. Ransom, after that devastating week, had become wholly focused on the survival of his crew—at any cost. The secret of the *Equinox*'s rapid progress was revealed to be the wholesale slaughter of nucleogenic creatures, from whom they were harvesting bioenergy. This was how *Equinox* had enhanced their warp drive. They had crossed ten thousand light-years in a matter of weeks—and Ransom, and his XO, Maxwell Burke, were ready to sacrifice more to make the journey home. And I was going to do anything to stop him, particularly when we came under attack from the nucleogenic creatures, intent on a very justifiable revenge.

It's disheartening, to say the least, that it took an encounter with our own species and civilization to draw out the most mistrustful and savage behavior from us on our voyage home, as if coming face to face with our own baser selves was too much to stand. I certainly lost my bearings somewhat in this encounter—I'll admit that. Some of the decisions I made in my desire to bring down Ransom and the *Equinox* crossed the line. My interrogation of Noah Lessing went too far, as Chakotay told me at the time. I even went so far as to relieve Chakotay of his command, when he questioned my decision to fire torpedoes on the *Equinox*. The deletion of the Doctor's ethical subroutines by Ransom's crew (a flaw we quickly corrected) allowed him to explore aspects of human behavior about which I am sure he would have preferred to remain ignorant. I know his memories of his interrogation of Seven of Nine disturbed him greatly. In the end, Ransom, seeing the error of his ways, and removed by his own XO, ended up fighting back against the mutineers, and sacrificing himself—and his battered ship—to save *Voyager* from the alien assault.

I flatter myself that I would not have made the same mistakes as Rudy Ransom, but it's fair to say that I wasn't tested in the same way. I cannot and will never condone the choices he made but speaking as the only other Starfleet captain who knows a little of how he felt, I can see how his desire to protect his crew and bring them home might have brought him there. The road to hell is paved with good intentions, after all. I'm just glad I never had to set one foot upon it. Rudy made good in the end: we should not forget that. He was himself again, before he died. The five surviving crew members of the *Equinox* came on board *Voyager*: I stripped them of their ranks, put them under close supervision, and limited their privileges. And I will state here for the record that they gave exemplary service for the rest of our journey. Not everyone is beyond redemption.

Chakotay and I had some repairs to make to our relationship after these events. Truth be told, I was grateful for him—grateful to have a man of principles beside me. I should always remember that about Chakotay—it was principles that drove him to the Maquis, not profit, or vengeance. He was my true guide home. But still, as we picked up the pieces, I had to wonder—and how I wondered—what the next day might bring, and the day after, and the day after, and whether I might face a week of hell bad enough to make me cross the line for good.

✦

I have faced numerous criticisms over the years about the extent to which I allowed use of the holodeck during *Voyager*'s journey home. Let me say that critics always find something to complain about, and this seems to me another in a long list of decisions that other people are sure that they would have made differently had they been the captain. Besides, I've heard it all before. Torres and Tuvok both complained about how much time people spent on the holodeck for, as Tuvok put it, "frivolous reasons," although I suspect that B'Elanna was glad sometimes that Tom had a hobby, and I know that Tuvok used it on occasion for meditation purposes… with B'Elanna, too, now I come to think about it! But their points were fair. Nevertheless, I was the captain, and this was the decision I made. For good reason too: morale, notably in the early days, was low. In discussions with both Neelix and the Doctor, I was convinced that permitting people regular use of the holodeck was a good way for them to relieve the unusual stress and isolation of our situation. I'm sure that any inventory of holodeck programs on board *Voyager* would have revealed a high proportion of simulations simply named "Family" or "Home." We were so far away, and there was a strong possibility we would never see the people and places that we loved again. I considered this use of resources worth it in terms of the effect it had on crew well-being.

As for the other programs—damn it, they were fun! They helped people relax and unwind, and, given the precariousness of our situation at times, this was also necessary. I knew there was a risk that people might slide into holo-addiction, a well-documented phenomenon, and we did monitor use. Detractors can also be sure that I kept a close eye on what proportion of resources the holodeck was consuming. There were indeed times when I had to cut use down to almost nothing. But when the going was good, the holodeck was an important part of keeping the crew functioning. Tom Paris proved most adept at constructing scenarios which gave his colleagues great pleasure over the years: Sandrine's was a great creation and, of course, Fair Haven was a place very close to my heart. Even a captain needs time away from her responsibilities. What does the poet say? Humankind cannot bear very much reality... We all needed to take some time away from our situation. We all needed a break.

I will not deny that there were occasions when I wished I'd shut the damn thing down at the start of the voyage and never switched it on again. Let us say that I never expected my role as captain to expand into acting. You will note that my account of my childhood does not document a sparkling theatrical career, and indeed that career had more or less peaked with the dying swan. I hadn't acted since junior high—when I was a lackluster and frankly not convincing Juliet, more suited to comedy than tragedy—and was not prepared to have to extemporize the role of evil queen. (You can skip the jokes—the crew made them all at the time.) How did this all come about, you might you ask. Tom's holoprogram, *The Adventures of Captain Proton*, was a great favorite, and one which he and Harry played by preference. On this occasion, they were forced to leave the program running when *Voyager* became trapped in spatial distortions. As we tried to break free, a species of interdimensional aliens who took photonic form crossed to our dimension, entering through the *Proton* program. And so the story became real. The aliens, when attacked by Chaotica, were genuinely at threat from his photonic weaponry, which was harmless to us, but could harm them. We decided to enter the story, to help the aliens defeat Chaotica, and to free ourselves. Tom, it turned out, had a specific role in mind for me.

I defy anyone else to have brought such authenticity to the part of Arachnia, Queen of the Spider People. My task, it transpired, was to woo Chaotica so that he agreed to lower the lightning shield to allow Captain Proton to disable the death ray. I would like to think I inhabited the role convincingly.

Perhaps my theatrical career is not yet over—I guess I'll need something to do in retirement. The crew rewarded me by adopting a new catchphrase, generally used after I'd issued a dressing-down. You don't want to know the number of times I heard muttered behind my back: *"Ha! You're no match for Arachnia..."* Well, they were right—they weren't.

There seems to be a subcategory of alien species unable to distinguish between fantasy and reality, and our next encounter with such gave me much more insight into the mind of our Emergency Medical Hologram than I might have preferred. The Doctor, it transpired, had been using the holodeck to daydream—all very well, I encouraged both him and Seven of Nine to explore the limits of their personhood, and the holodeck was an ideal environment for this. The Doctor's daydreams, however, tended toward the grandiose, and he had constructed a fantasy in which, as the "Emergency Command Hologram," he took charge of the ship. The Doctor might have been able to continue with this undisturbed, had not a passing ship, crewed by members of what we only knew as the Hierarchy, used a form of scan which enabled them to pick up the Doctor's program, mistaking the simulation for reality. Our knowledge of this came when a panicked junior crew member contacted us, explaining the mistake, and hoping we could save his skin.

The solution was for us to act out the deception for real, persuading the attacking Hierarchy ship of the reality of our "photonic cannon." My considerable trepidation over allowing the Doctor to use his Emergency Command routines was matched only by my sense that a small amount of rough justice was being dealt out. Nevertheless, he carried out the task with considerable aplomb, and I must admit that I was impressed at how the Doctor handled being in the hot seat. I could see some practical use to the ECH, and I reconsidered my decision not to devote formal research time to the project. I suggested that we assemble a team to explore it further. A change of heart that I am glad to say paid off in the long run.

✦

One adjustment that I had to make over these years was the extent to which my crew was now considerably more experienced than it had been at the start of the mission. Even my newest ensign, Harry Kim, by now had nearly half a decade's service behind him. In Harry's case, these years were marked by dedication, quietly getting on with the job, and being one of the most diligent crew members on board ship. I suppose at some point he was going to assert himself in the face of my authority, and the occasion arose when we made contact with the Varro. We were intrigued to learn that they had been inhabiting their generation ship for over four centuries. The ship was now in need of assistance—which we were certainly willing to give, on the principle of paying it forward; we were often in need of assistance ourselves. The situation was complicated somewhat by the mistrust of the Varro: they were, not to put too fine a point on it, a xenophobic people who would much have preferred not to have contact with us. But their need outweighed their distaste for strangers, and we were permitted access.

A generation ship was naturally of interest to me, since it was certainly one possible future for *Voyager*: if the ship's capacity diminished past a certain point, our progress might slow down to such a degree that the journey would take much longer than the life span of at least some of us. Who would crew the ship then? Naomi Wildman could hardly do this single-handedly (though that kid was determined enough that she would have given it her best shot). At the back of my mind, I was always wondering whether I needed to do more to encourage my crew to settle down, create families, treat our ship less like a place of work and more like a moving village. Not an option for the captain, of course, but a possibility for others. I was therefore interested to learn more about how the Varro's society worked. We discovered significant tensions: a dissident group had emerged, separatists who were discontent with the closed and insular life on board their ship, and who wanted to leave and follow their own path.

Usually we would not have involved ourselves; unfortunately, our hand was forced. Harry Kim, in what seemed at the time to be an unusual disregard for instructions, appeared to have fallen in love with a Varro scientist, Tal, developing some kind of physiological bond with her that was disrupting his behavior significantly, and manifested as physical symptoms. I was extremely angry with Harry over this, not least because we had no idea whether this could be a biological threat to the Varro, and because he might have disrupted our working relations with them too. Harry insisted that he had genuine feelings for Tal; I reminded him he had broken regulations, and I regretfully entered a reprimand onto his record. Poor Harry, unblemished service until then. We ended having a frank discussion about his actions: I believed he was suffering from a condition which needed treatment; Harry believed he was in love. With the unerring way in which the young know how to wound, he asked whether I would've taken a hypospray if it could have finished my feelings for Mark. I was fortunately not obliged to answer this question.

In the end, the dissident group, including Tal, were allowed to leave their ship and move on. Harry was bereft at her departure and, while the Doctor offered him a means to alleviate these emotions, he refused. I told Harry that this could not interfere with his duties, and that the reprimand stood. And I had to admit that I was surprised that it was him, of all my crew, who had behaved this way. Well, as he told me, he wasn't that fresh-faced ensign any longer. Five years is a long time—everyone changes. I think Harry learned from this, grew from this. That's all you can ask for, in the end.

There were other examples during this time of my crew asserting themselves, and on one occasion I ended up having to dish out more than a reprimand. The ship came in range of a quite extraordinary sight: a world entirely covered with ocean. Even more remarkable, this world was inhabited. Initially its government, the Monean Maritime Sovereignty, was suspicious of us; I was able to persuade their spokesperson, Burkus, that we were not hostile, and invited a deputation to visit *Voyager*. During this visit, we learned that the Moneans knew very little about the ocean upon which they lived, and that, in fact, the Waters, as they called them, were beginning to shrink. Paris, who had attached himself to this visit, said that *Voyager* could help. I guess I should have seen we were heading for trouble, but I allowed him to take the *Delta Flyer* down to investigate the problem. Meanwhile, Chakotay reported that the rate of the reduction in the world ocean was extremely rapid, and likely to result in its dissipation within five years. I was surprised that Burkus was more concerned about the politics than the reality of this situation; perhaps I should never be surprised of the short-termism that some politicians bring to global crises.

Tom's exploration revealed that the oxygen-mining operations of the Moneans were leading directly to the dissipation of the Waters, but Burkus was clearly more concerned with the political ramifications of the news. It was plain he was unlikely to do anything with this information, leading to an angry outburst from Tom. After Burkus left, I reprimanded Tom—in hindsight, locking horns with him was probably a mistake, since it only reinforced his tendency to rail against authority. Next thing I knew, he had taken the *Delta Flyer* back down, to carry out some kind of radical act to secure the safety of the world ocean. We were able to stop this in time—who knows what could have gone wrong—and when Tom came back on board, I reduced his rank to ensign and gave him thirty days in the brig.

At the time, I was bitterly disappointed in Tom, and very angry with him. All his hard work, it seemed to me, was in danger of being thrown away; the huge strides he had made controlling his impulsive streak... This was, so it seemed, a serious regression. I am so very glad that this turned out to be a momentary lapse. I had nothing to complain about after this incident. But I understood Tom better as a result. He would always, I had to recognize, rail against certain Starfleet strictures. The usual frustrations that we all have with the chain of command were heightened by the fact that they also represented his psychological struggle to separate from his father and to earn Owen's respect. Over the years, Tom seemed to find a working solution to this, and I guess I can forgive him his mistake. Nevertheless, I am extremely grateful that I was able to restore his lieutenancy before we were in real-time contact with home. And, in retrospect, I can see now that this marked the end of the old Tom, the last gasp, in some way, before a more mature version became fully established.

My other most impulsive crew member, B'Elanna Torres, had her own parental demons to deal with—almost literally, in this case. Returning from an away mission and hitting an ion storm, B'Elanna had a near-death experience in which she believed she was travelling on the Barge of the Dead to Gre'thor, the home of the dishonored dead, with her mother. Returning to consciousness, B'Elanna was completely convinced of the authenticity of her experience, and that her mother was on board the Barge of the Dead as a result of her actions. Against my better judgement, I authorized the Doctor to induce an artificial coma in B'Elanna, to allow her to learn more. That was a frightening time, but, when B'Elanna finally awoke, I could see from her eyes that the risk had paid off. When we talked about her experiences later, B'Elanna told me that she offered to take her mother's place on the barge and go to Gre'thor, but that this was shown to her as a version of *Voyager*—a metaphor for stasis, perhaps, of being stuck somewhere. B'Elanna needed to move on. I cannot comment on the truth or otherwise of these experiences. But they were true for B'Elanna, and whatever happened to her during those hours of unconsciousness, something had plainly been released in her. There were many more bumps along the way, but she was beginning to let go.

We had an entirely unexpected encounter with an old friend whom we had believed had long since outgrown us. Out of the blue, we were contacted by Kes—but this was someone to whom the intervening years had not been kind. She was weary, aged—and angry, stalking through the ship and attacking engineering. Many of these events are hazy to me, part of the local time distortions Kes created in her fury; suffice to say that I found memories returning to me that I did not know I had. She had come back in time, right back to her initial days on *Voyager*, and told us about her sense of loss after leaving us. That her powers were out of her control. That she had been a child when we'd allowed her to leave—and we had failed in our duty of care. As my memories returned, I remembered this encounter—and what we had done to stop it. As we came again to the moment when Kes approached us after her long absence, we evacuated engineering, and, when she arrived there, showed her the message she had left for herself. Her young self, begging her to remember what it had been like, and to leave us in peace. It helped, a little. It was sad to see Kes like that: that gifted and sensitive being that we had sent on her way with such love in our hearts. I hope that whatever happened next, she found a way back to that essential part of her: her clear sight, her curiosity, her courage.

✦

It seemed a long time now since we had received those messages from Earth, and yet it turned out that we had an ally back in the Alpha Quadrant, a man whose tendencies toward obsessive behavior could only work in our favor: Lieutenant Reginald Endicott Barclay III, Reg to his friends, and he will always have friends among the crew of *Voyager*. Barclay had become obsessed with our story, spending more and more time in holosimulation with the crew, and convincing himself that he could establish communications with us. He was working on the Pathfinder Project, which, as we were to learn, was a project spearheaded by Owen Paris trying to contact us and bring us home. It sure helps to have friends in high places—and an admiral's son on board. I knew I was right to bring Tom Paris along.

I've heard various accounts of the lengths Reg Barclay went to make his dream of communicating with us a reality; suffice to say that while I might not want to be his direct superior, I am eternally grateful for his devotion to our cause. The first we knew of his efforts was when we detected a microwormhole and then a communication signal which Seven identified as Starfleet in origin and transmitting on an official Starfleet emergency channel. Well, the speed with which we moved to clean up that signal! And then, blissfully, almost unbelievably—nearly a full minute and a half of two-way communication with home… Just time for a few words (expressing a multitude of emotions), to transmit our logs, reports, and navigational records back to Earth, and to receive some technical advice on modifying our comms to keep us in more regular contact. And Owen Paris, bless him, letting us know that they were doing everything they could to bring us home.

You can bet there were more than a few tears that day. I felt mostly joy. I'd hit rock bottom in that encounter with the *Equinox*; I'd nearly lost myself entirely. Now I knew I was going to find my way back home.

CHAPTER ELEVEN

ENDGAME—2377-2378

LOOKING BACK, ONE ASPECT OF OUR JOURNEY THAT I HAD certainly not anticipated was how many children would fall into our care. A Starfleet captain should be prepared for anything, however, and anyone who cannot manage to organize their ship to help their people with caring for their offspring is in the wrong job. Naomi Wildman, my fine assistant, had slotted right into our ship. My heart was naturally in my mouth on her behalf whenever we met with hostiles (and whatever agonies I went through were surely nothing compared to how Samantha must have felt). But her presence on board gave us perspective, and reminded us of why we kept on going; we all lightened up around her, we all wanted to bring her home to her other parent.

In the latter stages of our journey, moreover, some wholly unexpected charges fell into our care. When the *Delta Flyer* was intercepted by a Borg cube, we went to bring home our away team, and found the cube using an odd attack strategy. There was a reason for this: the entire crew consisted of five children, neonatal drones, as Seven explained, assimilated young. We found a baby too, in a maturation chamber, tiny implants on its little face… Truly our encounters with the Borg brought some terrible sights, but those lost children, wandering in the void, loyal to a Collective which, it transpired, had long since cut them loose, are among the worst. The eldest of this group, whom we only knew as First, cut off from the Collective, was now feeling the full effects of his reemerging adolescence, making him dangerous and erratic. He intended to keep our away team until we gave him *Voyager*'s navigational deflector. I was not inclined to bargain, not least as giving them the deflector would have allowed them to communicate with the Collective. I had enough Borg on my hands. I asked them to come on board *Voyager* instead, invited them to become individuals.

First was unpersuaded, and it fell to Seven to inform this little group that they were indeed completely abandoned, cut loose. The Borg do not tolerate imperfection—and they were imperfect. The shock was enough for the younger children to turn to Seven for aid; not First, though, who died insisting that the Collective would come for them. We brought the four surviving children on board, of course. The Doctor started to remove their implants, and Seven began the process of locating their real homes and families. The elder boy was Icheb, a Brunali; the younger twin Wysanti boys were Azan and Rebi; the little girl, Mezoti, was Norcadian. We put out calls to their people and their worlds, letting them know that we had found their strays. And while Seven thought that Neelix would be a better carer, I knew it had to be her. Who else could help them through these changes they were experiencing? Who else on the ship understood? I sometimes wonder what bedtime stories she told them. I should not forget that we had a baby to look after—if only for a little while. We were very quickly able to locate her home planet and return her to three relieved parents. Yet again, *Voyager* had found itself acting as a nursery in space. We might not have anticipated this extension to our responsibilities, but we carried it out with great success.

I am so proud of Icheb, and I know that Seven of Nine too became deeply attached to this unusual and gifted young man. It was therefore a significant wrench to us to discover the world from which he had originally come, and to learn that his parents were still very much alive. I could see no good reason for Icheb to remain on board: at first, he was deeply hostile toward this change in circumstances, not least when confronted with the realities of his home world. This was a rather isolated and technologically backward place where the local population had to work hard to make the land produce enough for them. Both Seven and Icheb were concerned about the impact this would have on his ability to further his studies in astrometrics, for which he had real talent. But Icheb's people, the Brunali, turned out to have hidden depths: they had developed sophisticated techniques in genetic engineering, in part to assist their farming efforts. After some initial missteps, I watched with relief as Icheb began to move from hostility toward his parents to an acceptance and beginnings of trust. But I could only feel regret for Seven of Nine, whose attachment to Icheb had been a serious bond for her, and who was now going to have to say goodbye.

She struggled significantly with this while we were in orbit over the Brunali world, and so I must forgive myself for initially doubting her when she came to me to express misgivings about the account given us by Icheb's father, Leucon, about his son's assimilation. She told me that Mezoti had spotted discrepancies in Leucon's story, and while it seemed to me that both of them were looking for reasons to bring Icheb back to us, she argued in return that if there was the slightest chance that Icheb was in danger, we had to go back and make sure. I looked deep into the eyes of my most unusual crew member then, and I saw how much she loved this boy—and that she would not remain on board *Voyager* if I denied her the chance to find out for sure. I took the ship back.

And only in the nick of time. Seven's instincts had proven correct. The Brunali's genetic-engineering skills were not only to help their food production: they had created a weapon to infect the Borg. The problem was in the delivery mechanism—Icheb. He had been infected with a pathogen, and sent out to meet the Borg, infecting the first probe that encountered him. A truly sickening use of this boy. There was no question over whether or not we would intervene. We took Icheb back on board (it was a close shave; a near miss with a Borg cube) and learned the whole truth—his parents had not simply infected him. He had been genetically engineered to carry the pathogen, made to be a weapon, born to be a sacrifice. I remembered the old Greek tale, about the tribute sent from Athens to King Minos of Crete, of seven young men and seven young women, offered to the Minotaur to save their city. Not this time. We had Icheb back, more precious to us now than ever before, because we'd come so close to losing him. I'm glad that I was willing to listen to the instincts—the hunches, if you like—of one little girl, and one young woman, who could tell when something was not right.

Seven of Nine's educational techniques initially left something to be desired (if I never hear the words "punishment protocol" again, it won't be too soon); the children, however, took matters into their own hands, and I eventually observed a relaxation in her disciplinary strategies. She would often say that she was not suited to this task, but when the time came for Rebi and Azan to go home, taking Mezoti with them, we all felt the loss, and Seven most of all. Was there a tear? Seven insisted that her ocular implant was malfunctioning, and, indeed, this proved to be the case, and a manifestation of a very serious problem. Seven's cortical node was breaking down, causing symptoms such as dizziness and convulsions, and preventing her from being able to regenerate. In simulation after simulation, the Doctor was unable to perform a procedure that would not result in Seven's death.

My crew rallied around her, of course: Neelix came to see her in sickbay and, when she left there, I understand she had a conversation with B'Elanna Torres about the afterlife. Severed from the Collective, she could see no way that her unique experiences would live on. B'Elanna had her own wisdom to impart here. None of us would forget Seven. I was glad to think of these two women, under my command, turning to each other in friendship, at this difficult time. I myself went to speak to Seven, to assure her that we would do everything we could, and found her viewing images of Earth. I promised to take her to Bloomington when we got home—and learned that she had no expectation of surviving that long. Worse, she seemed to think that she had disappointed me, that she had failed to meet my expectations in her journey toward establishing her individuality. Oh, Seven! As if that was the case! In all ways, you have exceeded my expectations.

In the end, it was Icheb who saved her, donating his own cortical node, and relying on his comparative youth and genetic resequencing to coax his own body into surviving without the node. It was a risky gambit, and Icheb was ill for a while afterward, but it paid off, and Icheb was able to return to his studies and work toward his dream of sitting the entrance exam for the Academy. I gather there was a moment, talking to Icheb as he recovered, when Seven believed her ocular implant was malfunctioning again: this time the explanation was much simpler.

✦

Surely the most important feature of the final year of our voyage home was the establishment of regular, direct face-to-face communication with the people at the Pathfinder Project. It had been a great and continued relief to me, since our first contact with the project, to know that there were so many people back on Earth working to bring us home. And while a solution to this was, according to their reports, a long way off, they had also been working hard to establish communications with us. At first, we only had the letters: those first tiny contacts with our families and friends that so rocked our little worlds. Then we were able to receive recordings. And now—miracle of miracles!—the people at Pathfinder believed they had worked out a new method to speak to us in real time.

Again, we should acknowledge the work of Reginald Barclay, our great advocate in the Alpha Quadrant. How strange to think we had met him as a (quite inaccurate) hologram before most of us spoke to him face to face! The real Barclay was far less confident, much less a raconteur (and, not incidentally, not hijacked by Ferengi for a quick profit). Since returning to the Alpha Quadrant, I have had many conversations with Deanna Troi about Reg Barclay, and I understand a little more about the obsessive tendencies and various oddities that made him so devoted to our cause. What can I say? There's a place in Starfleet for everyone, and oddities are right at home on *Voyager*. We made him an honorary member of our crew right back when those first messages from Pathfinder arrived, and he still remains a part of the crew, as far as I am concerned. The breakthrough he made that let us all speak to each other directly for the first time in years was a hugely significant piece of work for which he has been rightly honored.

You try to be conscious, in a situation such as this, that you are participating in a historic moment. The first transgalactic two-way communication! In truth, we were all very close to being overwhelmed by our emotions. How I felt for Tom, seeing his father on-screen for the first time—seeing what was completely, undeniably, and unconditionally, sheer relief and pride on Owen's face. And how could we not have been moved by that most precious sight—those real-time images of Earth, our home, straight from McKinley Station, so white and blue and familiar. I could see North America; I could almost fancy that I saw Bloomington, my home, the country lanes and the white picket fences. So close I could almost reach out and touch… Still thirty thousand light-years away. God, that moment will remain forever in my mind. I knew without doubt that it had all been worth it: all the long years, the fears, the losses. I was bringing my ship and my people home.

With the connection made, we now found ourselves able to communicate with Earth for eleven minutes every day. Sounds like nothing, doesn't it, but it was an embarrassment of riches to us. Naturally we had to devote part of this to official communications with Starfleet Command, but I argued (and won my case) that, in particular during these early days, we should turn over the bulk of the time to letting my crew speak at last to their loved ones. Of course, that's not much time to spread across one hundred and fifty people, and Neelix organized a lottery and then the rotation. When my turn came up (of course I didn't pull rank; I was about thirtieth, which was pretty good, all things considered), I stood nervously waiting for the communication to start. I was a little conscious of Seven of Nine standing behind me, but the moment my mother's face appeared on-screen, everything around me was forgotten.

"Mom," I whispered.

"*Oh Katy,*" she said. "*Oh, my darling girl!*"

I thought I was going to cry. Nearly seven years of keeping myself under such tight control, knowing that I was the one who always had to be strong… Well, we are all susceptible to the sight of our mother, aren't we? I'm only human, after all.

"It's so good to see you," I said. "I can't begin to say…"

She looked only a little older. Some more silver in her long hair; a few more worry lines around her eyes. "*I knew you weren't dead,*" she said. "*Owen Paris came to see me. I said to him, 'Owen, I'm not giving up, and neither should you.' He was trying to persuade me, and I ended up persuading him!*"

We both began to laugh. My mother—that was where I had gotten the stubborn streak! I could imagine her, listening to the visiting admiral, nodding politely as he spoke, and then saying: *No. This is how it is.*

"Between you and Reg Barclay, we have had some great allies back home."

"*I've heard from Owen about the Redoubtable Reg. I might invite him here for dinner.*"

"From what I gather about him, he won't accept!"

"*Well, let's not talk about Reg Barclay. Are you all right, Katy? Have you been looking after yourself?*"

"Yes, Mom, fruits and vegetables at every meal."

I saw her eyes drift past me to where Seven was standing. "*I'm sorry about Mark.*"

I brushed it aside. "Water under the bridge."

"Hmm." She didn't look convinced (I'm not sure I sounded convincing), but this wasn't something to discuss on a line like this. *"Your sister sends her love. Yianem too, and the girls. They want to speak to you next time around. The new one is very excited to speak to the famous family member! She's mad about Starfleet."*

Amelia: the latest addition to their family. I laughed. Sounded like she was a Janeway through and through—and she was, as you shall learn. "Three months," I said. "I hope they can all hold out that long!"

"All of us will be here. Oh, Katy. I'm so glad to speak to you again!"

"Me too, Mom."

Behind me, quietly, Seven said, "Thirty seconds, Captain."

"Not long enough," said Mom. *"Well, Katy, hurry home. We have the lamp lit, guiding you home."*

"Get the coffee pot on, for God's sake," I begged her, trying to sound cheerful. "I'm desperate for a decent cup of coffee!"

"I'll get your grandfather on it."

"Ten seconds, Captain," said Seven.

"Goodbye, Katy! We'll speak soon!"

"Goodbye, Mom," I said.

And then she was gone. I took a moment or two to collect myself and turned to see Seven contemplating me.

"Are you... all right, Captain?" she said.

"I'm fine, Seven." I took a deep breath. "You must have seen a lot of this now. Is there anyone back in the Alpha Quadrant that you're planning to speak to?"

"My father had a sister," she said, doubtfully.

"Try her," I said. "It might be worth it."

And I believe that she did. I'm not sure I can imagine how this conversation must have gone: her aunt would remember little Annika, no more than six years old. Seven of Nine was no longer that little girl. I hoped the aunt had the sense and the grace to accept her on her own terms, and not wish to have Annika back. I believe they began to communicate regularly; at least, I didn't hear of anyone accepting Seven's slots in the rotation. I wondered whether she would get in touch with her, once we were home.

This was a tumultuous time for us all: I often passed people in the corridor having a quiet cry. We had all been starved for conversations with our loved ones. The letters had been like field rations in comparison with being able to speak to them face to face, in real time. All of us were changed, of course: Harry Kim was no longer the fresh-faced new ensign who had left his clarinet at home. (I had a very nice letter from his mother about how grateful she was that I had looked out for her boy. I didn't mention this to Harry, although I did play up those night shifts, when he had been in command of the ship, for her benefit.) Even those of us with very close family ties were finding our feet again after seven years. And other relationships were starting over completely. I know that Tom always had B'Elanna with him when he spoke to his mother and father, as if to insist that this was who he was now, and that his father needed to get to know him on these terms. B'Elanna in turn had made tentative contact once again with her estranged father. How hard, to try to rebuild that relationship under these conditions! To be able to speak only every few weeks, and then for no more than a few minutes at a time! But B'Elanna was tenacious, and once she put her mind to something, she stuck to it, and she had decided that this relationship was plainly worth salvaging.

Of course, there was a very good reason for this. Our lovebirds had married at the start of our seventh year: I must say that was a typically outlandish proposal. They were participating in a race, on board the *Delta Flyer*, and the flyer's warp core had been sabotaged. I gather they thought they had about ten seconds to live when Tom popped the question. This was… very like Tom, shall we say. But he'd meant it, and they married—and before we had all got used to having this married couple in our midst, B'Elanna discovered she was pregnant. The Doctor warned us there might be emotional outbursts. Several people joked (not entirely kindly, I think; I put a stop to this) that they weren't sure how we would tell. In fact, this was a very difficult time for B'Elanna. It has been my observation that pregnancy, and imminent parenthood, make people reflect on their relationships with their own parents. I guess this is in part because they don't want to make the same mistakes—and they're worried that they won't avoid them. But at the same time, people seem to want to reconnect; they want their child to know where they came from, to know their grandparents.

For B'Elanna, this time was marked by a real coming-to-terms with what it had meant for her to be half Klingon. When she and Tom saw that their little girl was going to have the distinctive facial ridges, many unhappy childhood memories came back to her. Kids can be ghastly, after all; they'll always find something to pick on, and B'Elanna's physical differences had attracted some teasing. Worse than that, she believed that it was the Klingon part of her that had driven her father away. These emotions naturally surfaced now; she must have feared that history would repeat itself with her own daughter and husband. (As if Tom would leave her: the man was besotted with her. He'd stuck beside her through thick and thin.) She asked the Doctor to perform genetic resequencing to delete her fetus's Klingon genes and make her more fully human in appearance. The Doctor initially refused to perform such a drastic procedure on the grounds that it was not medically justified, but then later seemed to think that it was not just necessary but urgent. Tom, however, had his suspicions, and these turned out to be warranted: B'Elanna had tampered with the Doctor's program to get the diagnosis that she wanted. We stopped the procedure just in time.

I know that B'Elanna was, once she had taken a little time to think through what was happening, filled with remorse at interfering with the Doctor's programming. However, she had the means to make good. Ever since her pregnancy had been—I hesitate to say announced; *broadcast* was more like it—she and Tom had been plagued with offers from people who wanted to be godparents. (I know pregnant women often complain about finding themselves communal property: poor B'Elanna had this dialed up to the nth degree. Everyone on *Voyager* was invested in this child.) But there was only once choice after these events. I gather the Doctor takes his responsibilities in this respect extremely seriously.

Again, I must reflect on how I had never predicted the extent to which our ship would become so concerned with the nurturing of children. That last year or so, they seemed to take up more and more of our time. Not just our Naomi, whom we all loved very much. Not just our communal investment in Tom and B'Elanna's baby. Not just our Borg children, of whom we were so proud while they were with us, not least Icheb, who remained and was proving to be a most responsible, thoughtful, and careful young man. On top of all this, I found ourselves charged with looking after a recalcitrant, undisciplined, and annoying adolescent: the offspring of Q, Q Junior, unceremoniously dumped on us by his hapless father.

If ever an apple had not fallen far from the tree… Junior had no sense of the consequences of his actions. He caused havoc on the ship, even stripped of his powers, stealing the *Delta Flyer* and running into trouble with a Chokuzan vessel (or so we thought). His actions put Icheb's life in danger, and it was only then that we saw a glimpse of understanding from Junior: confronted again with the Chokuzans, he admitted that the events were down to him, and asked them to help Icheb. Of course, this was all revealed to be a situation generated by his father to teach his son a lesson. Games after games; always the same with the Q. After all the trouble those wretched Q caused us, you think they might have had the decency to send us home. No chance of that: Q provided information that took a few years off the trip, Junior gave me some roses, and with that I had to be content. I understand that I am the Starfleet captain with the most varied experience of the Q Continuum. All I can say is that I would happily have passed on this honor…

✦

There were many other ramifications of our increased contact with the Alpha Quadrant. Speaking for myself, regular contact with Starfleet Command had both pros and cons. Knowing that I was now able to speak to colleagues and superiors, to get advice and support, was a great help to me. I received regular messages from both Owen Paris and Parvati Pandey and their reflections on matters that were troubling me. Being able to share the burden of the command was a real relief. There were downsides, however. I have an independent streak at the best of times, and, for more than six years I had, in effect, been answerable to nobody. The chain of command had been severed—and now it was back. There were significant downsides arising from this, which came into sharp focus during our mission to locate the lost *Friendship 1* probe, which our superiors believed to be close to our current position.

It meant a detour, for one thing, when all we wanted to be doing was getting closer to our families and friends, and I had some misgivings about whether the crew would be happy about this. It turned out that the mystique of the missing probe was lure enough— most of us were Starfleet, after all, with curiosity in our blood. The mission itself proved to be distressing, a textbook case in the perils of sharing technology. The probe, equipped with antimatter reactors, had arrived on a world only for the antimatter technologies to be used for purposes of war. By the time we arrived, the world—and its people—were suffering from a nuclear winter, and the local population blamed us for what had happened to them. One of their leaders, Verin, taking our away team hostage, demanded that we help evacuate the population—but this would take us three years, time we could not afford. Here was my problem, then, with taking on missions such as this: we were there as representatives of Starfleet, but we could not operate as if we were Starfleet. Back in the Alpha Quadrant, I could have called in specialist ships. Here, I was operating under orders, but alone.

As it turned out, we were able to adapt photon torpedoes to explode nanoprobes in the planet's atmosphere, setting off a chain reaction that not only dissipated the nuclear winter, but neutralized the radiation. But the mission had cost a crewman's life: Lieutenant Joe Carey, part of the away team, murdered by Verin. I regretted every life lost on *Voyager*'s journey, but, looking back, this one hits hard. Had we known how close we were to getting home I would have argued against taking on this and any other mission. The priority, after all these years, had to be the safe return of all our crew. The fact that we were now in regular communication with the Alpha Quadrant gave Carey's death a bitter coda: I had to speak directly to his parents, and explain why their boy was not, after all, able to speak to them. I had some stern conversations with my superiors after this. Yes, we were Starfleet, and back within the chain of command—but the chain of command is a reciprocal relationship. It cuts both ways. We could take orders, but help could not be sent. Starfleet Command needed to remember this. We might be on the other end of the line, but we were still a long way from home.

✦

Our Doctor, now in regular contact with the Alpha Quadrant, characteristically made an immediate impact, electing to use his allotted time to speak to the publishers of his magnum opus, *Photons Be Free*. I am being a little unfair here on our estimable colleague, since he admitted that this was a first draft and, having received feedback from the rest of the crew, was willing to carry out significant revisions. You may have sampled the earlier version (I understand that a few are still out there), and so you can imagine my thoughts when I first saw Jenkins, captain of the *U.S.S. Vortex*, murdering a dying man. I do not doubt the Doctor's sincerity when he said that he did not intend the crew to represent us (although I might have a few things to say about his naivety). What was most wounding was that we couldn't help but think that this was, in some way, the Doctor's opinion of each of us. Tom Paris, I know, was very hurt: he had come a long way in the years on board *Voyager*. Well, Tom is hardly one to disappear and lick his wounds; he came back fighting, reprogramming the holonovel, and showed the Doctor exactly how it felt. This was when the Doctor agreed to revise his tome, realizing at last not only the hurt he had inadvertently caused, but how much damage could be done to our reputations, should the novel be widely circulated.

Of course, nothing can be straightforward when the Doctor is involved. The situation rapidly escalated, and I found myself involved in a tribunal to judge whether or not our EMH was a person. Imagine having to do this across the distance of thirty thousand light-years, with only a dozen minutes a day to present arguments! His publishers, Broht & Forrester, represented by Ardon Broht himself, were arguing—and this is not to their credit—that since the Doctor was not legally a person, he had no rights over his book. Sometimes I do wonder how some people sleep at night. (They publish the Dixon Hill novels – I shall never read one again.) As ever, when faced with a legal conundrum, I turned to Tuvok, who tried to argue the case that, leaving aside his personhood, the Doctor had to be considered the author of the piece, and therefore had rights as an artist. It seems ludicrous to me that the arbitrator did not simply rule that the Doctor was a person. The legal definition of "artist" even includes that word! But no: it seemed that our arbitrator was not prepared to set a precedent that day and ruled narrowly in the Doctor's favor as to his rights over his work—but not over his rights as a person. Downright cowardice, in my opinion. What more evidence did we need to provide? The Doctor has exceeded his programming—even his creator, Lewis Zimmerman—admits that. He feels, he loves, he changes—he creates. He is as much a person as any of us—he is more of a person than some people I meet!

There's a twist in this tale. The original version of the Doctor's book got loose among a community of EMH Mark Is who had been decommissioned as medics and were working as miners. They read the book as a piece of subversive literature—a call to arms, no less—and put down their tools and went on strike, the first act in what we now call the "photon rights movement."

I wait with considerable interest to see what the Federation lawyers make of this—and I hope they show a little more courage this time.

There was one more effect of our regular communications with the Alpha Quadrant that is worthy of mentioning, since it brought to the fore an issue which many of us believed resolved, but which I realized, as a result of these events, might need further thought and planning. I refer of course to the old division, which I myself no longer saw, between our Starfleet and our ex-Maquis crew members. These latter suddenly found themselves the victims of unprovoked attacks that left them comatose. It turned out that the attacks came from an entirely external source, albeit using one of my crew. A letter from Tuvok's son, Sek, sent via data stream, had, it transpired, been tampered with. Underneath the message from Sek there was another message embedded, from a fanatical Bajoran vedek, Teero Anaydis. Teero had worked with the Maquis in counterintelligence but had been forced out after experimenting with mind control. Tuvok, under Teero's influence, had carried out the attacks, and was struggling to regain control over his own mind. Put in a position where Tuvok had to choose between loyalty to his former Maquis colleagues, now themselves under Teero's influence, and his loyalty to me, I'm gratified to say that Tuvok chose his captain, and was able to mind-meld with Chakotay and the others to restore them to themselves.

Reflecting on these events afterward, I was chiefly saddened at how quickly the old suspicions had come back. I was grateful, however, to have been alerted to the fact that our increased contact with the Alpha Quadrant was causing many of them to worry about what the future held for them, and I held one-to-one conversations with all the crew who had been Maquis. These fears, it turned out, were very real. What was their reception in the Alpha Quadrant going to be? Would they face charges for their activity, even go to prison, as some of their comrades had done? To my mind, the previous half a dozen years had wiped the slate completely clear. But I could see how some back in Starfleet, still sore over the multiple defections, and without my firsthand experience of the courage and loyalty of these people, might think differently. I realized that this was something for which I needed to prepare.

✦

There is an interlude that I want to put down, because, in retrospect, I can see that when it occurred, I was so very close to home, and yet was nearly lost for good. I'll say this for Quarren labor law: the working conditions and pay were good. It was their recruitment policies that left a great deal to be desired. Their advanced industrial civilization had a chronic labor shortage, and some companies had resorted to a dubious program of systematic forced removal of aliens, giving them new memories along with their new lives. *Voyager*'s crew— or, at least, some of us, were taken.

My memories of this time remain intact—I was the same person; I simply didn't recall my true past life. I found myself a good job, and I found myself a good man, Jaffen. We moved in together. Others of my crew fitted in well too—Seven, inevitably, proved the most adaptable, slotting straight into her new role as efficiency manager at the station where we were working. Others were less successful—a shout-out for Tom Paris, who more or less got himself fired within a few days, and wound up in a bar, making conversation with a lovely woman named B'Elanna…

I would have stayed there quite happily, but part of our crew had been absent when the Quarrens took us: Chakotay, Neelix, and Kim had been on an away mission, returning to find *Voyager* empty, only the Emergency Command Hologram on board (I didn't, after all, regret allowing our Doctor to pursue this research program). Chakotay and Neelix infiltrated the plant, targeting us, and, through our conversations together, bringing our memories back. This rash of "dysphoria syndrome," among so many people of the same species, who had arrived at the plant at the same time, alerted a young doctor to our plight, and the scandal was brought to the attention of the government. We were able to depart, but not before I had to say goodbye to Jaffen.

The trouble was—he had not been kidnapped. This was his real life. He had met a woman whom he liked, and could well have loved, and he had been ready to start another chapter in his life with her. But she wasn't real. I wasn't that woman. I was *Voyager*'s captain, and I was never going to stay.

Still, I had been happy there.

✦

This whole period I recall as one of people getting to know their friends and family again. But we had one sad goodbye to say, to our dear friend and traveling companion Neelix. We were celebrating First Contact Day, Neelix-style, when we received news of a Talaxian settlement hidden within an asteroid belt nearby. I sent Paris and Tuvok, with Neelix, in the *Delta Flyer* to investigate, but the shuttle was shot down and crash-landed. They were rescued by the Talaxians, who had reached the asteroid after many years of exile, and after failing to establish a home elsewhere. We welcomed visitors from the Talaxians aboard *Voyager* to demonstrate our friendship. I could see that Neelix was becoming close to one of them, Dexa, a widow with a young son, Brax, of whom Neelix was also plainly becoming very fond. I wondered, watching them, whether this might be the end of Neelix's time with us. There were numerous complications, however: a company of miners was laying claim to the asteroid belt and trying to get the Talaxians to leave. But having at last built a home there, after many false starts, they were not willing to go. And I was caught up in the Prime Directive: I could not actively involve *Voyager*.

But Neelix, of course, was not bound by the Prime Directive... as Tuvok, so it turned out, had made clear to him. This understanding between my outlandish and certainly very extroverted morale officer and my staid and utterly introverted chief tactical officer was one that I had noted on various occasions, although I think neither of them quite knew what to do about it. I have wondered whether it was some aftereffect of the merging of their DNA so early in our voyage. Neelix irritated Tuvok; Tuvok perplexed Neelix. And yet when it came down to it, Tuvok proved to be Neelix's staunchest ally on board ship, and the one who came up with the solutions that brought Neelix a very happy ending, as far as his story on *Voyager* was concerned.

Prompted by Tuvok—I learned later, much later—Neelix realized that he had, over the years, become a little more than a chef and a host. "The most resourceful person I have ever met," Tuvok said to me later. He had that right—and I daresay Neelix had learned a trick or two from us along the way, even as he taught us many things (if not, yet, managing to persuade Tuvok to dance). Neelix devised a plan for the Talaxians to defend themselves against the miners—a successful plan, with perhaps a little last-minute intervention from the *Delta Flyer*. The miners were beaten back, and the Talaxian colony left in peace.

And yet Neelix decided to stay on *Voyager*—out of loyalty to us, and not wanting to give up on his friends. I could see it was breaking his heart. He had been away from his own kind for a very long time —an exile surely at least as painful as any that the rest of the crew were going through. And, at heart, he was a family man: he loved children—and Naomi was growing up now; she didn't need a babysitter —and he wanted companionship. This was plainly the wrong decision for him: But how could he put his loyalty to us to one side?

Tuvok, in fact, came up with the idea: that methodical mind of his must have been sifting through to work out a solution. "It seems to me, Captain," he said, "that as we draw ever closer to home, and put the Delta Quadrant behind us, we might benefit from having some kind of ambassador here. Someone whom we know well, and whom we trust."

By Jove, he had it, and when I put the idea to Neelix, I could see the sheer joy and relief on his face. He could have everything: company, fatherhood, and our continued friendship through the new transgalactic communications techniques. It was a deeply moving occasion, saying goodbye to him, and I am proud of my crew, and the honor that they showed him, lining the corridors to say farewell. I saw Naomi Wildman, standing beside me, wiping away a tear, and I have to say that if I had an ocular implant, it would have been on the fritz that day. Last of all, Tuvok stepped forward, and gave the softest of soft-shoe shuffles, and said those words that his people had said in greeting to mine, all those long years ago:

"Live long—and prosper."

And so we said, not goodbye, but—till we meet again, to our first and best friend from the Delta Quadrant. Till we meet again, our dear Ambassador.

✦

Of all the pigheaded, stubborn, and downright frustrating people whom I encountered during these years, there was none to compare with my own damn self. *O wad some Pow'r the giftie gie us, To see oursels as ithers see us!* You've got to wonder about someone willing to pull rank on herself. Damn woman. But in the end, Admiral Janeway, my future self, helped bring us home—like she, like I—had promised, all those years ago.

She travelled back in time to come and offer us a route back via a Borg transwarp conduit, but it seemed to me that our priority was to destroy the transwarp network and protect the Alpha Quadrant from Borg attacks. I was not unaware that I was facing, yet again, a choice very like that which had stranded us here in the first place: to use alien technology to take us home, or to destroy it and protect others. The admiral complicated matters greatly by revealing details of her future to me: twenty-three years in the Delta Quadrant (dear god, the prospect…!), the deaths of Seven of Nine and twenty-two others, and the horrible thought of seeing my friend Tuvok's faculties decline… But the crew were prepared to take these risks, if it meant destroying the network. The future is never fixed.

In the end, there was a sacrifice—the admiral took her shuttlecraft into the transwarp hub, in search of the Unicomplex, the center of Borg operations and the lair of their queen. I can only guess at how that encounter unfolded, and what my future self must have suffered. But she was our Trojan horse: she was carrying with her a pathogen that, when released, devastated the Unicomplex, causing it to be destroyed. For a while we believed our plan had succeeded completely. We entered a transwarp corridor, and then saw we were being pursued by a Borg sphere. As we shot along the corridor, I took *Voyager* into the center of the sphere and, just as we came out—a mere light-year from my own home system—I detonated a torpedo that destroyed the sphere.

We looked out on a fleet of ships—Starfleet vessels, all. Our friends; our comrades.

We had found the straight path. We were home.

✦

The ships that had been sent to fight the Borg were now an honor guard. They took us to McKinley Station, where *Voyager* had launched all those years ago, and we docked our ship. Earth was so close I could almost touch it. We were all in a hurry to leave the ship—but first I went to sickbay, to check on the newest member of my crew: Miral Torres Paris, a fine, healthy little girl. B'Elanna was beatific, if exhausted; Tom looked blitzed. I think neither of them had entirely registered that we were home. I don't blame them. There's some question whether Miral was born in the Delta Quadrant or the Alpha Quadrant. To my mind, she's the product of both: the first truly transgalactic child. I guess if our voyage was to have a legacy, it would be this: that the time we spent there as Federation ambassadors, as representatives of Starfleet, would mean that when others visited, there would be places where we would be remembered fondly, and in friendship.

I waited until everyone had left the ship to join their families and friends, and then I sat for a little while on my bridge. It was hard now, after everything, to say goodbye. Chakotay came to find me.

"Kathryn," he said. "Your public awaits."

I stood up. I went to join him, standing in front of the dedication plaque, and we embraced.

"Thank you," I said.

"Kathryn, it's been my privilege to serve."

We left together. I had a date—with my first real cup of coffee in seven years, and with my mother, and my sisters, and the four little girls in their care.

CHAPTER TWELVE
WHAT YOU BRING BACK—2378... AND BEYOND

HOW DID WE ALL FARE, ON OUR RETURN? How did we find life back in the Alpha Quadrant, once we had achieved our hearts' desire? I've thought, many times across my life, that you should be careful what you wish for: not everything turns out to be as you expected. As a child, I wanted more than anything to visit the stars, to be whisked, like Dorothy Gale, away from the quotidian to a marvelous land, but the reality proved very different. Much more of my life among those strange new worlds turned out to be everyday worries: about resources, and maintenance and repairs; about the psychological well-being of the people toward whom I had a duty of care. Life in Oz turned out to have a lot of housekeeping! So what about the return home? Some of us settled back very quickly into our old roles and lives; for others, the adjustment proved more difficult—they had begun their lives on *Voyager*, or else come into their own there. How might the Alpha Quadrant suit them now?

The first few weeks were extremely odd. Given how limited our communication time had been, what none of us had entirely realized was the extent to which, since the Pathfinder Project had made contact with us, we had become celebrities. (The folks at Pathfinder had decided not to apprise us of this, thinking we had enough worry about making the journey home without adding the sense that the whole Federation was watching.) As a result, we came home to learn that people knew our names, our faces, and our stories. The news of our arrival home was greeted with enormous public interest. There were the usual official functions, meeting ambassadors and dignitaries, top brass and all the rest of it, but there were also ticker-tape parades, public meet and greets, invitations to speak… I was granted the key to the city of Bloomington, Indiana, a great honor. Wherever we went, even simply walking down the street to get a cup of coffee, we were stopped. People wanted to get a holo-image, explain how they felt about us, tell us where they were when they heard we were home. It was deeply touching, such as when, for example, you were told how our voyage had been an inspiration or had helped someone find hope. At the same time, it was very disconcerting. You felt strangely… *watched*. (I noticed how many of us who had the option suddenly grew beards, and there were some significant alteration in hairstyles across the board too.)

I was extremely recognizable, and I guessed that, as the captain, and the face of *Voyager*, this wasn't going to go away. I had a faint inkling of how it must have been to be Neil Armstrong, back from the moon, with everyone wanting to have a chance to speak to him. Foolish, intrusive questions, sometimes: What shirts did we wear? What food did we like? Who were we not looking forward to seeing again? It was hard sometimes to keep up one's public face: if you were just trying to get home after a long day, and someone stopped you, hoping for an inspirational moment. I tried my best, and I sincerely hope no one was ever disappointed. I increasingly found that I preferred to spend a lot of time around Starfleet facilities, and I knew that I was going to have to find a remote place to set up home—my old apartment in San Francisco had become too well known, and people would drop by at all hours "just to say hello." A shame: I liked that place, but it wasn't practical any longer. For the short term, I relocated to quarters within the Starfleet Command complex, which were quite sufficient for my immediate purposes, and kept intrusion at a minimum. I was bombarded with many requests for personal appearances, not all of which I could accept. I should note one that was a very special honor: my invitation to address the Amelia Earhart Society. What a speech to be able to give! How incredible to think that this woman was, surely, still alive and making a future with those colonists! That was an extraordinary evening, a highlight of my public career. *Voyager*'s logs changed people's perceptions a great deal.

While I negotiated the highs and lows of celebrity, I should note that my family had quite a tough time in the first couple of years: Mom was deluged by uninvited visitors at the farm, although she was quite brisk and mercenary about the whole business, using it to promote awareness of the situation on Cardassia Prime, where she had become involved in the relief effort and postwar reconstruction. Phoebe and Yianem found this period very hard, trying to protect the girls' privacy, and there were several occasions when stern words were sent from Starfleet on their account to various journalists who were hoping to make their name from catching an image of them. We got the public on our side here, and the girls were declared off limits. I think they often used Yianem's surname when they were traveling, rather than identifying as Janeways.

There was one meeting that I did manage to keep completely private: with Mark. A few messages had passed between us on our return, and I think we both hesitated as to whether this was a good idea, or whether we were simply opening old wounds that should be left to heal. In the end, we both agreed that we needed closure. We decided on an impersonal setting, one of those comfortable but anodyne lounges that are all around Starfleet Command. I was glad of the familiarity of the setting, since this was a very difficult meeting for me. I did not, and could not, and *would* not blame him for finding someone else: for God's sake, the man had been widowed once already. I will not describe the details of this meeting and keep them for me and Mark alone, but there were tears on both sides, and many regrets, but there was also, as we had both hoped, healing. In the end, neither side had meant harm. We met again afterward, and this time I met his wife, a good and lovely woman who has made him very happy, and his little boy. And I was reunited with my beautiful Mollie. Mark's son was devoted to her, which made me shed a few tears. Love me, love my dog. I took one of the pups from Mollie's next litter. I was glad to see Mark so happy, and we remain in touch. But it was hard not to feel regret for the life together that we had lost. I asked him whether he would like the copy of *The Divine Comedy* back—it had been an engagement present after all. "Oh, Kathryn," he said. "I would have followed you anywhere—if I'd only known where you were. It's yours, and always will be."

It was easiest to throw myself straight back into Starfleet. Its protocols, rules, and regulations had been such a support throughout our time in the Delta Quadrant and were a source of continuity on my return. Naturally there was an extensive debriefing, on both sides. I for one was learning about the rapidly changing situation in the Alpha Quadrant in the wake of the Dominion War.

We had received detailed briefings during our latter months, after two-way communications were established, but the reality of being back, and seeing the impact of that brutal conflict not just upon Starfleet but upon the wider Federation, and beyond, took some readjustment. I found Starfleet to be a twitchier, more paranoid organization than the one I had left, and I had to realize the extent to which the (rational) fear of infiltration by Changelings had fundamentally altered the culture. As I say, nobody these days would skip a weapons' sweep when welcoming an admiral aboard. And then I would learn of the deaths of old friends and colleagues, people whom I had hoped to catch up with on my return, killed by Jem'Hadar. We have all said, at our regular crew reunions, how disorientating it has been, not to have this shared experience. The whole quadrant had changed in our absence.

On the other side, Starfleet Command was extremely keen to talk to me and my crew in detail about our time in the Delta Quadrant. I was now the Starfleet captain with more experience of both the Q Continuum and the Borg than any other, and there were hours of sessions devoted to these encounters. Our adaptations of Borg technology also formed the topic of many a discussion—and a dedicated team was put together to work on these innovations. Seven of Nine was naturally a person of great interest. There were lengthy sessions over specific incidents: the fate of the *Equinox* was a real concern, and I know that this case study now forms a significant part of an extended and compulsory course at the Academy on the Ethics of Command. I think we were all shocked at how rapidly the situation had broken down there. All cadets now attend at least two compulsory simulations which place them in environments where they find themselves with limited resources and no expectation of backup. I should note too that, following our reprogramming examples, it is no longer possible to delete the ethics subroutines on any EMH, or, indeed, any other kind of emergency hologram. I spoke privately to Ransom's family, whom I felt needed to know the full story. I am pleased to report that the five surviving crew members, who acquitted themselves faultlessly during their time on *Voyager*, have gone on to good things. Marla Gilmore was the only one to remain in Starfleet, and she has had a fine career. I am glad that this impossible situation in which she found herself, at the beginning of that career, under commanders who lost their way, has not blighted her potential in any way. We remain in regular contact, and I understand that she will be overseeing the cadet course on the *Equinox* next semester. She will, I think, be an inspiration to those students. She learned the hard way, and she has indeed learned. If anyone can teach these students to appraise themselves honestly, it will be her.

As for those of the crew who had been members of the Maquis: that war was long over as far as I was concerned. Nonetheless, a few of the top brass, predominantly those who had served out in the DMZ or who had personally been let down by Maquis defectors, were considerably more resistant. They argued that due process should be followed, and a dangerous precedent set if it was not. The matter was resolved quite simply: I threatened to resign my commission in the most public way possible if full amnesty was not granted. It's amazing how quickly that focused everyone's minds. All my field commissions were reconfirmed, and those former Maquis crew members who wanted to remain in Starfleet were able to do so without any repercussions. Many, however, were eager to return to their home worlds, to see how they had fared since the Dominion War. We see less of these people than we do others at our reunions— but they do stay in touch, and even drop by, every so often.

There were naturally debriefing sessions where my own judgement came under scrutiny, not least my decision to separate the DNA of Tuvok and Neelix at the cost of Tuvix. What can I say? I myself am unsure of the rights and wrongs of that decision, and thinking about what I might have done differently will continue to haunt me for the rest of my life. I also felt a deep and continuing responsibility toward the lives lost during our voyage home, and especially the crew members lost on that first, terrible day in the Delta Quadrant. I paid a visit to the relatives of each person that I lost, to return personal effects, and to bring home memories of them too. People like Joe Carey, Lyndsay Ballard… Even Lon Suder had a mother who'd missed him. Visiting the family of my old friend Laurie Fitz was by far one of the hardest things I have ever done. I have never stopped regretting asking him to come aboard *Voyager*. He was a fine doctor, and a good friend, and his death is one of the biggest regrets of my life.

✦

While there was no question for me that my future lay in Starfleet, this was not the case for many others that served on *Voyager*. I would say that no more than a third of the people who returned to the Alpha Quadrant continued in Starfleet, and most left within the first eighteen months of our return. Speaking to some of these at our regular reunions, they tell me that they found it hard to fit back into the old routines, and the distance between their own experiences, and those of colleagues who had come through the Dominion War, was too great to bridge. *Voyager* had been their home, but Starfleet no longer felt that way. They would have continued to serve under my command, but that was not an option. *Voyager*, my fine ship, was decommissioned shortly after our return. The wear and tear of those seven years had been too hard on her, and what had been state-of-the-art technology had fallen behind the rapid technological advances necessitated by the Dominion War. *Voyager* had served her purpose, even as she retained, in the minds of those had served on her, her status as home.

But even without a ship, and even as so many of us moved on, we have kept a kind of cohesion as a crew. We have regular reunions, and even a kind of base. Tiring of my pleasant but impersonal quarters at Starfleet Command, and realizing that it was time to have a real home once again, I have found myself a place on the Irish coast, in County Clare. A fine old Georgian country house, with plenty of bedrooms and a roaring fire, where you can "tuck up warm," as the locals say, after a day walking along the Wild Atlantic Way. (Those coastal paths are marvelous for walking the dog.) We hold all our reunions there, and of course the house is open to any of my old crew, whenever they need it, whether I am there or not. A haven—not Fair Haven, perhaps, but better, because it is real. The crew of my first command remain just that— My Crew—and I hope they know that their captain will always be there for them. Our experience was unique, and while a great deal has been written about us, or said about us, it's only we ourselves who understand what it was really like.

Some, like me, have stayed in Starfleet. Surely the most successful of these was Harry Kim, now captain of his own ship. My last act as captain of *Voyager* was to give him a long overdue promotion to lieutenant. I would have skipped a couple of ranks if I'd been able: Harry surely deserved it. (His speed of promotion since has made up for it, however.) I finally met his parents, and apologized for not picking up his clarinet, and also his fiancée, now his wife, Libby. I would say that of all of us, Harry has had the most success integrating back into his old life in the Alpha Quadrant. To some extent, I think that this was because such a substantial part of him was always still there. He was the one who had set the most store by returning home, who was young enough to keep his optimism alive, when the rest of us on some level believed we were stuck for good. But Harry's trust paid off in the end, and he's a father of four now. That keeps him out of trouble.

Tuvok too had no trouble returning to his old life, although this was for slightly different reasons from Harry. His family life and career in the Alpha Quadrant were so well established that seven years was a relatively small part of the whole. Tuvok always kept things in perspective. He had been married for many years, his children were more or less grown-up, and, while he missed the birth of his granddaughter, she was still young when he returned (I was there when he met her, and I am sure that I saw something suspiciously close to a tear in his eye). He was there for the arrival of all seven subsequent grandchildren. I am very glad to be able to report that the degenerative neurological condition that the Doctor diagnosed shortly before our return to the Alpha Quadrant was indeed cured quickly after a mind-meld with Sek, and that there have been no side effects or recurrences. Tuvok has had a long career at Starfleet Intelligence since our return, although he spends increasing amounts of time in meditation back at home on Vulcan, and I suspect that his retirement there is coming soon.

What of *Voyager*'s unlikely lovebirds, Tom Paris and B'Elanna Torres? Who would have believed that a relationship that began against the backdrop of a Maquis ship, was sparked by being flung together seventy thousand light-years from everything familiar, and was watched avidly by all their colleagues, would have had such success? And their marriage has been by any measure a tremendous success. Tom Paris was one of those who decided that Starfleet was no longer for him—or, perhaps, in his case, he no longer needed it. Tom, returning to the Alpha Quadrant, found that he had no need now to prove himself to his father. More than that, the desire was no longer there. The physical distance had been enough to establish the necessary emotional distance. He could love his father, and respect him, but he no longer had the desperate need for his attention or approval that had sent him off on such a destructive path. Tom's service on *Voyager* spoke for itself. Within six months he had resigned his commission. He and B'Elanna have a home in the south of France, near the coast, where Tom looks after the children and now has a successful second career writing holodramas (my mother was of help here), and flying whenever he can. You'll of course know him as the creator of *Captain Proton*. Altogether, it's a good way of life for Tom. He is completely content. I hear on the grapevine that he's thinking of renovating an old movie theater…

It is B'Elanna who has stayed in Starfleet, finding that her experience on *Voyager*, and the seniority and respect it earned her, has more than wiped away the disappointment of her time in the Academy. About a year after our return, she confided in me that she was self-conscious of the fact that she had not, technically, graduated from the Academy. You know, the thought hadn't even crossed my mind. If anyone has graduated from the University of Life, it's B'Elanna Torres. I put her name forward for an honorary doctorate, based on her service on *Voyager* and her exceptional work as my chief engineer, and I am glad to say that the Academy accepted the nomination with alacrity. It was a source of great pride to me to be able to give the citation, to see her in her finery accepting her degree, Tom bursting with pride alongside her, little Miral clutching their hands. This honor was the least that B'Elanna deserved. After her difficult and confusing childhood and setting herself on a course to self-destruction at nineteen, she has matured into a bold, fierce, intelligent, and capable woman, the heart of a loving family. On her return to Earth, she was able to reconnect with her father, John, and reestablish that relationship. She has found a large family back on Earth: cousins, and their children, all of whom have welcomed her.

Tom and B'Elanna have a son now too, Eugene Owen, and he is the apple of his mother's eye. Dear lord, all of those who know B'Elanna as stubborn, cranky, and entirely immune to flattery marvel at the sight of her with her son. She melts like butter when he is around. With Miral she enjoys a bond so grounded in love that even the tumults and clashes that inevitably come from putting two strong-willed women in the same household cannot shake it. It is as if B'Elanna has had the chance to revisit and rework her relationship with her own mother in a way that has allowed her to transform it. There are quarrels, of course there are, but Miral has never doubted that her mother loves her, and that makes all the difference. Besides, she has Tom wrapped around her little finger. She has a huge amount of his charm, as well as his daredevil approach, and a fine dash of his confidence. I have no doubt that whatever she chooses to do in life, she will make a huge success.

What about Owen, my old captain, now Admiral Paris? I wondered, when Tom announced his resignation from Starfleet, whether Owen was putting on a brave face about the news, but, having spoken to him about it, I know that this is not the case. He is genuinely, unconditionally proud of Tom—and completely besotted with Miral. Watching them, I see how grandchildren have the capability of transforming the bonds between parent and child: in Miral, Owen is given a chance to make good the mistakes he made with Tom. He can encourage her, and, most of all, he can *enjoy* her. She is not, ultimately, his responsibility—although she is his joy. Miral may yet choose Starfleet— although she is as stubborn as her mother and as wild as her father. I think she would make a superlative test pilot. When I see her, I remember twelve-year-old Tom Paris, having the time of his life on the flight simulators. Maybe Aunt Kate can take her out there soon. It comes in handy sometimes, having an admiral or two in the family.

What of those crew members who only existed because of *Voyager*, who would not now be living their lives had it not been for the fact that we brought them into existence? What about our Doctor, for example, who came online after the death of my dear Laurie Fitz, and who has surely exceeded whatever expectations his programmers might have had? I think the Doctor might be the one who has most embraced life after the Delta Quadrant. And why not? His mobile emitter allowed him to travel wherever he liked, and the matter of his sentience was resolved as soon as the Starfleet tech experts encountered him… I naturally hesitate to say "in the flesh," which would surely be offensive; in person surely covers it. Could anyone, meeting the Doctor, doubt his personhood? Recognized as sentient, recognized as his own person, the Doctor was able to do whatever he chose. He promptly resigned from Starfleet and has taken up the cause of photon rights (my mother, ever the activist, has been a great help, and they talk about collaborating on a children's book, explaining the issues involved). It is surely only a matter of time before the law catches up with the reality. He lives a very full and busy life, attending concerts, playing golf with Reg Barclay, driving a very fast car. Of all of us, he's the one that most embraced his celebrity status. It helps his cause, and, it must be said, he enjoys being in the limelight. I see no relationship on the horizon. (A side note here on Reg Barclay, our honorary crew member, who fought in our corner for so long. I was proud to be there to see him collect his Daystrom Prize, for his work in establishing the first two-way transgalactic communication. An honor richly deserved.)

Perhaps the person that I worried about most was Seven of Nine. Our arrival back in the Alpha Quadrant, and the subsequent disbanding of *Voyager*'s crew, meant that her "collective" was coming to an end. I was always concerned that this would be a kind of second trauma for her, the removal of support structures that had helped her in those first few tentative steps toward regaining her humanity. Her nascent relationship with my first officer, while short-lived, was crucial here, giving her some continuity with her *Voyager* days, while allowing her to make the transition to a new way of life. With Chakotay, she made a journey back out to the world where she grew up, and with his guidance, was able to lay a few ghosts of the past to rest. Although she has never discussed this with me directly, I understand obliquely from Chakotay that Seven has passed through what was surely a necessary stage of anger with her parents for their part in her assimilation into the Borg. She should never have been on that ship with them and, while she cannot change the past, she can come to terms with it.

Seven has reconnected with her family, most notably her aunt, although the gap between the memory of six-year-old Annika and the reality of Seven herself must have been a hard one for Irene to come to terms with. Seven spends a great deal of time with Samantha Wildman's family, remaining as close as ever to Naomi, who is, in effect, a much-loved younger sister. Samantha's spouse, Greskrendtregk, has accepted this extension to his family with equanimity. But where Seven has truly come into her own is through her work. She is, of course, of tremendous importance to Starfleet, not only as their special advisor and expert on the Borg, but also because of her phenomenal skills and talents. She is a key member of a significant Federation think tank, where she has access to whatever resources she requires. This is a fascinating group (I understand there are several augmented human members), although Seven does not often speak of their work in detail. And of course, there is still Icheb, whom I put in her care all those years ago, and for whom she has always come through.

And what of my first officer? What of Chakotay? How has he fared on his return to the Alpha Quadrant? I was not surprised, when the moment came, to see that it was the special circumstance of *Voyager* that allowed Chakotay to become Starfleet again. He resigned his commission after eighteen months back in the Alpha Quadrant, whereupon he and B'Elanna took a journey out to the old DMZ to pay their respects to their fallen Maquis comrades. Since then he has spent a long time traveling around North America, and also around colony worlds settled by Native Americans. He sees himself as doubly dispossessed: his ancestors forced from their lands when my ancestors arrived, and then his own family removed from their home when the DMZ was formed. He has found himself a task in life, reconnecting these places, learning about their histories and traditions, healing, perhaps, some of the wounds caused by those multiple evictions. He often drops out of communication for months at a time, suddenly turning up again, sending me a message from wherever he is, or arriving without warning at my mother's farm (my mother likes him very much). Sometimes he accepts a university post, where he will teach history for a while, before returning to his travels. When he is on Earth, we see each other every week, as we always did; he comes to my home in Ireland for dinner, and we talk about how life brought us together, and where it might take us next. My dog loves him.

✦

I am, of course, Starfleet till I die. I dreamed of captaining my own ship as a little girl, and I worked hard, kept dreaming, and turned that dream into reality. Being a Starfleet captain turned out very different from how I imagined it would be. I made many mistakes along the way, and there are some decisions to which I am still not entirely reconciled, but I did my best in unusual circumstances. I hope history won't judge me too harshly.

What of my life now? It is full, it is busy. I am an admiral, with all the responsibilities and headaches that entails. There are perhaps too many briefings in my life, and not enough ship time. Still, I would not have it any other way. When I am weary of talking to others, or listening to others, or have become tired of being inside, I walk down to the academy campus, where my career started all those years ago, and I find the rose garden. Sometimes Boothby (yes, he's still there) steals an hour or two of my time to help him, and I feel better for it, as I always did. Whenever I visit, there are roses on my desk the next day, as reward for my efforts. I go whenever I can.

I will be there later this morning, not in my capacity as under-gardener, but in dress uniform, as Admiral Kathryn M. Janeway, where I shall be giving the commencement speech to this year's new crop of graduates. I have done this speech two or three times in the past: I love this task above all. What a joy to see these young people, at the very start of their careers, so full of life and hope and ambition. It reminds me that my job now, above all, is to create the conditions whereby they can flourish in Starfleet and have long and productive careers, marked chiefly by exploration rather than by conflict. I find it a great responsibility.

I shall speak to them about courage, and how life can take you around the long way, and how they might find themselves having to answer questions that they never anticipated, and that they may not like the answer that they come up with. But most of all I want to tell them that there is no better job, and no better life, and that if I had my time over, I would do the same again. Every graduating class is special, but forgive me if this one is particularly special, because this time the audience includes one Ensign Amelia Janeway.

She is, of course, my daughter. My mother and Phoebe, believing me dead, and receiving all my worldly goods, including my frozen eggs, could not help themselves, and decided to have something of me live on. Phoebe and Yianem have brought her up among their girls, although she has always known who she is, in truth. Three mothers: how lucky can one girl be! Not to forget all those others who will be looking out for her across the years, within Starfleet and without: Commanders Torres and Tuvok, Captain Kim and Admiral Paris, Tom and the Doctor and Seven and Chakotay. They would do anything for her. Later, after she has graduated, our whole family—my mother, her daughters, her granddaughters, all the grandparents—will gather together and celebrate her success. Tomorrow morning we will go flying together, and that evening she will join me and Chakotay for dinner. Life is full of surprises: you can be whisked away at a moment's notice, and then come back to treasures that you did not know you had left behind. This life of mine has been a good life—and will, I hope, long continue to be so.

EDITOR UNA'S ACKNOWLEDGMENTS

My grateful thanks to:

Cat Camacho—for fine editorial guidance, and for giving the trolley solution to the Tuvix problem.

Max Edwards—for being such a mensch.

Daniel Tostevin—for long years of *Star Trek* gossip, and most of all for Pulaski.

Dayton Ward—for niftily dodging the Warp 10 dilemma.

And, of course, all my love to Matthew and Verity—for everything.

The pop-up books described in chapter 1 are based on two beautiful books by Robert Sabuda.

ABOUT THE EDITOR

Una McCormack is the author of the *Star Trek* novels *The Lotus Flower* (part of *The Worlds of Star Trek: Deep Space Nine*), *Hollow Men*, *The Never-Ending Sacrifice*, *Brinkmanship*, *The Missing*, the *New York Times* bestseller *The Fall: The Crimson Shadow*, *Enigma Tales*, *The Way to the Stars*, and *The Last Best Hope*, and the *Doctor Who* novels *The King's Dragon*, *The Way Through the Woods*, *Royal Blood*, and *Molten Heart*. She lives in Cambridge, England, with her partner of many years, Matthew, and their daughter, Verity.

For more fantastic fiction, author events,
exclusive excerpts, competitions, limited editions and more

VISIT OUR WEBSITE
titanbooks.com

LIKE US ON FACEBOOK
facebook.com/titanbooks

FOLLOW US ON TWITTER AND INSTAGRAM
@TitanBooks

EMAIL US
readerfeedback@titanemail.com